The Heaven Factor

Ten Commandment Edition

David C. Sloan

PublishAmerica
Baltimore

© 2002 by David C. Sloan.
All rights reserved. No part of this book may be reproduced in any form without written permission from the publishers, except by a reviewer who may quote brief passages in a review to be printed in a newspaper or magazine.

First printing

ISBN: 1-59286-116-4
PUBLISHED BY PUBLISHAMERICA BOOK PUBLISHERS
www.publishamerica.com
Baltimore

Printed in the United States of America

To my wife, Brenda
For all the years and all the help

Acknowledgments

Cover by

Wolf Creative Services
www.wolfcs.com

Inside page illustrations by

Loaves & Fishes
Inspirational Artwork
14232 Cloverdale Rd.
Rogers, AR 72756

Table of Contents

List of Ten Commandments	9
Introduction	11
Truth of Riches	17
Musical Illusions	41
Future Attitudes	61
Tradition	79
Extreme Reflections	111
Prairie Sunrise	133
Broken Promises	151
Choosing Your Price	169
A Stagecoach Mystery	187
Interstellar Missions	215

Ten Commandments

Ex. 20:3	"You shall have no other gods before Me."
Ex. 20:4	"You shall not make for yourself an idol."
Ex. 20:7	"You shall not take the name of the Lord your God in vain."
Ex. 20: 8	"Remember the Sabbath day, to keep it holy."
Ex. 20:12	"Honor your father and your mother."
Ex. 20:13	"You shall not murder."
Ex. 20:14	"You shall not commit adultery."
Ex. 20:15	"You shall not steal."
Ex. 20:16	"You shall not bear false witness."
Ex. 20:17	"You shall not covet."

* From New American Standard Bible

Introduction

The Heaven Factor is the end result of a decision to pursue a long-time dream of writing a book that might someday be published. Writing a collection of short stories served my purpose perfectly. I wanted to approach this project in a way that would be both entertaining and have substance for the reader. None of the stories are intended to be preachy or cliché. Science fiction is one of my favorites to read and watch in movie form. The problem with most of what I see is that God seems to be left out. There is also the problem of believability in what I see. I was taught at a young age that good science fiction always had an essence of believability. This is why two of the stories are with a science fiction twist. I hope as you read these you will feel each do contains the qualities that I just outlined. I also have a passion for history and was born and raised in south-central Kansas. Thus two stories are set in late 19th century and on the Kansas prairies.

Why did I name this book *The Heaven Factor*? The answer goes back to allowing heaven's influence in our lives. Most of us do not spend near enough time pondering the effect God has on our lives in the modern day and time. The term "factor" is found in the mathematical discipline of multiplication. Factoring heaven in our lives has positive results. Look at Jude 1:2: "Mercy unto you, and peace and love, be multiplied." 1Peter 5:2: "Grace and peace be multiplied unto you through the knowledge of God, and of Jesus our Lord...." I want all of the grace, peace and love God has for me, so I am working to apply this principle into my own life and encourage it in my family.

I am a pretty ordinary person but in the process of putting this project together I had a couple of very good lessons on exactly what this book is about. The characters within these stories are pretty ordinary and reflect various attitudes toward God and heaven. Some find themselves in extraordinary situations where they need help and are forced to factor God into their equations. Other characters have close friends or family members that pray for God's intervention into the scene. I do not intend to offend anyone who reads this book by any ideas, themes or method of writing. Instead I hope a sentence, a paragraph or an entire story within this book will spark a thought but mostly be considered a positive way of spending some of your valuable free time.

Feedback

I would like to invite each reader to send me your comments by e-mail. Tell me what you liked and didn't like. Don't worry, I will not be offended. I am interested in your opinion.

My address is: Dcbsloan@aol.com

Thanks for your input.

TRUTH OF RICHES

"You shall have no other gods before Me."
Ex. 20:3

One

"Here we are in the middle of a big field that has nothing in it but grass, Stephen. What are we doing here? I rode in that Jeep of yours for an hour to get here to what you said would be our future." Elli repeated these words in various ways for the next several minutes as she walked, ran, kicked the ground and pulled grass out at the roots and threw it at the sky.

Stephen just let her go on with her protest, and when she looked as if she were about to pass out he started to explain. "Elli, dearest, this is our future. We will be building a fantastic future for you, our children and for every person that takes part in our plans for this place. This is not just acres of dirt and grass, this is a place where people will live in homes we will build for them. Businesses will come in and life will be going on here."

"What do you mean by all that, Stephen? There is nothing within an hour of here. We are out in the middle of nowhere. No one will move out here so far from their jobs and town." Elli was confused by this latest of Stephen's "entrepreneur" projects, as he would call them. Most people would just call them "schemes." Oh, Stephen always had the best intentions to provide for his family and to make it big in whatever he did but he was always changing from one project to another, never giving the first idea enough time to take off and work. Stephen's basement is still full of shirts with Y2K designs printed on them. When none of the expected catastrophic problems came on or after January 1, 2000, Elli laid the law down. From that point on Stephen was to concentrate on his job, family, their church and that would be final. No more of these projects that promised to make them rich or even just make a good chunk of money in a short amount of time. At first Stephen actually seemed to be relieved and did follow exactly what Elli wanted. On the surface he seemed to be happy or at least okay with the whole idea. He started teaching a Bible class at their church for college- and career-age people and seemed to enjoy it a great deal. Stephen seemed to relate with the young people in the class and they respected what he had to say.

For the next nine months the Phillips family lived a pretty normal life, but then one day Stephen walked in late from work after meeting with a "friend" for dinner. He was more excited than he was after signing up to sell long distance phone service for one of those network-marketing companies. The subject of all his excitement was inside the brown box that was tucked under his right arm. This small box carried a rather large and demanding item that would affect the future of Stephen's family. It was a correspondence course on becoming a real estate agent. Stephen came in the house talking as if he had just inherited a million bucks and unfortunately he just might have thought this had happened. As he showed Elli all the material from the tapes to the books she began looking at him while shaking her head. It was as if she was trying to tell him "no, no, no." Stephen just kept going on about being able to study in his spare time and then he would be able to take the test for a real estate license. He promised not to even look at a video or crack a book until the girls were in bed. He could have the quality time with the family then hit the books to learn about the "booming" real estate market.

Ell began questioning Stephen with a slight sarcastic attitude. "Okay, how much did all these fantastic books and tapes cost us, and who was it you met tonight?"

Stephen took a big swallow then proceeded, "This is the best part of the whole thing, Elli. This is not going to cost us anything and I promise it will not interfere with the college and career class at church."

Elli stopped shaking her head and gave Stephen a look that would burn a hole in a solid steel door. Stephen knew this look well and knew he had to keep moving to avoid any burning of flesh. "And the person I met was Dan Townsend. You remember Dan from the company party we all went to three years ago. I introduced you to him and we spoke to him off and on all night."

Elli was not happy and she did not remember any Dan. "How should I remember a guy I met three years ago and hardly spoke to?" She had news for Stephen; even though he answered her first two questions she was not going to let him do this latest project. She was determined to win on this one. "I don't care if this Dan that I don't remember gave you the money to buy a sky scraper. You will not do this!"

"Elli, listen to me for just five minutes, and I know you will get just as excited as I am about all this."

"No, you promised no more schemes. You were going to get down to basics of working your job and coming home to the girls and me. What about the class you started teaching at church? I will not let you do this." Elli was shouting so loud by now both girls, Kelly and Christy, who were in the back bedroom watching TV, had come into the living room to see what was going on. "Go back and watch TV, girls," Elli said. "We are just talking...."

Kelly interrupted, "Talking about another one of Dad's wacky ideas?"

"No, not at all," Elli rebutted. "Go back to your TV and let your father and I talk for a while longer." Both girls knew to obey immediately whenever their mother used the phrase "your father." After they were out of the room Elli turned to Stephen and in order to save time and her voice she told him that he had "five minutes" and that is all.

"Elli, Dan and I have been talking a lot at work, you know, during breaks and lunch. He knew about some of my extra money projects and he asked if I had ever thought about real estate. He has this rich uncle who would like to invest some of his money to buy and develop some property. He wants to build a place for people to live away from the hassles of the city, but he wants to attract high-tech businesses to relocate either next to or very close to the project so we can develop an ideal community: safe, pollution free, noise free and ideal for raising children. Dan wants me to be part of this because I know so many people in the area and the lay of the land you might say. I already have several locations I want to show Dan and his uncle that have great potential for this sort of thing. He told me his uncle is William Hemingway III. He is one of the movers and shakers that make things happen. I'm not sure why he lives in this town, but that is beside the point. The thing to concentrate on is that he will go with whatever Dan says on who to bring into this deal and Dan has already sold him on me."

Elli interrupted with, "But do you know anything about actually buying and selling real estate?"

"Well, no. I don't know all the legalities of the business, but that is why I have this course. I do have a knack for picking out hot spots to build new stores for my company and Dan knows this. Every store that is built on the site that I recommended is doing great. A few days ago at lunch Dan and I drove to a couple of areas that were close, and after looking them over for just a few minutes I knew they weren't right for this project. From that point on Dan has been after me to help him with this. I just thought since Dan gave me all this and I can do it and keep my job that you might go for it. If nothing else learning more about something like real estate might help us make a better deal on our next house."

At this point Stephen moved in real close and started to put his hands around Ellis' waist while kissing her first on the right cheek then the left. She started to show weakness when she said, "I don't know. You have tried so many other things. How will you make money with this?"

That one question was the open door for Stephen and he walked all the way through it. They spent the next hour and a half going over the entire idea just as Dan laid it out for him. By the end of the evening Elli had given in and Stephen was busy reading and watching videos on how to be an expert at real estate. He was flying high and on his way to what he thought was his one last chance to make it big.

The next day at work Stephen went to Dan first thing and told him that he was in on the real estate deal and they needed to get to work hard and fast. Stephen took to real estate as if he were born to it. He zoomed through the tapes and books and even passed the test for a state license to be an agent in record time. With that out of the way, Dan arranged for Stephen to meet with his uncle so they could get down to planning the next phase of their business. The meeting was set for the following Friday night, 6:00 p.m. sharp. Elli was supposed to go but she ended up saying she couldn't find a babysitter and stayed home. In reality Elli just did not want to go. She still did not believe in this idea and decided to adopt the wait-and-see philosophy. She also decided to quietly pray for her husband and Dan. She had been raised to believe in prayer and had done it off and on all her life but really hadn't taken it seriously. Now she decided she needed to do just that, take it seriously.

She started getting up early each morning before Stephen and the girls and spent time in her overstuffed chair under a table lamp in quiet solitude. At first she didn't know how to start so she would just get quiet and ponder her life, then go to thinking about the girls and then Stephen. With time she would grow with the process and find great inner peace.

Friday evening came and Stephen found himself standing in front of a set of solid oak French doors attached to a large and intimidating stone mansion. Dan drove that evening and picked Stephen up. He felt it would be more impressive to his uncle if they came together and it would guarantee they both would arrive on time. As they waited for someone to answer the door Stephen noticed beads of sweat on the palms of his hands and his forehead. He started to shiver slightly. Dan noticed this and gave him some last minute encouragement about being the man for the job and all the sort of schmoose talk that went with pumping another person up.

When the door opened a very large man was on the other side ready to greet them. He was silhouetted by light coming from behind. This made him appear larger then he really was. Dan's Uncle reached out with his right hand as he said, "Well hello, Dan. How are you, glad you and your friend could make it tonight."

Dan reached out and met his uncle's hand half way with a strong and vigorous shake. They exchanged the usual about how good it was to see each other. Dan turned toward Stephen and began the introduction. "Stephen, this is my uncle William Hemingway III, one of the wealthiest and most powerful men in the country."

"Now that is enough, Dan," Mr. Hemingway said. "I just want to meet this man you have told me about and be able to talk with him not scare him. Hello, Stephen, Dan has told me a great deal about you and all good I might add. I was very impressed with how you completed your real estate study courses so quickly." Mr. Hemingway had to pull his right hand from Dan and immediately made a sweeping movement with the same hand toward Stephen.

As Stephen nervously shook the uncle's hand, he gave his appreciation for the kind words. He informed this new friend the same source had told him a lot of great things about his uncle. There did seem to be an immediate rapport with this man as if they had known each other for years. Uncle William had a rule pertaining to business meetings that he wanted to apply to this potential new business opportunity. If they meet they eat. With this they sat down to a fabulous dinner.

After dinner they moved to the library and had their coffee and other adult beverages and talked real estate. After the drinks ran out they were still talking real estate into the early morning hours. By the time Dan dropped Stephen off at home plans were made and they all had their tasks to complete. Stephen would be busy looking for the perfect site for their project and when they all agreed on the site and all the legalities were done, Stephen would be in charge of selling the idea to the community. Dan would be in charge of planning and actually getting streets and curbs cut and formed and taking care of all other construction challenges. Uncle William would take care of building permits, inspection and the most important part of funding the entire project.

The meeting went on for hours and when Stephen was finally able to go home it was so late he found everyone already sound asleep. One of Stephen's favorite parts of each day was bedtime. The girls always seemed to come to life in a special way as they talked and giggled. He carefully slipped into their room and stood by their beds looking as if he was memorizing their innocent faces.

When he crept toward his bedroom he noticed a light under the door. He opened it to find Elli sitting up in bed with her arms folded and a stern expression. Stephen felt the best way to approach the situation was with kindness and enthusiasm, so he walked over to her and slowly kissed her on the cheek as if to express the fact that he was sorry. He then proceeded to prepare for bed and slipped under the sheets next to Elli. He was there for several minutes when he tried to break the ice by saying, "The girls are so sweet when they are sleeping, why aren't they always like that?"

"They are, but their father is never around to notice," Elli snapped back.

"Elli, that isn't true. I'm home almost every evening and weekends. Can I help it if things are tough nowadays and I have to work at coming up with extra money all the time? Elli, what is really wrong here?"

By this time Elli's jaw was clinched so tight it seemed like she had to thaw herself out before answering with, "Stephen, you know the answer. It's the usual problem that I have with all your projects. How long will you be excited about this one? How much will it cost us? How will you do this and keep your job all at the same time?" It seemed as she talked faster with each question.

"I will ignore all but one of those questions. How will I do this and keep my job at the same time? Well, all the work that I need to do can be done on my lunch hour, before, after work and on weekends. Nothing will be taken away from the quality of my job."

Elli looked up at him from bed and went on with more. "Okay, when will you be able to prepare for your Sunday Bible class, and when will we get the first check from this great idea?"

Stephen thought for a second before answering. "I will get up thirty minutes early every day and do my preparation for Sunday and we won't be getting a check from the project until we start selling lots to people who want to build homes or businesses on the site."

Elli persisted, "How long will it take to start selling to people?"

"It will start happening as soon as all three of us in the partnership agree to the site, we'll buy the property and get all the legal paperwork completed and our plans approved by the county. Then we will be able to start selling."

"I don't mean to be a nag, but how long will that take, Stephen?" Elli was going to make Stephen accountable as she has never before.

"Well, that is difficult to say. There is a lot of red tape, but I would say in a few short months."

"Months, months." Elli did not sound surprised or disappointed. She knew there was nothing she could do to stop Stephen now. She asked him, "Have you found a location yet?"

"We are close, it is between two sites now. We should be able to decide this Saturday. All of us will be going to both sites and back to Mr. Hemmingway's home to go over the pros and cons of each one and make our decision."

"But I thought you had the talent to decide on the site and that was your job," Elli chimed in with a bit of sarcasm.

"You're part right and part wrong, oh wise woman of motherhood. It is my job to give my best recommendation, but all three of us have to agree or we will not do anything. We will quit everything if we are not in total agreement about what we do." This was interesting to Elli because it made sense to her. Maybe this will work out. She was still on a hold pattern till that first check arrives.

The Saturday meeting came and went with their first community site agreed on. Their plans were to develop a family home project of the future. They had gigantic plans of building homes with the latest energy-saving technologies and to attract Silicon Valley type of people and businesses to help establish the project. They were to build a model community with the best of the past, present and future in mind. They were also planning that a community like this would make all three very rich. Of course in Mr. Hemmingway's case he will become wealthier and the other two would, hopefully, become rich for the first time.

After this meeting Stephen knew if he were to keep going he would need to quit his job and go full time selling. After Dan left from their meeting Stephen asked Mr. Hemmingway if there was any way he would be willing to pay Stephen for his services from that point on and when the lots started selling he would accept a commission. This way he could quit his job and work full time on the project. Mr. Hemmingway agreed to everything, even the amount Stephen said he needed to live till the commissions started coming in. As Mr. Hemmingway put it, "I really am impressed with your talent and ability, Stephen, and I know you will pull this off and make it worth all the sacrifice. I just want you to understand we are all counting on you and will expect 125% on a 24/7 basis. If I am going to pay up front I will need to be able to call upon you and your services any time day or night. I have got to tell you something I have not told even my nephew. I want you to go into the negotiations when we talk to the companies we want to bring in to be part of the community." Stephen tried not to look shocked, then his eyes grew rather large with excitement because he knew this would mean big bucks for him. It will be better than selling small home building lots even though he was sure he wanted to do that also.

"Well," Stephen suddenly hesitated, "sure, of course, Mr. Hemingway. I'm 150% behind the project. You can count on me. I just need a little time to break the news to my wife and my boss."

Mr. Hemingway was getting into his shiny black Mercedes as he said, "Go ahead, Stephen, and let me know when you are ready to go to work for me full time, just make it soon."

The next Saturday Stephen and Elli made their trip out to the field where the new community would be built. He was hoping after showing her the site and explaining the entire vision to her Elli would accept him quitting his job a little easier. After Elli had become exhausted after kicking and pulling grass out of the dirt, Stephen walked her to a cold, clear stream running through rough and jagged rocks. The scene seemed to quiet Elli and Stephen both.

"We plan to have a park in this area, and a few hundred yards that way we plan on selling lots to build houses backing up to the park. Over there just below those bluffs we plan on having a country club with a P.G.A. approved golf course. Don't you love this, Elli?" Stephen held his breath and fixed his eyes on hers. He could tell exactly what direction she would go by reading those eyes.

"You know, Stephen," Elli began. "I do love this area, but why do you think people will come out here to live?"

"Elli, they won't just come out here to live; they will also come out here to work, play and raise their kids." He started seeing her direction go south on him, so he kept going with something he thought would impress her. "The best part of all is that I have convinced Mr. Hemingway and Dan that we need to find pastors that are willing to start new churches here and we will build the churches and they can reach people right here."

"I agree with that." Elli began to come around a bit. "How do you think you can get churches here and how do you know people will go to them?"

"Don't worry about that." He knew what to say next. "Just let God do the work. We are just instruments to do his work by his leading and I am getting convinced I am called to do this by God."

"Elli," Stephen swallowed, "there is another reason I brought you out here. I have something to tell you. Since I believe God is in control of all this and I know it will work I've decided to quit my job and work on the community full time. Of course Mr. Hemingway has agreed to pay me a salary that is the same amount I'm making at my job." He stopped and braced himself.

"Why am I not surprised?" Elli asked almost stoically.

Stephen was turning red in the face, and he didn't know what do at this point but to say, "What? Are you upset?"

"Well, I don't like it, and I think it is debatable if God has called you to do this. For one thing this is the first time you have brought this up. I am not totally stupid and I can see through what you are doing and I also realize I can't fight you on this anymore. I guess there is one part of what you have said today that is true, we have to let God do the work and I am going to pray He works to help you see the truth about what you are doing here. Have you already turned in your notice?"

"Going to Monday," Stephen replied.

"Well, okay, but you have to tell me some things so I know exactly what is going on from now on." She went on with more questions until Stephen began moving toward her and gently pushed her up against a large oak tree and then kissed her. A few seconds later he whispered, "Not to worry, we'll be okay. Just come along with me for the ride." They spent the rest of the afternoon by the stream among the place that would change their lives forever.

Since the next day was Sunday, Stephen had to stay up late the night before to prepare for the Bible class because he had not been able to do it all week. They made it to church on time and he was in the middle of teaching when the cell phone in his pocket started chiming. Stephen let it ring a couple of times, then asked the class to excuse him as he reached in his pocket and pulled the flip phone out. He turned his back to the class from the front podium. "Hello?" Stephen made it more of a question than a greeting.

"Hello, Stephen, is that you?"

"Yes, this is Stephen. Mr. Hemingway?"

"Yes, it's me, Stephen. We have some work to do today, I have a meeting first thing tomorrow morning with the county code office and we have a lot of work to do before then."

"Well, Mr. Hemingway I am teaching a Bible class right now, how about this afternoon?"

There was a moment of silence then, "That would be okay, if that is the best you can do. Tell you what, bring your wife and those kids for lunch so we can meet and size each other up. Then after lunch we will get to work. I will expect you here ASAP after you get out of church."

"You've got it, Mr. Hemingway," Stephen quietly answered. As he ended the conversation he turned around, sheepishly apologized to the class and picked up where he left off with the lesson. While they were on their way to the main worship service after Sunday school, Stephen told Elli what the call was about.

"Will you and Mr. Hemingway be working all afternoon?" Elli asked.

"Oh, I think he has some work for us but it won't take very long. I'm sure we'll all be home in a few hours."

After church the Phillips family found themselves driving down a country road on their way to the Hemingway mansion. Mr. Hemingway and his wife Margaret charmed all of the Phillips family with their wit, beauty of their home and a fantastic Sunday luncheon. When they had all finished eating, Mr. Hemingway suggested that Margaret should take Elli and the girls to their stables and show off their horses, and if they wanted they could even take a ride. That idea was a big hit with the girls, but Elli was not so happy about it. As the women prepared to go, Mr. Hemingway and Stephen proceeded to the study to get to work. As the afternoon went on Stephen would look at his watch seeing it go from 1:30 to 3:30. Suddenly the doors to the study burst open and all the women came running in. The girls were excited about riding horses in the country and how they all had a scare when Kelly's horse ran off and she was unable to control him. Margaret caught up with them and was able to do her magic to calm the horse down. They decided then to come in and Elli thought it would be a good time to go home. Mr. Hemingway agreed, but he did not want Stephen to go just yet. He suggested that Elli could drive home without Stephen and he would see to it that Stephen arrived home safely when they were finished. Elli reluctantly agreed and gave Stephen a kiss good-bye to be followed by Kelly and Chris doing the same. When they were all out of the study Mr. Hemingway and Stephen went back to work.

It was almost midnight when Stephen was dropped off at his own doorstep. As he walked into their bedroom Elli turned over and just looked at him, she didn't say anything. As she turned the dim light from the hallway came into the bedroom highlighting Ellis' blonde hair. Stephen noticed her eyes were red and filled with tears. The customary "where have you been" came from her mouth with an added quiver. Stephen gave the usual type of answer about how they were so caught up in work that before they both knew it the time was 7:00. Mr. Hemingway had dinner brought in for them. Then at 11:30 Stephen finally insisted on getting home. He was sitting on the edge of their bed by now and Elli had her arms around his waist while she impatiently listened. She had many mixed feelings and was trying to hide all of them but really wasn't doing a good job of it.

That week the work really began with the hours getting longer with each day that passed. Mr. Hemingway became more and more demanding. After the weeks of planning and approvals were over there were the promotions to plan and to get started. Mr. Hemingway did include Stephen in talks with the many different companies they were pursuing as he agreed to do. All this took weeks and then months. Every time Stephen would get more to do Elli would ask him what about Dan? Dan was doing his part, Stephen would reply, but he honestly felt Mr. Hemingway liked him and his work better.

Through it all Stephen still taught the Bible class on Sunday mornings but the time he had to prepare was less and less. The worse part of it was that he no longer had time to meet with members of the class outside of church. At one time Stephen told Elli those meetings were more important to him than Sunday mornings because he was able to show the students that he really did care on a more personal level. As the months went by several members of the class started to complain about the quality of Stephen's teaching and that he seemed to be losing interest in them. These complaints reached the elders of the church.

One evening when Stephen arrived home late as usual Elli gave him a message that he needed to call the church's education director. He returned the call from the master bedroom. Even though it was down the hall Elli could hear parts of what Stephen was saying and it was not very pleasant. When Stephen came back into the kitchen where everyone else was, he broke the news to them that he would no longer be teaching the Bible class. He told them about the complaints and a new teacher had already been recruited. Stephen was hurt and after a while he began to rationalize the change with, "Well, if that's what they want fine. I gave it my best and if that's not good enough for them that is okay with me. I was getting tired of those kids anyway. They were all just self-centered, caught up in their own little world. Always taking what I had but never gave back anything." Elli started to argue with him but decided it wouldn't do any good. Stephen kept going to church but would always have something to say about the education director, the sermon or something else. It only took a few more weeks for Stephen to announce to Elli that he was going to have to work every Sunday to get all the lots sold at the project and he wasn't sure how long that would take.

As the project grew so did the Phillipses' checking account. They were doing so good Stephen talked Elli into having a new home form them built in the community. They decided to sell their old home, build a new one that was twice the size of the old and Stephen was working almost round the clock seven days a week. On the surface it looked like the great American dream had finally come true for the Phillipses, but there was something wrong inside Stephen. There was something missing in all the success. The truth was flickering but he was fighting it all the way. He just kept on working and living this life he thought he had always wanted. Elli started noticing the scent of alcohol on Stephen after some of his long days. At first he explained he wasn't drinking, but he had to cater to his clients and when they wanted to drink he had to buy it.

Through it all Elli was becoming a real prayer warrior. At first she would spend just a few minutes each morning praying for Stephen, asking God to watch over him and direct his path that day. Then she started to sense that God wanted her to do something more. As time went on she kept on getting the impression she should pray that God would give her the strength to give Stephen up and let God take care of him. This meant, in her mind, not to worry about him and let him go where he thought he needed and to have faith God could take care of him. Pretty soon she was praying for all of the family in the same way. Most of all she would spend many hours each week in prayer for a large list of concerns for others. She started attending a woman's Bible study and was strengthened through the fellowship of other women. Elli was becoming the woman God wanted and this new character would soon be tested.

Stephen was going as fast as he could, fourteen hours a day five, six and seven days a week. He was making more money each month than the month before. He was also changing inside in a way that he would never admit to Elli or anyone else. Whenever Mr. Hemingway would come out to the project to see the progress Stephen and Dan were there. Whenever he would call for a meeting any time day or night they had to be there. There were meetings with the companies they were courting and the pressure was mounting on Stephen daily. One Tuesday evening, after the three partners had just sealed the biggest deal of their project that would guarantee they would be able to finish, they decided to celebrate. They were just around the corner from realizing the complete fulfillment of their dreams. Mr. Hemingway hadn't told Stephen or Dan, but he had big plans of expanding and duplicating this success story to other areas of the country. He knew he had the team in Dan and Stephen to carry out his plan. With this latest deal successfully being reached, Mr. Hemingway decided to share his vision with his team over a few drinks.

It was getting late and Stephen decided he finally had enough and needed to go home and tell the good news to Elli. He wasn't sure how she would take it, but he was sure he could sell her on it just like he had all the others. Mr. Hemingway confessed they were drinking a little too much and tried talking Stephen into staying the night. He could call Elli and tell her it would be wiser to stay there along with Dan since no one present was in any condition to drive. Stephen wouldn't hear of it and as he staggered out into the hall from Mr. Hemingway's fine study he made his way out the front door. Before he could make it to the steps of the front porch he decided to thank Mr. Hemingway for everything he had done for him. They met at the front door and as they talked Mr. Hemingway tried one more time to get Stephen to stay, but it didn't work.

"No," Stephen said as he turned to his car. "I'm okay, and I would rather go home."

He thanked Mr. Hemingway once again for everything as he left. It took several tries to get the car keys out of his pocket and he kept missing getting the key in the lock to open his door. When he finally got in and started the car he hit the gas and backed out of the drive, almost hitting a tree on the other side of the street. At least when he peeled out he was going in the right direction. Mr. Hemingway told Dan to call Elli and let her know he was on his way home. Elli thanked Dan for calling and when she hung up she had a strange sensation that she needed to pray for Stephen's safety and for him to be sensitive to the Lord that night. Elli wasn't sure why she needed to pray like this, but she felt the need coming from inside and obeyed it.

Mr. Hemingway lived in a remote area several miles out of town and the roads that would take Stephen home had sharp curves and the area was very dark and lonely. The speed limit was 55, but Stephen made it around each curve going at least 65. At one time he lost control for a moment and spun around to the other side of the road and landed with the front of the car going in the opposite direction. He cut the engine while still swirling in his own head and waited there until he regained some kind of sense about himself. Fortunately there were no other cars on the road that time of night.

When he finally got going again he drove a little slower but still swerved from side to side. A few miles further he started noticing something going on up in front of him. His headlights would catch a figure from time to time and he saw what looked like a flashlight being waved in the air. When he was about fifteen feet from the figure he could tell it was a young girl or a lady dressed in blue jeans and a red long sleeve top. There was a car parked behind her to the side of the road with the hood opened as people do when they are having car problems. Stephen pulled over and stopped more because he couldn't see good enough to pull around her than wanting to help her. He kept his head lights on her, and as she walked over to him Stephen rolled his window down and stuck his head partially out and asked, "What is going on? Do you need some help? What are you doing here this late at night anyway?"

"Oh, my car stalled or something." It was easy to tell she was nervous and scared. "I don't know what happened for sure. I was going down the road and it just stopped. I tried to start it again but it would just make a terrible noise. If you could help me I would really appreciate it." She sounded pretty frantic, but with the state Stephen was in at this moment it really didn't matter to him. If he couldn't get it started he could always give the girl a ride home.

"Let me try to start it, you might have flooded the engine is all." He only stumbled one time before getting to the girl's car. He decided to look under the hood to see if he could see anything out of place, but as he made it to the front he heard something or someone moving on the other side of the car. He couldn't tell what it was and didn't worry about it but asked the girl to shine the light under the hood. Everything seemed to be okay so he turned to go back to the side of the car but he heard another sound. He started to turn his head to the left and saw something move toward him. He didn't have enough time to be able to tell what was coming toward him before he felt a sharp pain at the back of his head, then everything went black. Stephen hit the ground while giving an awful sounding grunt and causing road dust and dirt to fly up. A man could be seen standing over him between the car's headlights with a large wrench in one hand.

One other man came from out of the dark and helped carry Stephen to his car and opened up the back door. They shoved him into the back seat and slammed the door shut. One of the men, the tallest and oldest, got into the driver's seat of Stephen's car. He told the others he would meet them where they agreed in one hour. Stephen was laying in the back seat of his own car with a throbbing bump to his head and unconscious.

A few moments later the throbbing became so bad it brought him back around. He struggled to pull his right arm out from under himself, and as he did this he let out a moan. He was feeling the car moving by now and realized someone else was driving but he wasn't sure if it was his car. He didn't know what happened and at this point was not remembering the girl that stopped him. He started rubbing the back of his head and brought his hand to where he could see it. Thank goodness, no blood. He just stayed there for a few moments trying to figure out what had just happened. All the alcohol he had consumed that night wasn't helping him to figure things out. He rose partially in the seat to try and see who was driving.

At the same time the man that was driving heard Stephen move and looked back at him. He pulled the car over to the side of the road, got out and opened the back door. He pulled at Stephen's legs until he could grab his shirt and got him out of the car and this time shoved him through the driver's door past the steering wheel into the passenger's seat. Then while the man got into the car he pulled a large gun from behind his back with his right hand. As he sat back down in the driver's seat he cocked the hammer and jammed it to Stephen's left temple.

Stephen barely got out "What's going on?" with a shaky voice.

The man pushed the gun into his temple more, then said, "What is going on is you are going to help me and my friends tonight." He brought the gun down and switched it to his left hand but kept it pointed at Stephen. He started the car and put it into gear and pulled back onto the road again.

"What do you mean?" Stephen was frightened but was trying not to show it. Thoughts of Elli and the girls immediately came to his mind. "Where did the others go?" Thinking they might be going to get the rest of his family.

"I'll ask the questions, you hear? Don't worry about the others; we'll meet them later. What I want to know is if you have the keys to your office tonight?"

"What for, what do you need that for?" Stephen knew what he wanted but could not contain the questions. As he started going down the road and talking, the driver laid the gun on his right leg but never took his hand off it. The end was always pointing at Stephen.

"Listen, we know who you are and what you do."

"How do you know all this? Who, who are you?" Stephen couldn't believe what he was hearing and what was going on. This guy did look sort of familiar, but between the alcohol and bump on his head he wasn't sure if it he was thinking straight.

"I know all this because we've been watching you and your buddy for the last several weeks." He began telling Stephen everything as if it didn't matter any more. "We have been following you from morning till night. We are going to that office of yours right now and making a collection."

At the same time the driver was talking, Stephen thought he heard something, a very small voice. He couldn't tell if it was real or just something in his head. It repeated the word "faith" several times. He figured it was from drinking too much that night.

The driver kept talking but Stephen broke in with, "Do you think we keep money at the office?"

"Well, what do you think I want, to steal the office plants, man?" He snarled at Stephen with this.

"I hate to ruin your plans." As he said this he vaguely remembered the name Adam being spoken during his abduction so he decided to use it as if it were the man's name. "I really hate to do this to you, Adam, but everything we do is either with checks or electronic transfers. That's it. We don't really have any reason to have cash there."

"How do you know my name, man?"

"I just heard the name somehow back there. Our office is a real estate office, we meet people there and take them out to the lots to show, but the transactions are completed at a bank or a number of other places. I'm afraid you and your friends have done a poor job of watching me."

Adam looked like his brain was on overload and his hard drive was about to crash. "You're sure there is nothing there?"

"I am the one in charge of most of the sales of the lots as you should know if you have been watching me," Stephen answered.

"We are still going there and you will have to prove it to me," he grumbled. "Do you have the key to get in?"

Stephen thought for a moment, and he didn't really know what to do. He finally answered, "Yes, I have it." Just then he heard another voice that sounded like it was coming from the back seat. This time it said, "Have faith" several times in soft tones. Stephen wanted to ask the driver if he heard the voice but he just sat there and waited until they turned into the office parking lot.

When they got into the office Adam forced Stephen to show him the safe. "If you don't keep money here, why do you have the safe?"

"We had it built in so if we ever took cash we would have it. But all we have in it now is papers, contracts and things like that but no money."

"Well." Adam was turning red in the face by now. He yelled, "Open it now!" Stephen was really getting nervous and he wondered what would happen when Adam saw that he was right. He wasn't worried about himself really. It was Elli, Christy and Kelly. If this gang has been watching him they probably knew all about his family and could probably get into the house and no telling what they might do in retaliation. While he was working the combination to the safe, Stephen heard that voice again. It was calming in a way and Stephen was hearing it more clearly now. The message was the same, "Have faith." He stopped for a second feeling a little more at peace. He finished turning the dial on the door of the safe and opened it showing Adam there wasn't money but just as he said, checks and other papers that would be worthless to him and the other two in the group.

"That kills that idea, doesn't it?" Adam looked at Stephen with a puzzled look but his gun was still pointed in Stephen's direction. "How much money do you have in your bank account?"

"Uh, I don't really know. Elli, I mean my wife, takes care of the family business." Stephen started thinking about all kinds of other things that could happen now.

"I know where your bank is," Adam said with a smile. "I've followed you and that pretty wife of yours when you go there. Do you have that ATM card?"

"I think I do, I usually carry it with me, but that won't get you what you want." Stephen was hoping his remarks would discourage him from carrying out his next plans.

"Well, it might not get me everything, but it will at least pay for some of the things I want."

They drove to the bank and Adam stayed in the background to avoid the cameras he knew were there. Stephen found there was little over five thousand dollars in the checking account. Adam wanted everything in their savings account, but Stephen convinced him this was impossible unless they could go into the bank and make a withdrawal from a teller, and it was too late for this.

After Stephen gave him the money Adam still looked worried. "I bet this was more than you thought you had in there. Are you sure this is all of it?"

"Yes, that is it," Stephen said softly.

"Then," Adam grabbed Stephen's arm and shoved him toward the car, "let's get back into the car and get going."

"Where are we going now? Are you going to let me go now? You can have the car, I'll just walk from here." Stephen didn't think this would work, but it was worth trying.

"No, we won't be letting you walk all that way home tonight. This cold, damp night air could be bad for you." Adam shoved Stephen back into the car through the driver's door again and pushed him all the way to the passenger seat. He jumped in and kept the gun looking at Stephen, slammed the door shut, started the car and took off across the parking lot and down the road back out toward the same direction they came from.

For some reason the air in the car was different now. Stephen couldn't explain it but he had never felt anything like it before. It was almost foggy inside the car but the sky and air were clear outside. About the time he started sensing the difference in the air he heard the voice again. The message this time was "I will take care of you." This was said only one time, but this one time filled Stephen with a sense that he and his family would be okay. He was no longer worried about anything or anyone. The power behind the voice had infiltrated his heart and he was no longer worried about anything or anyone. Stephen was wondering if Adam sensed the change in the air.

They were out of the city limits by now and traveling down those country roads that Stephen had traveled so many times in the last few months. His thoughts were going to his family and how things had been the last several months. He didn't want his life to end like this. Dan and Mr. Hemingway were probably safe in their homes right now. He wanted to ask Adam why they chose to do this with him, but it really didn't matter. The point is that it has happened and it was probably best if the others were not involved.

Stephen was pondering some of the things he had said to Elli the last few months to get her to let him take off on his venture. He had realized he was misusing God and what he knew about the Bible. At first he did think he could do both, serve God and work hard to make money for himself and his family. Then the money started to get more important and then he lost his Bible class and he just concentrated on making money. Everything started to make sense to him now. He would have given Adam every dollar he had if it would get him and his friends to let him go home to his wife and kids and know they were safe.

About thirty minutes later they pulled into a field just off a remote county gravel road through a grove of trees. By this time thick clouds had come in, so it was hard for Stephen to tell where they were. He thought they were somewhere close to Hemingway Meadows but he was not sure. He saw the other two and the car that was stopped by the side of the road earlier. They pulled up beside the other car and came to such a fast stop it caused a large cloud of dirt to roll up from below and behind the car. Adam looked at Stephen and waved his gun toward the passenger door as if to say get out. Stephen got out slowly and very steadily.

Adam got out on the driver's side and brought the gun up and over the roof of the car making sure he kept it looking at Stephen. "Let's go," he said nervously as he waved the gun toward his partners.

As they got closer to the others the girl asked anxiously, "How much did you get, Adam?"

"Shut up. You shouldn't call me by my name. He heard you earlier at the car." She gave him a very confused look. "I didn't get anything from the office. They don't keep money there. We went there and I had him open the safe to prove it."

At this time the other man seemed to come to life and blurted out, "What do you mean? We spent a lot of time on this and you promised we would make out big." The other man was shortest of the three, but Stephen could tell this guy had to spend a great deal of time in the gym working out. Adam was definitely the leader of the other two. They listened to everything he said closely.

"I know what I said, but that didn't work out. I did get a small consolation prize, however. We went to his bank and pulled everything out of his checking account. We'll have enough for a few days till we decide what to do next. We just have to carry out the last part of the plan."

The girl looked shocked. "Since the rest of the plan didn't work, why not just let him go?"

"You know we can't do that," Adam answered. "He knows what we look like and now he knows my first name. We have to get it done."

Stephen was standing there listening and knowing what they were talking about. He had been praying in his heart for the last several minutes. He was getting right with God because he knew what the end result of this night would be. The funny part was that after he got himself right he started praying for Elli and the girls, and it was as if God had him in His hands and was holding him even now while he was still on Earth. Stephen really was ready to die right there, but first he knew he had to do one more thing. At that moment he knew what he could do to make up for some of his past mistakes. He moved forward to the others and interrupted what they were saying and planning.

"I know what you are planning, and I know there is nothing I can do about it."

Adam shouted at him, "Shut up. We are going to take care of you in just a minute!"

"No, I won't shut up. I think you heard the voice in the car, didn't you?" Stephen had seen something in Adam's face when he said this.

"What voice are you talking about? Man, you're not just drunk, you're on drugs or something!"

"What does he mean?" asked the girl.

"Nothing," Adam said as he slung his left hand at Stephen.

"If you are about to take care of me in a few minutes, you might as well let me say what I'm going to say. What will it hurt then you can do whatever you want." At that time Stephen said the most important words of his life. Something came over him at that moment that gave him supernatural power. Words came to him that he hadn't thought about for months. He gave them the entire plan of God's salvation for every person of the world, but God was speaking directly to each of those three that night through Stephen. It only lasted about five minutes but it seemed like the longest hour Stephen ever spent. He told them of his mistakes and sins and how "God has and will forgive me for these through Jesus and because of what He had done for me on the cross and because of that I can forgive all of you for what you have done and are about to do tonight. You can gain forgiveness yourselves from God if you just ask Him for it."

All three were looking at the ground. Adam suddenly spoke up, "Okay, that's it, you've had your moment, and we need to get this done." He looked at the others as if to give a silent command. All three slowly aimed at a different place on Stephen's body. As the guns were lifted everything seemed to go into slow motion like in a movie. Stephen began to hear a high-pitch humming sensation in both ears. As he looked at his adversaries he noticed the same atmosphere that was in the car earlier. It was as if a blue cloud engulfed him, then he saw the faces of the others turning white with fear. Each of them dropped their guns and started backing up. There was a sound like wings fluttering around Stephen. He felt something almost feather like brush up against his face and arms. Stephen seemed to be held up by something invisible and he couldn't move from that spot. Suddenly all three of those so bent on doing harm to Stephen turned and ran to their car, got in and sped away from the field.

Stephen dropped to his knees in amazement in what he knew was a miracle. In shock more than anything he realized he had just been given a second chance. After some time he finally got up and made his way to the highway and began walking home. This was a remote area and it was late at night, but a man driving a red sports car soon pulled up just in front of Stephen. The driver rolled his window down and asked, "Are you lost, mister?"

A little paranoid and stunned by what just occurred Stephen answered,

"Well, no, not now, but I could use a ride back to town."

"I don't know what you mean, but I can get you back to town. Get in."

Still dazed, Stephen slowly walked around to the other side and got in. He managed to tell the driver where he lived, then sat back and pondered what he had experienced knowing his life would never be the same.

MUSICAL ILLUSIONS

"You shall not make for yourself an idol."
Ex. 20:4

Two

The beat was hard and drove the tempo of the harsh music right through the teenage crowd. This band was not just great it was *hot* and thousands were crammed in Millennium Stadium to see and hear the "new king" of rock and roll blast his songs out. Clint was in front of the largest concert audience of his life. It was a sold out night that broke all records for any concert in the country. The band was cranking out what the kids wanted to hear, making them wild and frantic. People were jumping and being tossed around on top of the crowd as if on waves on the ocean.

Maria and her three friends were front and center of the stage jumping up and down at the same time being pushed and pulled by the crowd. This was the first Clint Blackwood concert for all four girls, and they were loving it. Maria had been waiting for a whole year for this one night and she was going to get everything she could out of it. Being a typical fifteen-year-old, Maria was so excited about the concert she couldn't sleep the night before. She even got up early and spent half the day on the phone to all her friends and the other half getting ready for the night of rocking excitement. She had turned her room into a Clint Blackwood Hall of Fame with posters, photos, lyrics of music on posters and most of all his music blaring from the speakers of her stereo. Maria knew everything you would ever want to know about the rock star. To bring it all down to a bottom line, Maria idolized Clint Blackwood, and she was not alone. There were millions of other teenage girls doing the same all over the world. He was an international singer with record sales soaring higher than the Beatles and Elvis, the King himself. That is why he was being tagged as the "new king" of rock and roll.

Clint Blackwood had only been on the rock-and-roll scene for two short years, but he was able to get himself on the fast track to success with his style and willingness to do almost anything on stage to sell his songs and concerts. His parents were products of the 60s and he grew up with their generation's music and loved it. Clint was strumming an electric guitar and beating a set of drums by the time he was three years old. He was playing Iron Butterfly's "In-A-Godda-Da-Vida" perfectly on drums by the time he was five and attempting his own rendition of a heavy metal national anthem in the tradition of Jimmy Hendrix on the electric guitar. His heroes were people like Eric Clapton, Elvis Presley and Mick Jagger. His parents and all their friends loved this and encouraged Clint to go as far as he could. He was getting as famous for his "showmanship" as he was for his music. It had gotten to the point that one helped promote the other. If you asked most of Clint's fans what they liked best about his concerts, they would always say they couldn't make up their minds. The music wouldn't be the same without the action, and the action wouldn't be the same without the music. He was reaching millions of kids with his musical message, but was it the right message?

The concert had been going for an hour and Maria was feeling the heat and adrenaline of the crowd. It was as if every individual in the audience came together to become one living organism. The heat was rising from all the excited bodies jumping and screaming. They all breathed and moved together to the rhythm of the music and singing. Maria noticed the smoke all around her and the other different kids while they were passing out cigarettes. She had never experienced anything like this and she was getting caught up in the moment. At different times throughout the concert a group of kids on one side of the hall would pick a person up and start pushing them over their heads. Sometimes the kids on top would be pushed the entire width of the hall.

Toward the end Clint picked up the tempo and volume of the show. There was a beautiful black grand piano center stage that was being played all night. Clint ran around the front of the stage several times with a sledgehammer swinging it wildly above his head. On the last time around he ran to the piano and started swinging it. He kept on till the legs had broken down, the main body and top were smashed and the only part still in tact was the steel frame. After all this he walked to the edge of the stage and shook his whole body causing everyone in that area of the audience to be showered with all the sweat that was pouring from his body. This caused all the people on the front row to hit the stage. Some of them passed out and others pushed back causing fights to break out. Guards from back stage came out and brought the crowd under control and carried the hurt people to where they could get help.

In the middle of the concert Clint did a tribute to the rock-and-roll stars from the past. He would run off stage and come back in a few short minutes in a high collar costume similar to something Elvis Presley would have worn. Stagehands had set up racks with costumes that were like the ones worn by other rock and roll groups of the sixties and seventies. He started singing and moving as Elvis, then he would run to a rack and change into another costume symbolizing another singer and would go into their songs. The kids loved it and became even more excited. When he finished the last song Clint took a deep bow as to say thank you to the kids and ran off stage while his band kept playing.

Maria, exhausted but more excited than ever, began looking around and saw how she could make her way to a door that was partially opened that went back stage. She could see light coming through it to the hall. She knew she would have to move fast but thought she could make it to the door and back stage. Ducking and hoping no one else in the crowd would get the same idea, she moved quickly toward the cracked door. She had to push some people out of the way but did make it to the door and was able to squeeze through without opening it any more. Back stage was like another world. The lights were brighter than out in the music hall causing her to squint until her eyes became accustomed to the difference. It was chaos with people trying to get ready to tear down all the equipment and load it on the band's truck so they can move to the next city. Maria was able to move around without anyone noticing her while she looked for Clint.

By staying close to the wall she could sneak around easily. After sticking her head inside three rooms hoping Clint would be in one, she was about to try a forth when she felt someone grab her left arm and made her stop. She turned to see a very large black man with long braided hair in a black t-shirt and jeans. He bent over and said, "You aren't on the crew. Who are you and what are you doing here? How did you get back here?"

Maria looked up at this intimidating person and sheepishly replied, "Looking for Clint Blackwood. I was hoping to see him and ask for his autograph."

"Well," the man's grip on her arm loosened and the tone of his voice became more congenial, "sorry, but you'll have to go back outside. Clint is gone. He leaves as soon as the concert is over. Let's go." He escorted her over to the same door she came in and gently shoved her out and shut the door.

Back out on stage the band had stopped playing and the lights were starting to come back up. Maria made her way back over to her friends that were looking for her. She told them about where she had been and how she almost got to see Clint. She didn't really believe Clint had left, but she couldn't do anything about it. All her friends couldn't believe she would go back there, and she was suddenly lifted up to hero status.

All four of them made their way through the trash that was strung all over the arena to meet Maria's mother. They had a place to meet her in the parking lot so she could take them all home. They were all going full speed emotionally because of the entire evening and didn't notice the kids in the hallway still on stretchers being attended to by paramedics.

Once they met Maria's mother and were safely in the car, all four girls seemed to talk all at the same time. Maria's mother couldn't see how they could understand each other, but she also remembered how she was at the same age. The next day was Saturday and Maria spent half the day sleeping and the other half on the phone again to her friends going over the events of the night before. Her father came into her room early in the evening and told her it was time to come into the dining room for super. When he opened the door to her room she was on her phone talking to a friend, but when she heard her dad's voice she went through a personality transformation.

She looked up at him and said, "Dad, I'm not hungry. I'll be okay. Can't I eat later? I'm on the phone, why do I need to eat with you guys now?"

"Just hang the phone up and come on down. We are waiting on you. Don't wait, just hang up and come down now, young lady." As he was walking out of the door he said, "Your concert is over and we need to get back to some kind of normalcy around here."

Her dad, Bill, really didn't care for her room and he fought the idea of all the Blackwood stuff all over it but Alice, his wife, was able to convince him to give it some time and let Maria have a little freedom. Alice told him to think about what he was like at Maria's age but finally just had to tell him to keep his mouth shut on this for a while, and he did.

The following weeks around the house appeared to be pretty calm and peaceful on the surface. Maria was an only child and had always been active doing a lot of outdoor activities. Being the only child and having a dad that loved to go camping, hiking and fishing, the whole family would usually be drafted to go on weekend trips as well as on long camping vacations. When she was a little girl, she liked going on these trips and became a pretty good camper and outdoorsman. Since she became interested in rock and roll and more specifically, Clint Blackwood, her interests were starting to change.

The next time they were scheduled to go on a weekend camping trip and it was time to start packing, Maria asked if she could spend the weekend with a friend instead of going with her parents. They were taken back by this and sat down to talk this through. They decided she was growing up and it might be a good idea for her to spend the weekend with a friend. After all she was developing her interests and deserved time to herself and with other friends. The friend Maria wanted to spend the night with was Liz and was one of the three she went to the Blackwood concert with. Alice said that since she and Bill didn't know Liz's mother, she would call and get a feel for her and talk to her about Maria staying for the weekend. Bill reluctantly gave in and they dropped Maria off at Liz's house on their way out of town. They weren't out of the city limits when they looked at each other and exclaimed at the same time, "What did we just do?"

That Sunday afternoon Bill and Alice left camp early and broke all speed limits to pick Maria up. Of course they didn't act as if they were concerned about anything when they arrived, but they were very nervous but relieved when they found she was okay. That evening around the dinner table all three discussed the weekend by taking turns telling what they did. Alice and Bill did a little embellishment in order to hide their boring weekend. When it was Maria's turn to share how her weekend was, she just said, "It was okay, we didn't really do much." The parents felt like there was more to her weekend than this but didn't think it would be a good idea to push it. They all finished dinner and basically went their own way with Maria going straight to her room. While in her room Maria would listen to her Clint Blackwood collection of CDs on her stereo while reading an article on Blackwood in the latest issue of *Rolling Stone*. Her parents watched a *Star Wars* movie on TV, not wanting to push in on Maria's turf. They figured she needed her space, so they let her have it.

That next week at school Maria started showing some strange behavior. Several of her teachers noticed she was not paying attention in class and not having assignments completed on time. They became concerned quickly because Maria was a good student. She always completed her work with good grades. Her attitude had always been positive and even enthusiastic about learning. Her math teacher, Mr. Albertson, decided to call Maria's parents and let them know of this development. Their conversation went okay, until Alice started to cry some.

Nothing was said about the phone call that night until after dinner. Maria went up to her room right away for her usual rock-and-roll session. That night she listened to other CDs besides Blackwood. Bill was in the living room looking at that day's newspaper. He was not really reading, just going through the motions. Alice came in after washing the evening meal dishes and sat down next to him on the coach. She started talking. "Bill, I think we have a real problem here with Maria."

Bill came back with, "I think I agree with you for the first time in quite a while, Alice."

They looked at each other as Alice continued, "What are we going to do about it?"

Bill thought for a second then said, "I didn't want her to go to that Blackwood concert, but you overrode me on that one just like you did this past weekend. I noticed a big change in her the very next day. I never thought Maria would sneak back stage like she did that night. Her attitude is what concerns me the most. Do you think she is on drugs?"

Alice got sort of a sick look on her face as he said that last sentence. "I hope not. I don't think she is, surely she wouldn't try anything like drugs. I don't know, Bill. What do you think?"

Bill was feeling the same and said, "I don't know, but I do think we need to find out somehow. I'm going to go up and talk to her right now and find out just what is going on with our daughter." As usual Alice attempted to calm Bill down, but it didn't work this time. He told her she could come up with him or stay downstairs, but he was going to go to Maria's room and talk to her.

As he went to Maria's room he first knocked on the door but there was no response. The hard rock-and-roll sounds and drum beats seemed to make the door vibrate. He tried opening the door but it was locked so he knocked louder with no answer. He finally started to beat on the door and yelled, "Maria!" Still no answer, so he unlocked the door with a small tool he always kept above the door. When he got the door unlocked and opened, he found Maria in the middle of her bed with her phone to her ear along with the music blaring. He ran over to the stereo and punched the off button. The silence came so suddenly Bill thought he saw the walls relax and sag with relief. Maria just looked at him but kept on talking on the phone. Bill told her, "Stop talking and hang up immediately."

"Liz, my dad is here and I need to hang up. See you tomorrow."

Her dad sat on the edge of the bed looking into Maria's eyes and asked her, "What are you doing in here? I mean what is really going on here, Maria?"

"I'm talking to my friends and listening to music, Dad. What's wrong with that?" she replied. "What do you think is going on?"

"I don't know, but whatever it is I don't like it." Bill went on, "I've noticed a big change in you ever since you started listening to this Blackdeck's music."

"Dad," Maria moaned. "It's Blackwood, Clint Blackwood. Why do you do that all the time?"

He paused for a moment to collect his thoughts then continued. "Okay, I don't care what his name is, I don't like what is going on. I want it to stop."

Maria countered with, "Look, I'm not taking drugs, Dad, and I'm not having sex with anybody. All I'm doing is listening to music that I really like. What's wrong with that?"

"Maria, look around you and tell me if this is normal." They both looked around the room and at the same time Maria's mother walked in the room.

"What's going on?" Alice asked.

Bill started, "We are discussing what is going on in this room and I want it stopped, Alice. I want all the Blackwood stuff off the walls and I don't want my daughter dressing like this anymore and listening to this garbage she calls music. I also don't want her to talk to these people she calls her friends."

"Then who will I talk with and do things with, Dad?" Maria was yelling by now.

Alice tried to sort this out and make peace between the two, but they went at it for another hour. Finally there was a compromise struck with Bill winning on all the Blackwood posters coming down but one that Maria could leave on the wall. She could ware some black clothes but had to mix them with other colors and she would be limited on time on the phone with her friends. Maria was not happy but she agreed to everything mainly because her parents presented a united front and she saw she didn't have a choice. If she kept fighting them they might take everything away from her. One more thing that was part of the agreement was that Maria had to bring her grades up by at least one point by the end of that quarter.

After they left Maria, Bill and Alice went down the hall to their room and talked. "What do you think about all this, Alice?" Bill looked stumped.

"Bill, just think about how you were at fifteen. Don't you remember how you were?"

Bill didn't give up. "Alice, what's going on here is Maria almost worshiping this guy and his junk they call music. I have liked music and listened to rock and other types of music but never got into it like Maria. It's not healthy for her to go so far with this. You know when she went back stage at that concert was not like her, she never did anything as bold as that before."

Alice had been debating about telling Bill about a friend of hers who had been talking to her about problems like this. Elisa was giving Alice information on today's rock and roll stars and also giving her pamphlets that talk about church, God and the Bible. Some of them had gotten Alice's attention specially when it came to problems with raising teenagers. She was hesitant to tell Bill because he was always opposed to organized religion and never would listen to anyone who tried talking to him about it. Maybe this was the right time. Elisa had invited Alice and Bill to her church for anytime they might want to come. She had been telling Alice how free she is now that she had her life going right with God. Alice could see something new in Elisa.

"Bill, a friend of mine at work has been talking about things like what we are going through tonight. She has given me some brochures on this and other problems that we are going through." She had gone over to her purse, turned back around to Bill and handed several of the brochures to him. He reluctantly took them from her hand.

After looking at the front page of several of them he glumly said, "Oh, these are about church and God."

"That's right, they are about those things. Elisa has talked to me about Maria and what she is going through. Not sure how you'll take this, but one problem is with you and me."

Bill looked at her with astonishment. "What do you mean by that, Alice? Look at what has just happened in Maria's bedroom. I took the initiative to get her to agree to the changes we just made. So what is wrong with me and you?"

"Bill, I know you have been concerned about Maria. You are a good father, nothing is wrong with you or me when it comes to our love for her and each other. The problem, Bill, that Elisa keeps telling me is that we are leaving an important element out. She says Jesus is the answer. I'm not sure what she means yet, but maybe she has something here."

Bill thought for a moment and then exclaimed, "We go to church, don't we, and we pray sometimes before we eat and we even read the Bible sometimes. So what does Jesus have to do with this?"

"Calm down, Bill. At first Elisa was sort of getting on my nerves, but the more I listened to her and watched her the more I wanted to know about all this. I've been reading these tracts and some of the verses from my Bible. I don't have all the answers, Bill. I just think there might be something to all this and we should take it seriously."

"Okay, Alice, if we look into this what would be the first order of business?"

"Well, you need to read all these tracts and think about what they are saying. I'm not sure how you'll take this, but we need to go to Elisa's church this Sunday. I know we go to a church sometimes, but our church is not what we need. We need to hear something else and we all need to go."

Bill looked around and gave the tracts an over view again. "Okay, I'll go one time and we will see what they have to say."

Alice gave him a hug and a kiss on the cheek then whispered in his ear, "It will be okay, it will be okay. Thank you."

On her way back to the kitchen she noticed Maria's door was partially open and the light was on. She slowly pushed the door open to walk in and give Maria a hug and tell her how she loved her as some positive reinforcement. When she walked in the room Maria wasn't there. Alice didn't think anything about it and she walked back and went to the kitchen. Maria might have gone some place else in the house, bathroom or even outside. After about ten minutes Alice went back to Maria's room and she was not there. Alice checked the bathroom and no one was there. She yelled for Bill and he came from the master bedroom.

"Bill, have you seen Maria?"

"No," Bill replied. "I've been reading these papers you gave me. What do you mean?"

"Maria isn't in her room and I can't find her anywhere." By now Alice was on edge.

They both went into Maria's room and noticed an envelope on her bed that Alice overlooked the last time she was there. Bill picked it up. Maria had written "Dad and Mom" on the front of it. It was sealed so Bill tore it opened. As he read the note that was inside tears started forming in his eyes with a stream starting to fall from his right.

"What does it say, Bill?" Alice was getting anxious and already crying.

"Maria has run off. Here, read it."

Alice read the note and grabbed Bill and buried her face in his right shoulder. Finally they both started thinking a little clearer and Bill managed, "She shouldn't be too far from here. We ought to be able to find her. Let's get in the car and drive around."

"Shouldn't we call the police first?"

"No, not yet, let's try to keep them out of it." Bill was reassuring to Alice, so they both got in their car and drove around the neighborhood. They were both working to hold back what they felt about the idea of losing their only child. They didn't find her on the first go around, so Bill decided to expand their search and they should split up. They both had a car and a cell phone and could cover more territory this way. They took off and went for a couple of hours. Their town wasn't very large and they should have been able to find her easy enough. Three hours had passed with no luck. Alice had called Bill earlier and they came up with a pretty good plan. She went to check all the places she knew Maria hung out at with her friends. Bill would go to the bus depot and several places around town she might be attracted to.

The bus stop was the last place Bill went. This was not really a true bus stop, just a counter inside a convenient store with a few gas pumps in front. There were a few benches in the front close to the counter that had an older man behind it that sold tickets and answered questions. Bill walked in nervously shaking and looked around. He saw the back of a small figure go behind a display. "Maria? Maria?" He walked over to the display and went behind it. Maria was standing there as if she was a little girl, playing hide and seek.

"Maria, what are you doing?" Bill asked with relief and a little anger.

Maria couldn't look up at her father but did say, "I'm leaving like my note said."

"Oh no you're not, Maria. You are coming home right now."

"But I already bought my ticket and the bus will be here anytime." She was holding the ticket up in the air, so Bill took it from her hand and went up to the counter and proceeded to threaten to call the police on the man for selling a bus ticket to a minor unless he was given a full refund. Bill called Alice to let her know he found Maria and they would be home immediately. Maria balked a little but left with him. She sat in the front seat next to her dad, but neither said a word all the way home.

When they arrived home Alice was already there. When Maria walked in from the garage Alice grabbed her and gave her a tight hug. No one yelled, they just sat down on the couch with Maria between Alice and Bill.

Alice went first. "Why did you do this, Maria?"

"Didn't you read my note?" Maria asked.

"Yes, but that didn't really say why you were running away, it just told us where you were going. In a way I guess it did because you said you were going to find this Clint Blackwood. You didn't think we understood you anymore, but you knew Clint would and that he would know what to do for you. Maria, your note scared us."

Maria was mostly looking down at the floor then finally said, "Well, you should listen to his music. The lyrics really speak to me. He really cares for all people, even kids. He says he has the answers to all our problems and questions."

Bill interrupted her, "Is that what his songs are saying? That's strange, I can never understand a word he is yelling. I mean singing. I'll tell you now, young lady, that you will never do this again. I won't have it. I have never heard of anything like this."

Alice stretched her arm out to Bill and placed her hand over his mouth. "Bill, wait, don't yell. Let's just discuss this and try to get to the bottom of it all." She turned toward Maria. "Maria, what do you mean about Clint's lyrics? I've listened to his music and I don't get that from the words."

Bill got up and went to Maria's room and found several of Blackwood's CDs and brought them into the living room. He opened them up and pulled the papers out that had all the lyrics of the songs on them. He started reading them and was pretty surprised about what they contained. He handed the first one to Alice then opened another and read the lyrics. Maria kept defending Clint, his lyrics and the music, but she finally gave up and told her parents she was going to bed.

A few minutes after she left the room Alice went and checked on her then came back and read more lyrics. They found explicit reference to sex and drugs. At first they were worried Maria might have been involved with drugs but ruled it out because she never showed signs of it. Maria told them she picked up on the lyrics that talked about love and visions Clint had of God where he was given special insights to truth and wisdom. He was using the music as a way of reaching people with what he believed to be God's message for the world. In other lyrics he was conveying how God told him to tell the young people of his vision because the adults were already lost and without hope.

Then Alice was going through Maria's bag and found a brochure that talked about the retreat Clint Blackwood had built in Colorado. It was open for anyone to come to and "find peace and truth" as the writer put it. They were both convinced now this guy was setting up a worldwide new age cult and he was able to reach millions of kids through his music.

After going through all the CDs that evening both Alice and Bill were convinced this guy was crazy and they had made a lot of mistakes by letting her listen to this stuff. Alice was waiting for Bill to remind her that he was opposed to this guy from the beginning but she wouldn't listen to him.

She was stunned when Bill looked up at her from the floor where he had been reading lyrics for the last hour and said, "Alice, our daughter has been deceived by this Clint Blackwood and we are at least partly to blame. We never read these lyrics. Where have we been, and why did we let our daughter get so involved with this?"

Alice had been trying to hold back her tears all evening and finally let them go, and with these tears streaming down her face she confessed to thinking this was all innocent and was to blame. She didn't think any lyrics could be as bad as they were when they were both teenagers. With the Viet Nam war going on during that time, all the songs were of rebellion, full of drug and sex related stuff. This was an eye opener to her. "I guess times do change and we have not kept up with them."

Bill reached out and took her right hand and said, "Maybe we need to start thinking about some of the things in those tracts you showed me today. Maybe we need to go to that church Elisa goes too. I am not sure if I buy everything in those things or even the Bible, but we need help. I've got a lot of questions and no answers." Alice was thrilled, she was like Bill because she didn't have a lot of answers, mostly questions. She was just grateful they didn't lose their daughter, and maybe this was a wake up call for Bill like it was for her. Alice and Bill walked toward the bedroom and spent the rest of the night in each other's arms with all sorts of mixed thoughts and feelings traveling in their heads.

The next morning Alice woke up first and remembered Bill deciding to go to church. She woke Bill up and went down the hall to wake Maria so she could get ready. Maria told her she didn't have to go to church, that she had her head on right and knew what she wanted. She proceeded, "If Dad hadn't found me last night, I would be on my way to Clint's right now. He has the answers to all my questions. No one at this church you want to go to will know anything, they never do."

By now Bill was up but not quite awake as he walked slowly in Maria's room. "Good morning, Maria, are you giving your mother some problems here? She and I decided last night we all need to go to this church that her friend at work told her about. We will all go and that settles it." With that he turned and left expecting everything to be okay. Maria just sat on her bed and let her mother choose a dress for her to wear that morning. Alice left the room after telling Maria that she had fifteen minutes to get ready and to come to the kitchen for breakfast. Maria gave them the silent treatment all through breakfast and during the drive to the church.

Elisa was in the foyer of the church visiting with some friends when she saw Alice and her family walk in. She went up to them with a smile and her arms open to Alice and they hugged briefly. Bill noticed a very worn Bible under Elisa's left arm. "I am so glad you could come, Alice. This has to be Bill and Maria?"

"Yes it is. I gave those tracts to Bill to read and we had a small incident come up last night that made us decide to come today."

They all walked into the sanctuary together finding Elisa's husband, Albert, and their kids, then got ready for this new experience. As the service started, Bill looked at Alice as if he was very confused and really didn't want to be there, but he told her they needed to at least try it. At this point he was there for Maria more than anything. Maria just sat there for the hour and didn't really hear anything the preacher said. She had her mind made up and to her all this was just a temporary setback. She would stick it out until the next time she had a chance, then she would go to Clint.

After church Elisa invited the whole family over to her house for dinner. After an awkward acceptance they all ended up at Elisa's home for the afternoon. Of course the conversation around the dinner table was on the sermon. Albert brought it up in a casual sort of way. Of course Bill brought up some of his doubts and even fears concerning belief in God and the Bible. He and Alice always considered themselves as pretty intelligent people and always thought Christianity was for the weaker types.

Maria was taking in all this and even spoke up at one point and asked her mom and dad, "If you don't believe any of this then what are we doing here?" That was the turning point of the afternoon for Bill and Alice.

Albert saw an opportunity and jumped in with, "You know, Bill, the bottom line of all this is God knows you and he knows what your fears and questions are. He can cut through all those things. He is not about rules and rituals; He is about love and providing a way for us to reach Him through Jesus. Without the sacrifice God made by giving up His Son, Jesus, it was the greatest act of love that has ever been performed. Bill, you only have one daughter. I know you love her, but how much do you love her?"

"A lot, well, I would give my life for her."

That is the type of answer Albert was hoping for. "I knew that, Bill, and do you realize God feels the same way about you? You are the only Bill Baker that God has. Don't you see God gave his own life for you when Jesus died on the cross for you? I don't pretend to know all the answers but I do know this is a free gift from God. He is offering you the ultimate gift of forgiveness and entry into His Heaven when the time comes. He is tugging at your heart right now. Bill, I don't believe it was no accident for you guys to be here today. "

With those words Bill's face turned pale and he felt something inside that he had never felt before. It was as if God was calling him. He asked to be excused from the table and made his way to the bathroom to get himself back together. It was a last ditch effort by Bill's ego to maintain control. While in the bathroom he looked in the mirror and what he saw completed the task. He saw a man that was struggling all for the wrong reasons. Bill walked out of that small room, looked at Alice and told her they needed to "get it right" and asked Albert what they had to do. Alice knew this was right because she was feeling the same way. They both begged Maria and hoped she would feel the same way, but she just sat there and refused to give up what she felt was the truth. With tears coming down their faces, Bill and Alice listened while Albert shared the same message of salvation. Bill and Alice bowed their heads along with Elisa and Albert. They both asked Jesus to come into their hearts and take their lives over so they could live for Him forever. Bill and Alice walked out of that home new people. They knew with the true God they could work things out with Maria.

The next several weeks were good, exciting and disappointing all at the same time. The believers at Elisa's church opened themselves for Bill and Alice. They took a class for new Christians and decided to be baptized there. This was a time of real spiritual growth for both Bill and Alice that also brought them closer together than ever. Maria went along with everything. She followed through with the agreement with her parents. She cleaned up her room, changed how she dressed and didn't call the same friends from home anymore. She still saw them at school and called from other places. She would sneak into the extra room late at night where the family had a computer with Internet access and go to Clint Blackwood's Web site, then to his chat room. There she would talk to other teens in the same situation with parents that were restricting them on how much of Clint they could be exposed to. Occasionally Clint himself would get onto the chat room after a concert while traveling and relaxing on his private bus. He would encourage the kids going through what they felt was a tough time in their lives. Sometimes he brought God into the conversation and reminded them that he had a special word from the god that spoke to him. He was enlightened and they just needed to continue to be patient and get what they could of his music and words. He would then mention his Freedom Compound, as it came to be known, and invited any of them to come whenever they could. He was careful about what he said about parents using subtle comments that could lead to undermining authority.

All this helped Maria survive the next several weeks of her parents insisting on her going to church, small Bible studies for kids her age and even reading the Bible together as a family. She went through the steps and acted out what her parents wanted to see but inside she was the same person as she was before.

Maria kept the act up and wasn't caught until one night when her mother had to get up in the middle of the night. She couldn't sleep and was on her way to the kitchen to get a glass of milk. As she passed the computer room, as they called it, she noticed more light than usual coming from under the door. As she pushed the door open and went in, she saw Maria intensely typing away. She didn't even notice Alice coming into the room. Alice quietly walked up to Maria and asked, "What are you doing up so late, Maria? What are you doing on the computer?"

Maria, realizing she was caught, quickly stopped typing and moved the cursor on the screen up to the corner where she could exit off the site and off the Internet. Before she was able to get completely off Alice saw part of the page title "Clint." "I just couldn't sleep," Maria stuttered. "Just got onto the Web for a while to look around."

Alice knew something was up and she said, "I saw the word Clint. Were you on a site about Clint Blackwood?"

"No, Mom, I wasn't on a site from Clint Blackwood. I wouldn't do that."

"Young lady, you need to get back to bed right now." Alice knew something was wrong, but it was too late and not the right time to do anything about it.

The next day Alice had Bill check the computer and found Maria had been going to the Blackwood Web site for some weeks. They never thought about checking this area of the computer because they thought everything was going well with Maria. She was doing everything they asked of her and they had trusted her. That evening, after Bill had come home from work, he and Alice confronted Maria about what they found. A heated argument followed with Maria saying a lot of awful things about her parents. She was tired of having to read the Bible and going to church. She said the only reason they were going to church and saying they "had Jesus" in their lives was to get her away from Clint. This went on for a couple of hours until Bill finally told Maria to go to her room and to bed. They took all her computer privileges away from her and would deal more with her the next day. He and Alice prayed for their daughter most of the night but Maria had other plans.

It was about 2:30 the very next morning after the big argument. Maria got up and packed a bag she got down from her closet. She quietly snuck out of the house without leaving a note this time. She walked several blocks to a friend's house. The friend came to the door half asleep, and when she realized who was at the door she let Maria in. Sandra was a big Blackwood fan also and believed in what he taught. She also knew about Freedom Compound and got onto the chat room a lot and spoke about going there some day. Maria told her, "I'm going to Freedom. I have had it with my parents and want to go where I can do what I want to do."

Sandra asked her, "How will you get there?"

"I've been saving and asking some other friends for help. I have enough money to get out to Colorado by bus. All I need is for you to take me to the bus stop tonight. I found out the schedule and there will be a bus leaving in about an hour. All I need you to do is take me so I can get out before my parents realize I'm gone." Sandra was sort of taken back. It was one thing to talk about doing something like this, but to actually do it was different. She was admiring Maria for stepping out, but at the same time Maria was only fifteen. Sandra was eighteen herself and didn't have her act completely together. Maria asked Sandra to come with her, but she refused. Finally Sandra agreed to take her to the bus stop. She made sure Maria got onto the bus and then went home.

That morning Bill got up early and was in the shower when Alice came in and banged on the shower door. "What is it? What's wrong, Alice?" He stepped out with a towel wrapped around his middle.

"Maria is gone again. I went into her room to make sure she was up and getting ready for school and she's gone. I checked all over the house and she's not here. I know she is gone. What are we going to do, Bill?" Alice was crying as she fell into Bill's arms.

"We will look for her like last time. We'll find her. We have to trust God will protect her and help us. Do you know how long she has been gone?"

Alice fought back tears. "No, no telling this time."

Bill thought for a moment and said, "Let me get dressed and we will find her."

Experience taught them it would be best to split up so they could cover more territory quicker. At the end of the day they came up empty handed. They were both in the living room exhausted and anxious about Maria when the doorbell rang. Bill found Sandra standing on the front porch. He didn't know who she was and asked if he could help her. She replied that she was a friend of Maria's and needed to talk. After letting her in. Bill grabbed her by the arm and rushed her into the living room. "Alice, this is Sandra." He looked at her and asked, "Do you know where she is?"

Sandra looked at both of them and, holding back emotional tears, began, "I know where she is going. I've been thinking about all this and finally decided you needed to know."

Alice interrupted her, "Do you know where she is? What happened?"

Sandra began again. "She came to where I live early this morning. She asked me to take her to the bus stop so she could catch a bus that was going to Colorado. She is going to Freedom Compound."

"What is Freedom Compound?" Alice asked.

"It is a place Clint Blackwood built for anyone that wants to come and search for truth. It's really a great place and Maria will be safe there. I took her to the bus stop and made sure she got on before I left."

Bill broke in. "She is only fifteen, why did you think you had the right to do this? You should have called us and kept Maria with you until we could have gotten there to get her. You are in trouble for this. Not sure what we can do, but we'll do something about this. So you are telling us Maria is now on a bus traveling to some place in Colorado that promises her everything she wants in life. This is a Utopia for anyone?"

"Well," Sandra swallowed hard, "yes, she is going there right now."

Bill left the room and came back in a few minutes with a map of Colorado. "Do you know exactly where this Freedom Compound is in Colorado, Sandra?"

"Well, I think it's close to Aspen or Ft. Collins. Not sure really, but you have a computer, don't you?"

Alice and Bill both said, "Yes."

They took her to the computer and Sandra looked up Clint Blackwood's Web site and found the town where the compound was close to. "What do you think you'll do now?" Sandra asked.

"Don't know," Bill replied.

"Go get her," Alice said.

"Yes," Bill agreed, "we'll go get her, but if we do, will she run off again?"

After Sandra left they sat down and prayed for guidance only a great God could give. This is something they wouldn't have even thought about just a few weeks earlier. This was the beginning of a long adventure that would take them to many highs and lows. It would teach them to trust the Lord even when the odds looked to be against them. Alice and Bill prayed for Maria and each other before embarking on a path that would teach them of God's greatest love for them all.

FUTURE ATTITUDES

"You shall not take the name of the Lord your God in vain."
Ex. 20:7

Three

The airways were really busy with people trying to get to work, parents getting their kids to school and thousands of others going to as many other destinations. When the weather is bad like this the airway department usually issues a travel warning and the air speed limit is reduced, but they haven't done it yet. The storm came up suddenly without warning. The clouds were darker than Carson had ever seen in his life. He was alone and trying to watch the traffic around him and the clouds at the same time, but then a big black bird, a crow maybe, came up in front of him and he had to maneuver his autowing to miss it.

"Oh my god! Get out of my way. How did that get through the tunnel field anyway?" Carson yelled this as he swerved the steering gear to the left and down just in time to get in front of a large truckwing that swerved upward to miss Carson. When the truckwing rear-ended an airbus loaded with kids going to school. This caused the driver of the airbus to collide with the skysport that was in front of him which in turn swerved to the left and went into the airway side rail causing major damage and several other auto-wings to pile up on the airway. Carson just sat on the side hovering and watching from his '76 Chevy Auto-wing. He couldn't believe his eyes with all the stuff he just saw. "Oh my god," he said softly to himself. "I better get out of here and get to work."

As he pulled back up to the main flight stream for wing vehicles, the storm hit with ultra high winds and rain that seemed to blow down from the clouds. "Oh my god, would you look at it rain." He had never seen a storm like this one before. He turned on his lights like everybody else. He turned his radio on and heard the air report on the wreck. "The cause of the airway accident that occurred on air-highway 869 South just 5 air miles east of the main intersection of Air Hydraulic appears to have been caused by a single, red 2176 Chevy Autowing. The driver is unknown and he fled from the scene. No one was able to get any identification marks, so the person causing one of the worst accidents in the greater Chicago auto-airways history appears to have gotten away." He turned the radio off so he wouldn't have to hear anymore. He couldn't believe it all started with a bird flying in front of him. Somehow the bird got through the electrical field that formed a tunnel for the flying transports. Fortunately the electric tunnel field kept the rain out, but it got dark enough for the tunnel lights to come on.

When he finally got to work he pulled into the parking building and taxied into his designated space. Everyone in the office was talking about two things, the storm and the big airway accident. Carson quietly made his way to his cubicle on the 89th floor of the Davis Worldwide Internet, Inc. headquarters. When he checked his e-mail there were over three hundred messages for him. "Oh my god, what's all this about," he said in a low voice.

"Hey Carson," he heard a voice come over the back wall of his cubicle. "What's going on, Carson?" The voice belonged to Ray Collins, an accountant for the company.

Carson looked over the wall at Ray. "Oh, nothing much. You know the same old thing. Get up in the morning and fight the airway traffic all the way to work. The only thing is I've got all these e-mail messages that will take all morning to return. Think I'll just delete them all and say I never got them."

Ray said, "Sounds like a good idea to me, better time management. That will really help our company keep ahead of the competition."

Carson sat back at his desk and took up his next business priority. He called his girlfriend, May Wills, in the advertising department. "Are we still on for lunch as usual?"

May answered, "Carson, you called at a bad time. I'm late for a meeting. I'll meet you at the entrance. See you then. Bye."

He worked through the morning and went to the company cafeteria down on the 80th floor. The company had a cafeteria for every ten floors in the one hundred story headquarters. He and May made it through the line and sat down by an outside window where the view of the city was breathtaking. They talked about the last weekend when they went to the Greater Chicago Jazz Festival. They also started planning their next weekend trip up to Toronto for the Winter Ice Festival. Before they parted to their respective cubicles they confirmed the dinner date for that evening. When he got back to his cubicle after lunch there was a message from his boss on his voice mail. He was being called to discuss a certain file of his. "Oh my god, I hate that file. It has been a headache for me from the first day I started this job." He pulled the file and made it down the hallway to his boss' office.

He came back to his desk, exhausted after two hours of trying to answer the boss' questions about this stupid file. There were more messages on his phone and the icon on his computer screen that warned him of e-mails was flashing red and meant an overload. "Oh my god, what am I going to do? Guess I'll do the old, 'I never got that message' routine again."

About 4:00 Ray yelled over the wall to Carson, "Have you heard about that tornado that came to the edge of the city this afternoon?"

Carson yelled back, "No, I didn't. What happened?"

"It came down out of that same dark cloud system that brought all the rain this morning. Dropped down right at the edge of the city and just stayed there in one spot. The news said it was at least a mile wide at the base. They estimated the speed should have been almost 100 miles per hour inside it. The only thing is there was no wind on the outside. People drove right up to it and nothing would happen and it stayed there for an hour. Isn't that weird?"

"Yeah, that is strange," Carson got up and looked over the wall, "have you ever heard of anything like that before?"

Ray came back with, "No, I haven't. They're saying it was an 'act of God,' but I'm not sure of that. Thought that type of thinking went out a long time ago."

Carson paused then answered, "I thought it went out too. Didn't the government finally outlaw any reference to religion about three years ago?"

"Yeah," Ray remembered, "I think it was called the Freedom of Thought Act. The main idea was to rid us of the restrictions religion places on our thinking. Some of the biggest advances in science have come since the act was signed into law. The penalties for being religious nowadays are really stiff."

"Well, Ray, I've got a lot of messages to return and the boss wants me to do more work on this one file before I leave today. Better get to work."

He made it through the afternoon, and on his way home on the airway he turned his car radio on to hear reports on the storm earlier that morning. All the clouds were gone now and the sunset was really magnificent with bright reds, purples and yellows intermixing. This really made the flight home more enjoyable than usual. He remembered when sky travel was first being introduced. There were two big selling points. The first one was, the time had finally come for every person to be able to fly the skies. This is what many of the science fiction movies of the early 20th century predicted would happen by the end of that century. The other selling point was the view each person would have anywhere he or she went by sky travel.

All the safety problems were overcome and of course the invention of the electrical field that created the tunnel was the biggest thing that helped the whole idea go over. When a traveler entered into the tunnel there was no way any weather problems such as rain could come in, and if there was a breakdown a person could land their auto-wing on special runways that were held up by the electrical field. There were auto-wing mechanics on duty 24 hours a day, seven days a week on these platforms and they could make any type of repairs and get you back on your way in no time.

Of course the tunnel also meant a boon for electricity to be produced all over the country and eventually the world. This brought about many alternative methods of producing electricity. Hydropower was the biggest and the best method ever devised to power the new age of travel.

The manufacturers of the modern autowing incorporated solar cells on the top of the flying auto along with a newly developed, ultra light and compact battery that could take a charge that would last for at least 100 hours of flying time. These two power sources along with hydropower made this the best way of getting around late in the 22nd century. During a sunny day the solar cells on the auto-wing would be charging the battery but you could also charge the battery by plugging a cord into any normal electrical outlet, and your battery would be charged in a few hours. Carson thought this was an incredible time to live, and he was thankful he was able to appreciate many of the finer things this life had to offer.

After getting home he parked and plugged his auto-wing into the garage outlet then ran in and jumped into the shower. While he was in the shower the light in his bathroom flickered twice. "Oh my god, what's going on now?" Carson said out loud. He was running late and needed to go pick up May for their dinner date so he kept going with his shower. A couple minutes later all the lights in the house flickered twice. He thought it must be something with the electric company having problems because of the storm that day. This time Carson finished his shower and got out while grabbing his towel at the same time.

He was walking fast toward his bedroom when he heard a voice say, "Carson, you remind me of Adam when I watched him get caught after Eve gave him that fruit to eat. Remember that from your daily Bible reading?"

As Carson came into his bedroom he was shocked to see a very tall, well-dressed man with shoulder length hair standing by his closet. He exclaimed as he jumped back in astonishment, "Who are you and how did you get in here?"

"Hold on, Carson. Didn't you see the messages that I sent you?"

Carson asked, "What messages?"

"You know, the ones I sent to you on your computer? I think you call it e-mail."

He remembered deciding to delete all those e-mails, didn't want to take the time going through them. "I don't remember seeing any messages from anyone saying they were going to break into my house tonight. Now you need to get out now and let me get dressed and I won't call the police."

The stranger ignored the last part of Carson's remarks. "Oh yes, I saw you delete all those messages, you were going to just tell everybody you didn't get them instead of doing what you should have. That's okay, Carson. I just wanted to see if you would respond to a little warning and make the adjustment without me coming to see you. Guess it didn't work. Look, why don't you get dressed and we can continue this discussion in the kitchen."

Carson was still standing with his towel around himself, dripping on his carpet. "Oh, I guess I could get dressed, but I'm going to call the police and have you hauled off to jail, and why are you going to my kitchen?"

"I think you need something to eat to calm your nerves. I never get hungry," the man replied.

After getting dressed Carson walked all around the inside of his home then went to the kitchen where he found his visitor making a smoked turkey sandwich. "I can't find where you came in. How did you get in here and who are you?" He was saying all this while he picked up his phone to call the police.

"You're just wasting your time doing that. The phone doesn't work right now."

He couldn't hear a dial tone and nothing he did would bring it back. "Oh god, the phone is dead."

This brought about a sudden shout from the visitor. "That is why I am here!"

"To fix my phone?"

"No, you have got to stop this severely offensive habit of yours."

Carson looked at him even more confused. "What offensive habit are you talking about and who are you?" Carson's voice was getting real stressed by now.

"Okay, Carson, I am someone you don't believe exists. I'm an angel sent to you from the God you don't believe in, but keep using the name of whenever you feel a little distressed."

Carson sat down with a sudden thud in a kitchen chair. He repeated what he just heard but with a monotone pattern. "You are an angel sent to me from the God I don't believe in, but I keep using the name whenever I feel a little distressed."

"That's right. You're starting to get it now, Carson." The angel started patting him on the back.

Carson looked calmly at him and asked, "Do you have a name?"

"I do, I have an angelic name and I guess you could say I have an earthly name."

Carson continued to ask, "Which one do you want me to call you?"

"You couldn't even begin to pronounce the angelic name so we better use the earthly one, Andrew."

Carson thought out loud, "This is crazy. I am listening to this guy that broke into my house but I can't figure out how. I can't use my phone to call the police because it isn't working but I don't know why and now you're telling me you're an angel named Andrew. Oh, g…I mean oh man! I am not having a good day." Carson just stared at a wall for several minutes and "Andrew," as he wanted to be called, sat down and remained silent until Carson broke it. "Okay, you say you are an angel, right?"

Andrew quickly responded, "Right."

"Don't angels have special powers?"

"I guess you could say that." Andrew knew what was coming, it happened on every mission he was sent on.

Carson turned and looked into Andrew's eyes. "Then do something. Perform a miracle."

"Carson," Andrew smiled, "I already have. I am in your house in spite of the fact that you have every door and window locked. I didn't have to open any of them to get in. The phone is another, and Carson, there was the storm this morning."

Carson's stressed voice managed to get out, "You caused that storm?"

"Well, I asked for it and He agreed. Believe me, it was a major effort on my part. I had to use every reason I could think of but it finally worked." Carson just thought of the tornado and asked if Andrew had caused that too. Andrew just smiled and slightly nodded his head.

A few moments later Carson finally said, "You caused the storm and tornado to warn me about saying 'oh, you know who'?"

"Yes and no, Carson. This is a major mission and we were trying to get the attention of everyone but it was also to start getting your attention. When

I saw the general method wasn't working I decided to use a more specific method with the e-mail, but when that didn't work I had to do this. By the way, the tornado was my idea. Pretty creative, huh?"

Carson still was not sure about all this. "I don't get this. Everybody says this, this phrase that I use. Why aren't you doing something about them?"

Andrew gave him a stern look. "Are you going to be like everybody else and tell Him how to do His job? I don't even do that, but you humans have the amazing attitude that you can tell God how to take care of you and what He should do for you. The big problem is that if He doesn't come through then all of a sudden you don't think there is a God. I know about the Freedom of Thought Act. Yeah, right. It was a great idea. Okay, Carson, let me explain it this way. The company you work for has certain expectations for each employee, right?"

Carson was hesitant but he finally answered, "Right."

"If you don't come up to these expectations right off does your boss fire you immediately?"

Carson thought for a moment. "No, they have steps you go through and they don't even do anything until the problem gets really bad. They are pretty patient with all employees, especially new ones."

That was the answer Andrew was looking for. "Good, Carson. Think of it all this way. God has very high expectations of all of you here on earth but he is very patient. Now what happens at work if you are given several chances but do not improve at what you do?"

"Well, your boss will talk to you and they will go through counseling steps. If you still don't shape up, they could fire you."

"Exactly," Andrew continued, "God has done many things to try to get everyone to change. He has taken you all 'through the steps' as you called them. He would like to call Michael over to blow that horn of his and call it quits, but He knows it's not time yet. He is wanting to see some change around here, and at least part of the change is going to start with you, Carson."

"Me?" asked Carson.

"Yes, you. Don't tell me you're just one person and you can't do anything. What you can do is influence the people that are around you every day and they can do the same. Don't think you are the only person we are visiting about this. There are more, but you are the key person here. So what do you think?"

Carson was staring at his ceiling by now. He didn't know what to think. He finally responded, "I don't know. I mean how do I really know you're an angel and what you are telling me is true?"

"I guess you need more proof."

Carson looked down from the ceiling. "I think so. Don't know what it could be though."

"Carson," Andrew came up with a question for him, "when you read your Bible as a boy do you remember Hebrews 1:14?"

Carson was getting angry now. "I don't understand why you keep bringing up my Bible reading when I was a boy. I have never read the Bible. I don't know what you mean by that."

Andrew knew this would happen. "Carson, you have let yourself forget what your parents tried to teach you. You are afraid of what might happen to you because of the law here about religion."

"I'm not afraid of anything," Carson snapped back. For the first time that night he noticed the clock in the dining room chiming 6:30. He was supposed to have picked May up by now. "I'm late, and you made me late. I have a date with May and you need to get out of my house now."

Andrew told him, "Okay, but I will be in touch, I can't give up. I have never failed at a mission yet." With this he slowly faded away without a sign he was ever there.

Carson shook his head and figured he and this angel, or whatever it was, had been talking for almost an hour. He attempted to get back on track for the evening and jumped into his car and on to May's home. He noticed a plumbing truck parked in May's driveway as he walked up to the door. When May came to the doorbell she greeted him with, "Hello, Carson. Where have you been?"

"Sorry I'm so late, May. Are you ready? I'll explain everything the best I can on the way to the restaurant."

"Well, Carson. I'm sorry, but I don't think we can go."

Carson looked a little shocked by this. "What do you mean?"

She said, "I have a leak under the kitchen sink and I had to call a plumber. I know these are ultra modern times, but pipes still carry water just like they did two hundred years ago. He's only been here for a few minutes but it might not take very long. Let me go ask him how much longer."

Something made Carson follow her into the kitchen. As they both walked in the plumber was half way under the kitchen sink so Carson couldn't see his face. May tapped his leg and asked, "How long do you think you might be, Andrew?" When Carson heard this and saw the plumber's face he shouted, "Oh my god. What are you doing here?"

May was taken back by Carson's behavior and shouted, "What are you doing and what do you mean by that, Carson?"

Andrew remained calmly seated on the floor and watched Carson as he struggled for an answer. "I mean, uh, I didn't realize you had a plumber in your kitchen. I'm sorry, well, Andrew, how much longer will you be?"

Andrew looked up at him and said, "Not sure yet. Might be a couple hours." May finally regained her composure and introduced the two men since she didn't know they had met or how they met. Neither of the men told her about what had happened earlier that evening. Carson didn't acknowledge May's introduction but instead insisted on leaving for dinner so he could get away from Andrew.

"Carson," May answered, "how can we leave? The pipe under my sink is leaking, water was pouring all over the floor and I had to call somebody to fix it and I can't just leave him here by himself."

Carson came back quickly, "Something tells me you can trust this man to leave him by himself to finish the job."

As Andrew was getting back under the sink he said, "I think it would be better if you stayed. I might run into a problem and will need your permission to do other work."

May agreed with staying. "I could always order something to be delivered in. I'll go look up places. What do you feel like eating, Carson, Chinese or Italian? What do you think?"

"What I feel like," Carson started, "is for us to go out and eat at our favorite restaurant as we planned."

"I can't do that, Carson. I need to stay here." She reached out to him and started stroking his back while explaining, "It's just one night and it will be okay." Carson couldn't resist it when she did that, so he agreed to stay and they would order Chinese.

After she went to the online communicator in the next room to order, Carson turned to Andrew. "How did you manage this? What are you doing here?"

Andrew replied, "I am here to serve and to fix this leak. I managed this, Carson, because I'm an angel. You wanted more proof, here it is. How many mortal men do you know could do what I've done tonight? Just read Hebrews 1:14 from that Bible you still have tucked away in your closet. You also need to remember what your childhood was like with your parents teaching you from the Bible."

Carson was getting pretty hot by now. "I don't remember anything like that, now fix the leak and get out of here."

With this Andrew completed his work and left the more traditional way, through the front door and left the couple to their Chinese dinner.

The next morning Carson was back on the airway nervously making his way to work. He was thinking about the previous day while watching closely for any other stray birds flying around where they shouldn't be. He was trying to go on as if nothing happened with the traffic, the storm and most of all Andrew. He had been under a lot of stress lately, so he decided to let it all go and not worry about it any more. The radio was on his favorite station and about the time he was starting to relax the music suddenly stopped in the middle of a song. He thought the radio DJ had come on at first, but he had never heard a DJ like this one before. He was talking about loving each other, then he talked about what love is. After this he said, "Even though many of you have been trying to forget God, He has not forgotten you. The greatest measure of love is to keep loving someone who does not love you back. You only love to misuse His name. He sacrificed His only son for you. Do you not remember?"

Carson thought the voice sounded familiar but he couldn't figure out who it was. He tried changing the channels but the same voice giving the same message seemed to be on every channel he went to. He noticed others doing the same thing in their carwings. When the voice had finished the music came back on the radio and Carson noticed a strange feeling in his carwing. It was as if there was a great deal of pressure within the carwing. It was like a small cloud forming over the front passenger seat. A familiar face with a mischievous smile started to form before his eyes, then a body appeared seated next to him. Carson started losing control of his car-wing and started to swerve into the one next to him when a hand reached out of the cloud and pulled the steering wheel back. The cloud and pressure went away after Andrew asked Carson, "What did you think?"

Carson yelled, "Think about what? I was almost killed just now. If I had gone into that other car-wing, we could have been killed. What are you doing?"

"Slow down, Carson. Everything will be okay."

Carson interrupted him. "I thought I got rid of you last night, and was that you on the radio?"

"Well," Andrew continued, "you haven't gotten rid of me because my mission isn't over, and yes, that was me on the radio. Pretty good, huh?"

Carson kept asking questions while attempting to maintain control of his car-wing. "Did you come on every station and radio or were you just on my radio?"

"The answer to both those questions is yes. I thought it might be a very good time management idea. You know, get the message out in the most effective and time efficient method? You guys seem to be big into that sort of thing nowadays, so I figured it would be okay. By the way, Carson, I haven't heard you say that phrase one time this morning."

"What phrase is that? Oh, where I use His name, right?"

"Yes, that's right," Andrew replied.

"I just thought it would be a good idea to do something else. You know, sometimes you wear a phrase out."

Andrew looked very seriously at Carson for a moment then said, "You still don't believe that I am an angel, do you?"

Carson kept looking straight ahead. "Not really."

Andrew asked him, "Then what am I? If what I have done so far has not convinced you, then what would it take?"

Carson just shook his head as if to say he wasn't sure what it would be. Andrew stopped talking, looked down, and shut his eyes as if he were meditating. He was in the position for several minutes then looked up at Carson. "I think we need to do something else today besides going to work." He reached for the steering and pulled it to make the car-wing go down. At the same time Carson yelled, "What are you doing?" Carson lost all control of his car-wing to Andrew as he drove it from the passenger seat. They went under all the air traffic down to the bottom of the tunnel; then without warning Andrew pulled on the steering again and they went through the bottom of the tunnel into open air. They sliced through as a razor sharp knife with sparks flying everywhere, but the car-wing made it without a scratch. Carson had read of accidents where others had hit the sides or top of the tunnel badly damaging their car-wing and becoming injured. He couldn't believe this was happening, but they were flying through open skies. He didn't know where they were heading and really didn't know who or what was driving his car-wing.

He finally worked up enough nerve to ask, "Where are we going?"

Andrew would just say, "Where you need to be. We have a long way to travel and we won't make it in time without a little help."

With these words something like a large clear bubble enveloped the entire car-wing and he saw the area below start to move by them at what might be called supersonic speed.

"This is really strange," Carson said. "It looks like we're going really fast, but I don't feel anything from the speed. How fast are we going?"

Andrew looked at him with a smile. "I'll just say we are going as fast as an angel can fly."

They traveled for about an hour before Andrew made another move that slowed their speed down to where they could make a safe landing. The bubble disappeared as they moved down and came to a soft landing.

"I don't know how you did this, but I still don't believe you're an angel," Carson stubbornly said as they came down. Andrew didn't say anything as he started getting out of the car-wing. Once they were both out, Carson started to look around. It was a beautiful country setting with rolling hills, trees and a small farmhouse in the distance.

"Do you recognize this place, Carson?" Andrew asked.

"Oh my," Andrew interrupted him, "now remember what this is all about?"

"Well, I'm still not sure what this is all about, but I do remember this place," he answered. "This is where my parents live. It is where I grew up."

Andrew continued, "We can walk from here. Let's go." Carson started to ask why they were there but he decided it wouldn't do any good. "You're remembering the last time you were here, aren't you?" Andrew asked a confused Carson.

"It's been a few years, and I never had a desire to come back."

As they walked up to the white siding and brick farmhouse, a familiar feeling came over Carson. This was the Jenson home where Carson and his brothers and sisters grew up. There was an older couple working in a vegetable garden just outside the house. The man was hoeing between the neatly planted rows, and the woman was picking choice red tomatoes from well-cared-for vines. The scene was something out of a different time that Carson was no longer used to. It was as if everything went into slow motion. Carson's head began to throb as a nervous headache came over him with every step he took and beat of his heart. Memories of a childhood he hoped to have forgotten flooded back. The smell of the garden and the voice of his mother interrupted the pain with, "Is that you, Carson? Arthur, Arthur." She dropped the tomato she had just pulled from one of the plants. She started walking to Carson and Andrew. "He's back, Arthur. You came back to see us. Carson, you've been gone too long." She reached out and with tears in her eyes and put her arms around an apprehensive Carson who didn't know what to do next.

He slowly placed his arms around her and finally asked, "How are you, Mother?"

The gray haired man stopped his work, straightened up and looked in disbelief. The son that left them in such turmoil so many years ago was now standing at the edge of his garden. He finally broke his silence. "Is that you, boy? What are you doing here?" He put the hoe down and walked over to the visitors. Tears came down the father's tired, worn face. He managed to ask, "Carson, what are you doing here?" He stood within arm's reach of Carson and his mother who still had her arms around him, but the father wouldn't reach out.

"I'm not sure myself," Carson answered. "This man, Andrew, brought me here, but I don't know why. Andrew," he turned to him, "why are we here?"

All Andrew would say was, "To heal." With this Carson's father moved closer and they all walked inside the small house while Andrew did one of his vanishing tricks once again.

Inside the house the air was filled with the aroma of an earlier breakfast complete with the rich, brewed coffee that both parents would consume every morning. Carson was still nervous, not really wanting or understanding why he was there. They all went into the kitchen and sat around the same table that Carson sat at while growing up. He looked at the surface of the table as he sat down and started rubbing both hands on the surface as if saying hello to an old friend. They were all silent until his father asked, "Where did your friend go?"

Carson answered. "Oh, he just disappears sometimes. I think he'll be okay."

His father continued. "Your mother needs you, boy. She has been going through a lot lately. This means a lot to her."

Carson looked at him. "Does it mean anything to you, Dad?"

He paused. "It means a lot to me too. I just didn't think it would work, that's all. My faith isn't what it used to be."

Carson wasn't sure of what he had just heard so he asked his father, "What do you mean? What has worked?"

"Your mother has been praying for weeks that you would come today. It's been five years you know."

Carson interrupted, "Dad, what's this all about?"

His mother had been anxiously watching from the side of the room and at this stepped up closer to Carson. "It's all about you and us. We have got to deal with our losses, heal and grow back as a family." It had been a while since he even thought of his mother's prayers, but it all came back to him. Carson's mother, Esther, had a very uncommon faith. She kept on. "You know it has been five years today since your brother Paul died, and we needed you here with us. That is why I started praying and God heard me."

Carson looked at both his parents and finally said, "Look, I can't really explain how I got here today, but I'm not convinced this is an answer to prayer. Haven't you people heard about the Freedom of Thought law? You can't talk about a God that doesn't even exist. Don't you know you could be arrested?"

His mother interrupted, "But it was God who brought you back today. You just have to admit it. That's a silly law. How can you outlaw God? Your father and I remember how it hurt you when your brother died. It hurt all of us and the day you left your words were harsh, but I know you didn't mean them."

Carson stiffened up on this. "I meant every word."

His father broke in, "Forget it, Mother. He didn't want to come here. It's a waste of time. Carson, just get back in that flying car of yours and go home. I don't want your mother hurt anymore. You don't understand what she's been through, the doctor." He froze as if he had let out a very important secret.

"Arthur." Esther looked at him with a cold, stern look. "Most of the time you don't say enough, but you've just said too much."

"What do you mean by the doctor, Dad?" Carson asked. "What's wrong?"

"Your mother is not well, Carson," Arthur started. "She's been sick for a long time and now the doctor is saying," he choked for a second. "He says now she won't be with us very much longer and she just wanted to see her son one more time."

"How long have you known?" Carson asked. "What does the doctor say is wrong?"

Esther answered this one. "A couple of months. That's when I started praying for you to be here today. He says it's some kind of rare blood decease. You know I was never good at medical terms."

"Mom." Carson's face showed his anger. "You talk about God and how He has answered this prayer about me coming home. What about needs that you have? They don't have a cure? You know they can cure every known cancer today. Why can't they cure this?"

"No, they don't have enough cases like your mother's to fund research," Arthur said. "That great government you believe in so much only spends money on things that get votes. That's why they passed that law about ruling out God."

Carson ignored his father on the last point and went to his mother. "Mother, how can you speak about a loving God when He allows stuff like this to happen? It was Paul first and now you. I feel like I did with Paul."

His mother started smiling. "You admit you remember everything now. You know God brought you home. Carson, you have to deal with all this. God does love all of us and He is a good God."

"Okay, I do remember everything. I remember getting the call from the policeman that told you Paul had been involved in that wreck and died before help could get there. That is your loving God. He doesn't love us. I don't even believe He exists. I know our government isn't perfect, but the people in it do try to help others when they can. Living for today is all I have, and that is all I believe in."

Suddenly they heard a racket from the roof just above the kitchen. It sounded like an animal fell on it and was scrambling to get up and was running all over it. All three of them looked up and then at each other. Carson was the first outside and the others followed. "What is it?" Arthur shouted. They all looked up and what they saw was nothing like anything they had ever seen before. It was not an animal, at least not like any animal any of them had ever seen. Carson recognized it was Andrew. It looked like he was tangled in a long robe that appeared to have feathers and was multi colored. While he was struggling to get up Andrew looked down seeing the three looking at him. "Hello, believe it or not this is not what I planned. Guess I dropped my left wing a little more than I should have." As he started getting up a foot slipped on wet shingles and he fell to the ground just in front of the three unbelieving humans.

"Andrew, what are you doing? Where did you get all this stuff you have on, and are you okay?" Carson asked all at once.

Andrew looked up at him. "I'm okay. Angels never feel pain. Just give me a moment."

Esther and Harold stood there silently watching.

Just as Carson was saying, "Why don't you get off this bit of thinking you're an angel," Andrew stood up and the feathers weren't just feathers. They could all see the feathers weren't attached to the robe. They seemed to be part of another arm coming out of his back, then it hit Carson, they were wings. "Where did you get those things?" Carson was pointing at the wings.

"Well, I was made with them. The God you don't believe in, Carson, gave them to me. Let me get up all the way and show you how they work." With this Andrew stood straight, his wings able to spread to their full capacity.

They seemed to fill the entire sky and were in the shape and color of Eagle wings. Carson and his parents couldn't move or talk while this was unfolding before them. Andrew appeared to gain in height as well as majesty. He looked at them and finally said, "You probably expected them to be white. Some are but not all. Don't you remember reading, 'Yet those who wait for the Lord will gain new strength; they will mount up with wings like eagles, they will run and not get tired, they will walk and not become weary.'" With this Andrew tilted his wings upward and soared into the sky. As they watched Andrew joined many other angels in the sky. The spectacle was so great it was beyond description. Their wings created a sound that was, well, heavenly. The three earthbound spectators were motionless until the skies were suddenly clear and silent with Andrew landing in front of them.

"Now, what do you think?" he asked. "Uh, you can all close your mouths now. Were we that bad?"

One by one the three spectators started to come to the reality they were in the presence of real, live angels. Suddenly the Bible verse Andrew asked Carson to read came rushing back to him. Hebrews 1:14: "Are they not ministering spirits, sent out to render service for the sake of those who will inherit salvation?" His mind and heart became filled with memories he had not had for years. Of course Esther started crying and Arthur was numb with both fear and awe. Carson was finally able to say, "Andrew, you win, you finally got through. Your mission is complete. I only have one question."

Andrew asked, "What is it?"

"Has everything that has happened for the last several days because of my mother's prayers?"

"You might say that was what got the ball rolling," Andrew answered. "Carson, you can't outlaw God. He is the same yesterday, today and tomorrow, and Carson, Paul wants you to know he is waiting for all of you. I know this is the most visual angels have been for a few centuries but the times call for different actions. Yes, this is and will be happening in other places and yes, Carson, your mother along with many others started it all. They were all concerned with more than just their own happiness. Carson, how will you be using the name of my Lord now?"

Carson looked up then at his parents. "With awe."

"Your mission is just beginning," Andrew replied. "Look to Him for your strength and our God will guide you."

TRADITION

"Remember the Sabbath day, to keep it holy."
Ex. 20:8

Four

Through the centuries sports have always been important to people of all cultures around the world, from the Olympic Games of Greece to current day athletic superstars of many different sports. Probably the most widely watched event today occurs on a Sunday evening every January. Two opposing teams fully padded and suited up run out onto a lined, green field before millions of spectators watching from around the world through the miracle of TV. This is not to say sports are bad or evil, but many times Satan does have the ability to take anything meant for good and create a way of using it as a distraction from God.

Just imagine the first meeting that took place eons ago between Satan and his demons just after getting booted out of heaven. They were probably brainstorming methods of keeping people from knowing the true God. The atmosphere had to be dark, of course, and the air was probably thick with hate, fear and shattered egos. "He thinks we have lost," Satan begins, "and we will not be able to do anything about His plans for the universe. I might not rule as I hoped but we can create lots of problems for one area of His universe that He loves very much. The earth is full of the people He created and we can devise ways of keeping those people from knowing the truth that He would want them to know. We need to come up with ways they can find my truth and wisdom instead. I need to hear ideas now." The demons began to shutter and grumble with many ideas, but Satan refused them all.

One demon from the back of the room raised his claw and quietly said, "Be subtle."

Satan thought he heard him but wasn't sure. "Who was that?"

A small and shy demon stood up and said, "It was me, sir. I said be subtle."

"What do you mean by that?"

The demon thought for a while then said, "You know, be subtle in all things. I think you could keep many from Him by attacking Him directly but you will be able to keep millions more from Him by giving people subtle distractions. Come up with new ideas about how to get to heaven but call it something else and how to live a meaningful life that lead people to you instead. Whenever there is something good that people do just help them to become so obsessed with the idea they never have time to think about Him."

Satan thought about all this for a while then finally replied, "That is a great idea. We will fan out throughout the world and whenever possible infiltrate thoughts and let people think they are on the right track but we will throw subtle obstacles in their path and throw them off course. That is a great idea, and in the end we will have the most on our side and we will end up winning." After this all the demons along with Satan must have held a celebration thinking they had the answer and would eventually win out in the great race for the souls of mankind.

The only thing Satan and his partners did not count on was that God saw this coming from the very beginning of time and already had everything in motion to provide the way for people to come to him through His Son, Jesus. Satan just didn't know it all like he and his demons thought.

The subtleties of Satan continue to this very day, which brings us all the way to the current day to meet the two players of our story, Leo Bertelli and Claire Henry. Both came from broken homes and were raised by single mothers. They could both count on their fathers to send an occasional check and to visit a few times a year, but that was about it.

Leo's mother recognized early that he was a natural athlete and encouraged him as much as she could. She sacrificed a great deal for him to play baseball, basketball and soccer. As he got older he took advantage of whatever else came with being a good athlete. When it was time for college he went on a soccer scholarship.

Claire excelled at academics all the way from grade school up to senior high and was able to attend state university on a full scholarship. She still had to work for extra things but she enjoyed the challenge and continued her academic goals.

While in senior high school both Leo and Claire experienced their greatest spiritual victory over Satan. A persistent Youth For Christ director took special interest in Leo and stopped him from speeding to a self-destructive end. His life was permanently changed at his third YFC meeting when Leo accepted Jesus as his savior. He always thought sports were the most important thing in his life. Sports were his way of coping with his life and he was hoping to go professional at some time, but after he met the one that gave him those talents he started looking at life a little differently.

Claire had a caring friend that kept inviting her to church to hear their youth director speak on how Jesus could change your life. She finally decided she needed Jesus in her life while attending church camp for the first time. Claire attacked Bible study with even more passion than her school studies and soon became a teacher on Sunday morning with children. She also gained what she believed to be a clear understanding of much of what the Bible has to say.

He felt certain God supplied this as the way to get his education so he went out for soccer and baseball and made the Dean's list for high grades. Claire was awarded several scholarships from the same school, but she would still have to work part time to afford everything. They went to the university for almost three years before officially meeting. Claire knew Leo from the sports but never really thought about meeting or dating him. She kept pretty busy with classes, studying and working.

On that special Friday evening in their junior years in college, Leo was going to the Baptist Student Union to see a movie. Since it only cost $1.00 to get in, he could afford to bring a date this evening. Jeannette was a beautiful sophomore with a perfect grade point average and from a very wealthy family. This was their first date, and Leo was thinking it would be their last. She talked about her ski trips and places from around the world that she had already traveled to with her family. Leo could only talk about the places he would like to go some day. He was in line waiting to get popcorn and a coke when he looked over in the line next to him and saw Claire for the first time. She was slightly shorter than Leo, had on a plain blue t-shirt under a pair of denim overalls. He really couldn't figure out what it was about her that caught his attention, but whatever it was he liked it. As the line moved Leo sort of froze and stared at Claire. She noticed him out of the corner of her eye. At first she thought he was looking at something else and just ignored him. When she finally realized that Leo was actually looking at her, she turned her head toward him and noticed he had a very nice smile and she couldn't help saying, "Hello."

For just a moment Leo felt like he had been caught off guard and didn't know how to answer her. He fumbled around for a second then finally gathered himself together and said a simple "hello" back to her. The ice was broken, and as they moved on up in line they started making the usual small talk about the movie and how long they had been attending the university. By the time they made it up to the counter and had gotten their orders, it was as if they had come as a couple for the movie and not with other dates. As they made it back into the movie they had to split to go to their dates.

As Leo sat down he was pretty stunned by the chance meeting with this girl. Then he suddenly realized that he didn't know her name and he didn't give her his name. As Leo sat next to Jeannette he noticed that the girl coming down the aisle in the row in front of them was the one he had just met. While Jeannette picked up the conversation as if Leo hadn't left, he wasn't really paying attention. He kept looking over at Claire wondering what her name was and how they could meet again. Finally the movie started and Jeannette stopped talking and they watched the movie, but Leo kept thinking about that other girl sitting just in front of him. When the movie was over Leo made sure he caught Claire's attention and started talking to her. He introduced himself to her date, Eddie, and introduced him to Jeannette. That is when Leo found out Claire was her name and he would never forget it. They kept talking and walked out the door together leaving Jeannette and Eddie to figure out what was going on together.

After they were all outside Leo came up with the brilliant idea of everyone going to a little restaurant that was just a block from campus, easily within walking distance. The weather was great and it would give them a chance to get to know each other more. Claire didn't hesitate at all; the others reluctantly agreed. As the night went on all four started talking more with Jeannette showing signs of being more interested in Eddie than Leo. This started when Eddie was telling everybody about the chain of sporting goods stores his family owns across the country. Jeannette told him that she was a big sports fan and started asking him questions about the stores. Pretty soon it was as if they were a couple. This was perfect for Leo, and before the evening was over he knew all about Claire from when she was born to where she lived along with her phone number. He ended up taking her home while leaving Jeannette at the restaurant to be infatuated with Eddie's chain of stores.

"This is not good," Satan grumbled from his lair as he monitored the situation. "We have done everything we knew to destroy these two all these years and to keep them from meeting. He had to interfere and they have found each other." He looked at the dark and damp earthen room filled with his servants and said, "We must do something that will split them up, but what will it be?" His eyes lit up in glee as the perfect solution came to him. He gave his orders to his evil helpers and they set about to do their miserable deeds.

Leo and Claire slowly walked back to the campus theatre and the parking lot where he had parked his very old but classic '70 VW Beetle. "I'm sorry this isn't a Cadillac or something more worthy for someone like you to ride in."

She smiled at him. "This is great. I love old cars."

Leo opened the door for her and had to reach in and throw a lot of books and papers from the passenger seat to the back before she could even get in. It took three tries to get the classic VW started, but they were finally able to get rolling down the road. Claire lived in one of the dorms on the other side of campus, so the drive would only take about ten minutes, they thought. Up until now neither of them had talked about their faith in God. What was about to happen would bring this part of their lives to the surface and will surprise both of our players.

The night air was warm, so they rolled the windows down and were enjoying a nice conversation. In order to get to the dorm they had to drive through East River Street that ran next to the river of the same name. Back about thirty years ago it was a very nice area of town. Now the businesses had changed to nightclubs where a lot of undesirables hung out. Leo wasn't very comfortable going there but it was the only way of getting to Claire's dorm.

When they came to the corner of East River Street and Elm, the traffic light was red and there were two other cars in front of them. They were still talking while waiting for the light to change when they both heard a rumble from one of the clubs to their left. They both instinctively looked to see what the problem was just as the inside of the building became illuminated with a sudden flash of light followed by a loud explosion causing glass to shatter from all the windows. The explosion blew off much of the front and roof of the building causing several people to be hurled through the air and out into the street. All the people that were outside froze in shock and disbelief at what was happening. Part of the roof flew up into the air and landed on top of Leo's Volkswagen. When he realized what was going to happen, he ducked to the right of the steering wheel just as the car roof came crashing down around him. Claire was able to open her door and jumped out and turned to find out how Leo was. The impact caused Leo to black out for a few seconds, but Claire brought him to by tugging on his right arm. She kept on pulling on his arm until he was able to get freed from under the roof and out of the car.

Dazed, they ran to the sidewalk on the opposite side of the street and fell to the concrete breathing heavy and sweating from both the heat of the fire and from fright. The scene was chaos with some people standing around still in shock and others running and screaming. You could hear sirens in the distance so somebody must have called for help.

Claire wanted to run with the others but at the same time Leo heard something from inside the burning club. It was a faint "help" and he was sure someone was trapped under debris and needed help. No one else seemed to be hearing the cry and the fire seemed to be getting worse. Leo was more of a quiet, leave-me-alone type and not a hero, but something inside him urged him to go in that building and try to help that person. What Leo didn't know was the real cause of the explosion, and the cry for help was still inside the building. No one else was responding to the cry because they did not hear it. The cry was intended only for Leo and Claire to hear. "I have to go and see if I can help whoever it is that is yelling for help," Leo said with a desperate look to Claire.

"No, the firemen will be here any second and they can take care of it," Claire said as she reached for him, trying to keep him with her.

Leo was standing by now but crouched next to Claire and placed his hand on her shoulder then said, "Claire, I'm not a hero, but I know I need to go. Pray for me." He turned and ran toward the burning building.

At first his words astonished Claire but then she started praying as Leo asked. When Leo was entering the front of the red-hot building he offered up his own short prayer. "Lord, protect all of us tonight and guide me to this person." As he went through the opening he yelled, "Where are you, I heard you scream for help. Where are you?"

A response came from the back of the room, "I'm over here!" He kept walking, stumbling over debris as he made his way to the back of the room where the bar for this club once stood. It was getting hotter as the flames became more intense and the black smoke was filling his lungs. When he was about half way to the bar he started hearing a sound like a hiss but he couldn't make it out with all the roar of the flames. Back behind the bar the end of a pipe was sticking out of the floor and the hissing was coming from it. This was the pipe that carried natural gas into the club and next to it was the cause of this catastrophe. One of Satan's demonic soldiers was carrying out orders that came directly from the rebellious one.

Leo kept looking for the person while going further into the flames. Not being able to see the spiritual creature that was standing next to the pipe, Leo went further into the room. Choking and gasping for air he yelled one more time, "Where are you?" At this very moment the demon moved the pipe to blow its death hiss towards nearby flames. A flash of light from what was left of the ceiling caused Leo to look up, then he was pushed down onto the floor by some powerful force but he did not feel hurt. As this was occurring he heard a terrible blast all around him that produced a shock wave that seemed to hurl him forward through the room up into the air and over the street where his car was now burning. He came down fast and automatically went into a tuck and roll position on the only soft and grassy spot in the whole block just behind where Claire had been praying.

Leo passed out for a few seconds and when he came to he was laying on his left side with his right hand holding the hand of a young lady that appeared to be passed out too. Her face was covered with smoke and her clothes were smoldering, but she was alive. Leo let go of her hand and slowly sat up while a crowd of people gathered around them. He heard many of the people say they had never seen anything like it before in their lives. They knew they had just witnessed a miracle when they saw Leo flying out of that exploding building holding onto the girl he had gone in to rescue.

Claire came running over to them and hugged Leo with tears running down her face. Ambulance attendants came running and placed the girl on their stretcher since she was still unconscious and Leo was up talking with others around him. One of the attendants came up to Leo and asked what happened. He watched the girl being carried away while trying to put the pieces together with people slapping him on the back and praising him for being a hero. Finally Leo exclaimed, "I'm not sure what happened! All I remember was a flash of light from above me then being pushed down onto the floor. The next thing I knew I was on this grass looking at that girl beside me. I don't know where she came from."

It was after midnight by the time Leo walked Claire up to the front door of her dorm building. After the explosion, East River Street became full of fire trucks, ambulances and news reporters. Several reporters found Leo after hearing of the miracle and persuaded him to tell his story in front of news cameras. He finally told the reporter from LIVE TV12 he would tell the story if he would give them a ride out of there. The agreement was made and in a few short minutes they found themselves in the quiet of the college campus once again. They were exhausted, excited and confused. Neither of them said very much all the way to the dorm. It was as if they were both trying to determine in their own minds exactly what took place that evening before they would open their mouths. Finally, after they had been standing at the door, looking at the ground for several moments Claire started, "What happened back there and what you did were beyond anything I have ever seen before in my life. You are a very brave man and I will never forget this night. I mean there were people all around us that were hurt and crying out for help and you heard this one girl over all the others clear across the street in that building. I still don't know how you heard her over all that chaos."

"Claire," Leo started, and then paused for a moment. He went over to a short block wall on the side of the sidewalk and they both sat down while he began. "Remember just before I went into the building and you told me not to go?"

"Yes, I remember that and I'm sorry if I…"

"No, you didn't do anything, at least you didn't do anything bad or to hurt me. Let me ask you something. Remember when I asked you to pray?"

"Yes, I do."

"Did you?"

"Yes, I did."

He looked at her and asked, "Why? Was it because I asked you and you were caught up in what was going on, or was it something else?"

Claire knew exactly what to say but she wasn't sure why he was asking these questions. She was afraid he might be questioning God because of all this and was not a believer. "Leo, I am a Christian, and when you asked me to pray I did. Leo, I hope you understand."

"Oh, I understand," Leo said with a smile. "I understand and am grateful that you prayed."

"You are?"

"Oh yeah, I am very grateful. I said a very short prayer just before getting into the middle of those flames. I think we need to understand a couple of things that occurred tonight that are wild. The first is that no one died from the explosion tonight. The second thing, Claire, is that I don't think we just met tonight by accident. Let me put it this way, I am a Christian too. Now don't get me wrong, I'm not a nut and think we should run out and get married tonight because of all this. I mean for some reason, and at this point I'm not sure why, but we were supposed to meet tonight. I'm not sure what really happened in that building either, but I did not see that girl until I came to on that grass. When I was in that blazing inferno, I felt something that I had never felt before. Claire, I've only been a Christian since high school, so I am still learning about God and what he is capable of doing. I am also learning God has an enemy and I was headed straight for that enemy at one time. It's the old saying, Satan had me in his back pocket, but I have never felt anything like I felt tonight. In that building it was as if," he paused and took a deep breath. "I felt as if I was seeing what hell would be like. I don't mean the heat from the fire, I mean I sensed a presence or something strange was in that building with me just before that last explosion. I can't lay my finger on it exactly, but all I know is that when I saw that flash of light I had not found that girl yet and all of a sudden something pushed me down but I wasn't hurt. When I was flying through the air it was as if something was holding me and then helped me tuck and roll when I landed. Claire, I didn't know what a tuck and roll was until one of the firemen told me about it tonight after I landed."

By now it was sometime after midnight and all of a sudden both Leo and Claire realized Leo didn't have a way of getting back to his apartment that was on the other side of campus. It was as if they read each other's minds on this, and when Leo started to bring it up, Claire interrupted him and said it for him. He used the phone in the lobby of the dorm to call a friend to come pick him up. When the friend pulled up to the front of the dorm he found our two players sleeping on top of the short block wall. He woke them up, and Leo said good night to Claire with the promise that he would call her the next day.

Back at the scene of the explosion, most of the people had left, and firemen were rolling up hose. The owner of the club had come to look at the damage to his building and try to figure out what caused the blast. There were others of the dark spiritual world also assessing the damage and what they referred to as their accomplishments. One of Satan's highest-ranking demons was there to gather information for reporting back. He saw much of what they wanted to accomplish was done but when he asked about Leo he was not happy with what he heard. He roared, "You know our main objective tonight was to ruin that human's life. Not to kill him, but to burn him enough to make him too ugly for that Claire to ever want to marry him. We were to be keeping these two humans from the destiny that He would have for them. You have failed us and for that you will be sent to the worse of places. I will see to that. We have to come up with another plan to give to Satan as an alternative. Now think and make it quick," he said as they both faded out of sight.

Even though they had busy schedules with classes, work, studies and sports, Leo and Claire made time to see each other. They would meet for lunch or study together in the evenings. At first all they talked about was that dramatic first night. Eventually other things took their places. This was a process of getting to know each other. Of course, one thing they talked about was faith in God and what that meant to each of them. The first snag in their relationship came during a discussion about their views on different areas of the Bible. "You know," Claire began, "I have a problem with the commandment about honoring your parents. I know I have always loved and tried obeying my mother but not my father. You can just forget that one. I mean, where has he been all my life? He wasn't around while I was growing up and still doesn't come around."

Since he was in the same situation with his dad he thought for a few seconds before answering her. He wasn't sure if Claire really wanted him to give her an answer. She might have just wanted him to listen, but he decided to share what he found that helped him get through the same problem. "Claire, I think I know what attracted me to you."

"You do?" Claire was a little surprised; she didn't know why Leo would bring this up at this point.

"Yeah I do. I have a theory about how all people get together. You are attracted to the person of the opposite sex, of course, because you have something in common. God plants something inside of us that is a common thread or a generic thought if you want to call it that. Now understand this is my theory and I don't think you will find anything in the Bible that will prove it. What I mean is that the first time I laid my eyes on you there was something about you that pulled and tugged at my heart. Now I know what it was. We have a common thread between us that originated from our past, in our families. I realize now what I felt was like a voice inside me. It might have been God, I don't know. I think one reason God put you in my path is because I could help you through a problem that is deep rooted inside of you."

Claire still wasn't sure if she understood all this but she listened intensely.

Leo went on. "While I was growing up, I had a lot of hard feelings about my dad too. My mother and I had it rough and needed help. My dad never came around and never helped with anything. Mom worked hard and gave up a lot to get me into sports and I'm glad she did." He continued with a sarcastic twist to his voice. "My dear old father was not around when we needed him. He never came to my games or other school things. For years I didn't think I was good enough, and if I worked hard and became the best at soccer and baseball then Dad would come around and want to see me play. I was hoping we could actually have a relationship. You know what, I was a great athlete in junior and senior high school, but he never showed up. I became angry and bitter.

"I had never really known my father, but that didn't matter, I was mad at him. I started hanging out with kids that were into drugs and alcohol and I was starting down that path. It was all in rebellion over what my dad had done. Even after I asked Jesus into my life I had problems with my father. Jesus saved me from hell and drugs, but I was carrying that old hate with me and it wouldn't leave.

"I was at a weekend retreat with my youth group from church the summer before I started college. Everything for the three days was centered on forgiveness. Before the weekend was over it was like God convinced me to forgive my dad for all those years of not being there. The biggest thing about forgiveness is that it really isn't for the person you forgive but for yourself. I put this to bed that weekend by praying the Lord would help me to forgive my dad. It took a while and more prayers and getting into my Bible. It's just like what others say about a great weight being lifted off my back. Besides the moment I asked Jesus into my life, this was the next biggest turning point in my life and, Claire, you need to do the same thing. It is like a process and you have to take the first step by praying and then follow through with more and have faith that it will work."

Claire didn't say anything for a while. Finally, "Well, I know you are right, but I have to do some more thinking about it. I guess I have other issues that I need to deal with first. To be honest I'm not sure if I am ready to forgive him yet. Does that sound weird to you?"

"No, no it doesn't sound weird. A little strange, but I wouldn't call it weird. I hope we can talk more about it as time goes on."

"Sure, we can do that. I guess if I hang onto the hate it makes me feel like I am punishing him. Have patience with me on this one, okay, Leo?"

"I can do that. If it is okay with you, I will even pray for you," Leo said with a slight smile.

As time went on, Leo and Claire grew closer together until one Sunday afternoon in the spring he decided to tell her how he felt. Claire had been able to move out of the dorm and into an apartment recently, and she had invited Leo over for lunch after church. Claire had brought up another Biblical topic that sort of fit the occasion, keeping the Sabbath holy. After all they had just been to church, it just seemed to be a natural for the day. Claire felt you should always keep one day each week special for God, but Leo had different thoughts on it. He had a commitment to God, but while growing up many of his sports events were on Sunday and instead of going to church his mother made sure he was at those games. "I just don't see the problem with playing a game on Sunday. Don't you ever watch basketball or football on Sunday?" Leo seemed a little aggravated by this discussion.

"Well, no I don't. I like those sports but," Claire thought for a moment then continued. "Ever since I became a Christian I've learned that God wants us to make one day a week special not just for ourselves but for Him also. This has been a big deal with me because I want to try and correct what I thought were mistakes from my family's past. When I was a kid we hardly ever went to church. We didn't have any guiding principles or traditions. I just think having those things gives special meaning to a person's life. If I ever have a family I want to do things different, that's all."

"I can understand that," Leo came back. "What about that verse though where Jesus says something about the Sabbath being made for man and not man for the Sabbath? I think that says everything for me. Anyway, I go to church on Sundays when I can. A lot of churches have services on Saturday nights now. What do you think about that? Are the people that go on Saturday nights sinners or something?"

"We are all sinners, as Christians we are just forgiven. So what you are trying to say doesn't hold water. I think going to church on Saturday is okay, but I also think there should be more to keeping a day special for God than just attending church. There is far more to it than just that."

Leo saw he was losing this battle, and he had not planned on talking about this in the first place. He wanted to let Claire know about his feelings for her so he decided to change the subject. "What did you mean about having a family?"

"What do you mean?" Claire asked.

"Well, you were just talking about having a family some day and how you want to do things differently. What did you mean by that?"

"Just what every young girl means when she says the same thing. I hope to meet a person of the opposite sex some day that will be the one for me, get married and have kids. You know, have the house with a high mortgage, two-car garage, fence, 2 ½ kids and a big dog. I want what I didn't have while growing up." Claire didn't realize where Leo was going with this.

Leo went on with his discussion. "That is nice to know. I mean I would like to have some, maybe even most of those things. Not sure about the kids, the dog sounds nice though."

Claire laughed and moved closer to Leo while sitting next to him at the dinner table then asked him why he was asking her all this. "Are you telling me you are all of a sudden being Mr. Domestic?"

"Oh, sure, why not. The only thing is I need somebody to be domestic with." He looked straight into her eyes and changed the look on his face from funny to serious. "Would you be interested in the idea?"

Claire dropped her fork onto her plate causing a load clang that seemed to wake her from a daze she went into for a second or two. "Who, me? I mean, what do you mean? Hey, I will not move in and live with you. I hope that is not what you mean. We have talked about that and you know how I…"

Leo interrupted her, "I know how you feel about that, and you know I feel the same. I'll spell it out for you. Will you marry me?"

Claire, starting to breathe fast and heavy, looked down at the table, out the window then back to Leo. "Uh, this is interesting. I thought first you need to love somebody before you ask them to marry you."

"Oh, does that bother you? That I haven't told you that I love you? Will you be the type of wife that wants me to tell you that I love you every five minutes or something?"

"No, I didn't say that, but most of the time I thought a couple would fall in love with each other then they would contemplate getting married, then talk a little about the idea and finally the man would pop the question. Isn't that how it should work?" She held her breath and looked at Leo beginning to anticipate an answer.

"You know something? Maybe you're just too traditional for me." He looked down at his plate with a sad look on his face. "No, I don't think that would work either. Claire Henry, I love you. Would you marry me?"

She was stunned and really didn't know what to say, so Leo decided to break the silence fearing her answer would be "no" and he didn't know what he would do then. "You know I love the way you get deep into a discussion. You are really an intense woman and I guess that is what I love so much about you." He repeated, "I love you for your intense spirit. The way you give everything you have to whatever you are doing."

"Stop." Claire reached out with her hand and put it over his mouth. "Leo, I love you too, and I will marry you. I love you and I want to marry you."

They both naturally kissed and hugged and kept talking about what they just did and what it would mean to get married.

Our two players were being very sensitive with each other, but they needed to be aware of the spiritual beings in the back of the room listening to the conversation. One was dark and gloomy, the other bright and hopeful. The dark one grumbled that he didn't like the way the two humans were continuing on with their relationship. "This was not in the plan, but I think I now have two weaknesses to use against them. Claire's hate for her father and this old argument that we have used many times before about this religious right of keeping the Sabbath holy." He thought all he had to do was to be patient and with time he will be able to cause a distraction that has worked for millions of others. The angel of light advised the angel of darkness that he would not win and to give up the effort as he reminded him it was doomed from the beginning. With this, the angel of light drove the demon from the home. "You can't keep me from them forever," he cried as he left.

The angel pursued the demon. "If you come back I will be here waiting." With this, he returned and maintained guard over our couple for the rest of the day.

Plans were soon underway for a wedding during the spring break from school, just before graduation. The idea was to get all their difficult classes out of the way before the wedding. Their last semester was for classes like photography, mountain climbing techniques and guitar. The next year flew by quickly with all the planning and usual showers, work and keeping up with classes. Claire and her mother became closer while they were working on the wedding.

One year later the wedding day successfully came and went. They enjoyed a fantastic honeymoon free of any demonic interference. Afterward our players worked hard at the routine of establishing careers, and striving for the typical American dream. Leo landed a position as the baseball and basketball coach at Thomas Jefferson Senior High School while Claire landed a very good position in the accounting department with the local branch of 1st National Bank. They moved into a very nice apartment that was part of one of the best complexes in town.

With the new job came 45-50 hours of work each week. Leo was busy building the athletic program at the high school. Between seasons Leo was spending all his extra time at other high school games and watching films of games from the past while making plans for the next year. Fortunately Claire and Leo found a good body of believers at the Church of the Shepherd before their wedding day, and of course Claire insisted they make time for Sunday to be the day they kept for worshipping the Lord. This helped anchor them to the spiritual truth and reality they both needed so much. Since they both could relate so well with teenagers, they were automatically recruited for the youth committee at church. Of course they couldn't have said "no" to any church project so every spare moment became filled. In spite of the busy hours they were very happy and did not think about anything changing for a long time to come.

With all the activity, it was once again difficult for our players to find time for each other, but they kept working at it just like they did in college. Early one morning the following September Claire woke up feeling bad. She became nauseous and ran to the bathroom from their bed. The same thing happened for the next several mornings. Leo had already left for work each day so he was not aware of the problem. After the third morning with this problem she decided to go to the doctor and find out what was going on. That afternoon, after her appointment with the doctor, Claire went by the high school and found Leo in the gym at basketball practice. Leo was surprised to see her walk into the gym since she was usually working at this time of day. Claire waved at Leo when she saw him on the other side next to the bleachers. They met in the middle of the floor, but with all the players working out around them they couldn't talk so they went to Leo's office.

As they walked into the office, Leo sat Claire in a chair to the side and went around to the chair at his desk. "Well, this is a surprise. What's going on? What brought you here today? Oh, I know you went to the doctor today. I forgot about the appointment. What did you find out?"

"Honey, I," she paused for a moment then Trent, one of the students, walked through the door of the office that was open.

"Hey Coach, what do you want us to do next?"

Leo looked up at him. "What have you been doing?"

"Running wind sprints in the gym."

"Well, do some more."

"More?"

"Yes, Trent, get out there and run more wind sprints!"

"How many do you want us to do, Coach?"

"I don't know, until I say stop."

"Really?"

"Yes, really. Now go, I'll be back out in a minute." He shut the door after Trent left. "Okay, Claire, now you have my undivided attention. What were you saying?"

"Well, okay. You were right about the doctor's appointment this morning. You know I've been feeling sort of bad lately, so I decided to get checked out."

Leo noticed she was starting to tear up at this point. "What's wrong, honey? Is it something serious?"

"Oh, no, yes, oh no. It isn't serious but, well, it could be, but it's mostly really great, Leo. Leo, I'm pregnant. I'm going to have a baby!"

Leo's mouth fell open and he turned a little pale. He leaned back in his chair as his eyes traveled down toward Claire's middle. He took a deep breath then jumped out of his chair as if he just realized what Claire said. With a half worried, half elated look on his face he went to Claire and put his arms around her. "Are you sure about this? I mean, could the doctor be wrong? Do you know what it is? Is it a boy or a girl?"

"Uh, yes the doctor could be wrong, but he's not with us, I mean with me. I'm pregnant, Leo. We are going to have a baby, and no I don't know if our baby is a boy or a girl. We will be able to find out later, but it's too soon."

By now the room was full of the electricity that was going on between our two players. They were clinging to each other and both talking at the same time. Leo finally calmed down long enough to let Claire finish what she needed to tell him. "I'm two months now. We have seven months to go. I'll have the baby after you finish the semester, you will be off for the summer and I will be on family leave from the bank. Isn't that great?"

Leo interrupted her again. "Wait a minute. Can we afford this? Do we have enough room? Should we buy a house? Maybe this is the time to get a big house? We need more room now."

"Leo, stop. We have time and we have to think about this, but to ask if we can afford this is sort of a bad question, isn't it?" Claire leaned back in her chair for a moment.

"Oh, I don't mean anything bad. I know there is no turning back and I want to be a father. It's just that we haven't had much time to be, you know, together without kids." Suddenly the office door swung open and about ten sweaty teenage basketball players huffing and puffing walked in.

"Coach." Trent was struggling. "Can we stop running these sprints, they're killing us!"

Leo looked at them all and burst out, "Hey, we're pregnant. I'm having a baby, I mean she's, Claire, is having a baby." All the guys looked at each other like they couldn't believe what the coach was doing and saying. "Okay, don't worry about sprints, guys. Go on and shoot some baskets, I'll be right out."

He looked at Claire and gave her one more hug then asked, "Are you okay? Do you need me to drive you home?"

"Leo I'm okay, and no, I don't need you to take me home. Go ahead and finish your practice. I was just so excited I needed to come tell you right away. Leo, I hope you're happy about it."

"Claire, I couldn't be any happier. I know with God's help we will be okay and we will have a great baby, and I don't care if it is a boy or girl. Why don't you go on home and I will be there this evening and we will talk more and work everything out."

Claire walked through the gym with all Leo's basketball players stopping and congratulating her. When she finally got out and to the car she drove home, stretched out on the couch and was soon fast asleep while experiencing the most awesome peace of her life. The same angel of the Lord that had been with them for months was hovering above her while he watched for the dark one that was about to come once again.

The next seven months flew by quickly with Lamaze lessons and planning their future as well as keeping up with jobs and church. They took the big plunge and bought a house and remodeled one of the bedrooms into a nursery. They prayed and worked together and formed a closer bond than ever. Claire decided she would definitely go back to work after the leave was over since a coach's salary would not be enough to support them and make the payment on the new house. About the sixth month, Claire was starting to complain a little about the extra weight and her ankles swelling each day. They had everything planned for when the delivery time came. They knew all the different routes from home to the hospital and they had alternative plans made out if the time came while Claire and Leo were at work, church or doing almost anything else. They thought they had everything under control.

One Friday about eight months into their new family venture, Leo surprised Claire by calling her at work and telling her he would be free that evening and asked her for an old-fashioned date. They decided to go to their favorite place, The Italian Gardens, for dinner and to a movie after. While they were enjoying their pasta and salads, Claire felt a kick in her side. "Oh…that was a good one." She placed her right hand on that same side of her stomach.

"Did our son give you a good kick that time?" Leo asked, confident they were having a boy.

"Our daughter kicked a field goal that time. Oh, there's another in the same place. I guess Italian isn't our child's favorite." She sat back in her chair trying to relax for a moment before continuing with her dinner. A few seconds later there was another pain followed by a small cramp that caused her to jerk.

"Are you okay?" Leo asked.

"I'm not sure, haven't felt anything like this before." Another jolt came and she was in severe pain. "Leo, I think I'm going into labor. I think I'm going to have this baby tonight."

Leo started to panic then remembered their plans. He reached in his coat pocket for his cell phone to call their doctor, but it wasn't there. He really started to panic with this. "Uh, dear, do you have the cell phone?"

Claire looked at him, as her pain suddenly grew worse. "No, I don't have it, you are supposed to carry it."

"Okay, that's no problem. I will go up to the cashier and borrow the restaurant's phone and call the doctor. Oh, honey, do you have the doctor's phone number? I left my organizer at home. I just didn't think about all this happening tonight."

Claire found the number for their doctor in her purse and made the phone call. They met the doctor at the hospital in plenty of time. They were both hoping this would be false labor, but it turned out to the real thing, just a lot earlier than planned. That evening, after several hours of intensive labor, our players became proud parents of a healthy baby boy. Now they were going to face the biggest challenge of their lives. This was the beginning of the non-stop marathon of raising children.

Leo brought the new mother and son, William, home a few days later where her mother was waiting to give a helping hand for the next few days. They compromised with William; Leo wanted Willie after one of his greatest baseball heroes, Willie Mays. Claire wanted something a little more formal so his official name would be William Bertelli, but they would lovingly call him Willie. From that day on, their lives were centered on Willie and meeting his needs. Of course Leo had his plans for Willie to start throwing and catching baseballs as soon as he could manage to hold one.

A year and a half later Claire gave birth to little Barbara Claire Bertelli who gave even more joy to this young family. Even Barbara had to have an informal name so they called her Barb most of the time. This time Claire was determined to fulfill a dream of your own to have a daughter that was involved in music. She didn't care if she played an instrument or sang, she just wanted Barbara to be the musical one of the family.

Even during the time of pregnancy and after having both children, the Bertelli couple remained very active in their church with the youth and anything else they could find time for. Claire was very happy with the way Leo seemed to have adjusted to maintaining a more traditional day of worship and family each Sunday. As they were growing together in a very busy time of life, there were forces at work around them that would go undetected until one event that would take place on one special day.

THE HEAVEN FACTOR

Several years later

Leo had been teaching Willie how to throw and catch a ball now for several months and had gone on to teaching him how to run the bases and even more advanced methods of playing the great American game of baseball. Willie was now six and was starting into the city T-ball league. His first season went great, of course, as they followed the tradition of officially not keeping score during each game, but privately the parents knew who won. Claire was letting four-year-old Barbara sit with her at the piano and seemed to be showing some aptitude for music. One afternoon while listening to a CD of a violin solo, Claire noticed Barbara really listening closely. When the CD had finished playing, Barbara started asking questions about the instrument. After a brief discussion it was decided that Barbara would take up the violin and even learn a little piano. The next year Barbara started private violin lessons and Willie went into peewee baseball. Occasionally Barbara would have a recital and Willie would have a baseball game on a Sunday afternoon. These events never interfered with morning church, but they had to miss a youth meeting from time to time.

The next year Leo advanced into the next level of the city league and Barbara was developing so well she had been invited to take part in a special citywide youth orchestra. All practices for both kids were afternoons during the week, but each had a ball game or concert on several Sundays during the year. Claire didn't mind taking some time out of their Sunday, but after ten years of marriage Claire and Leo had attempted to maintain the same busy schedule as when they were first married. They had talked about making changes in order to simplify their lives but were never able to decide exactly what to change. Claire had advanced in her job to a very nice and lucrative position that added a large amount of income to the family. This helped buy vacations, pay for the violin lessons for Barbara and baseball for Willie. Leo had become head baseball coach and moved onto being head of the entire athletic department of the high school. They knew they were having a great life, but things slowly started to change in another area. Without realizing it, the Bertellis gradually moved from devoting their Sundays to worshiping and serving God to eventually not going at all. They would miss some activities occasionally, but pretty soon there were more scheduling conflicts and church seemed to lose out almost every time.

Sometimes after a long day and they would be lying in bed, exhausted, Claire would ask Leo if there were a way they could slow down. Occasionally she felt a twinge of pain about the direction her spiritual life was going and that of her family. During each of their discussions Leo would usually calm Claire and turn her around to see his way with the exception of finding a church that had Saturday evening services. He was hoping this would solve the problem for Claire and the rest of the family. Claire was stubborn when it came to maintaining what she felt was a traditional Sunday and refused to change. The big problem was that by the time our players reached their fifteenth anniversary they didn't even have a remnant of a traditional Sunday as Claire had hoped to maintain. By this time Claire and Leo were busy with their two teenagers, careers and buying all the material items the world looks at as being good. Both dark and light forces were battling all around our special family and they didn't even realize it.

One night after the whole Bertelli family had gone to sleep, a dark force entered and began chanting an incantation throughout their home, but the white light of the angelic guardian intercepted the spirit and repelled his attack. On his way he laughed. "It's too late. They have already fallen for the lie and they are going to fall." The guard received orders to reinforce his presence with others for the time being and to watch for extra evil activity.

Spring break was coming up in a few days, and our players had developed a family tradition of traveling out to the mountains of Colorado for snow skiing. This spring break wouldn't be any different. They had all grown to love the mountains and all of them had developed to be pretty good at the sport. When it came to downhill skiing, they had all graduated up to intermediate slopes with Leo taking at least one afternoon for the more difficult slopes. While Leo was growing up he had always watched TV programs and read about downhill and cross-country skiing. He couldn't talk Claire into trying it, but as soon as he could get a set of cross-county skis on both kids they were off into the countryside. They would spend at least two days of their trip sliding through the valleys and up onto the mountains. Whenever they would take breaks they would talk about how they would love to be able to come up to the mountains and cross-country ski and camp in the snow for several days at a time. This gave Leo, Willie and Barb a chance to get to know each other and develop a bond in a way that most families don't have.

They planned this trip the same as all their trips. The Bertelli family had their traditions and they were not about to upset the routine they had carefully developed through the years. Each year they went to a different ski resort in the Rockies. They figured this way after several trips they could compare all of them and decide which one they liked the best and go to that one exclusively.

They always downhill skied the first three days, cross-country skied the next two days, then they would load up and go back home. This would give Claire two days to rest up and spend time in whatever shops that would be close by. She never worried about the others since she had such great trust in Leo athletic ability and his sound judgment.

The drive to the new resort was pretty uneventful with the exception of getting a flat about half way and having to empty practically the entire contents of the family van so Leo could get to the jack and spare tire. This caused a short detour and some time waiting on their tire to be patched, but Claire found a very cute little café and shopping area close to the repair shop. Out of all four of them at least Claire was enjoying herself. After they got settled into the lodge, they immersed themselves into the next three days of great powder on the slopes. There had just been a big blizzard in the area a few days before the Bertellis arrived, so the powder was good and deep. They were all looking forward to the best ski time ever.

The first morning after they arrived was spent getting to the ski slopes and learning where they wanted to go. The rest of the time for the next two days was spent hitting the slopes from daylight till dark. By Wednesday afternoon they were all so tired they quit early and spent time at the cabin they had rented getting rested up for the next two days of cross-country skiing. Leo had obtained topographical maps of the area weeks earlier and had already mapped out the courses they would ski on Thursday and Friday. They usually go for four hours in the morning, take an hour for lunch, then turn around and head home by back tracking the same exact route. The first day was probably the best time they had ever had for cross-country skiing. The scenery was the most majestic they had ever skied in. They were exhausted that night, but all of them were determined to go out for their last day.

The last morning always came quicker than any other during their vacations in the Rockies and this was no different from any other. They all drug out of bed and made it down to the kitchen for breakfast. Claire was sitting at the kitchen table with all the others and was really concerned about them being so tired. She asked, "Leo, don't you think you and the kids should stay here with me today? The weather man on TV said there might be snow later this afternoon. Besides, I think you need to stay and get some rest. All of you seem to be more tired than usual and there are some dark clouds out there."

"We might be tired, but that's just because we've had the best time that we have ever had. I think this is where we should come every year. We have skied faster and harder than ever and have really enjoyed it here." Leo looked over the table into her eyes and continued, "We'll be fine, don't worry about the weather, those guys on TV are wrong more than they are right. However, I will suggest a compromise with you. Since today's trail starts about a hundred yards from us, we'll go for three hours instead of our usual four and turn around and come home." He turned to Willie and Barb. "Is that alright with you, kids?"

"That would be okay with me, I am pretty tired, so just two hours would be fine for me," Barb said.

Willie nodded his head in agreement. Leo ignored the comment about two hours and finished his breakfast confident they would have a great day.

After breakfast, Leo, Willie and Barb got ready and left on skis since the trail was so close to the cabin. Leo had the route mapped out and mostly memorized but always carried a map in his daypack for safety. He also left a copy of the map with Claire with the route marked. This way if anything did happen on the trail and they needed help, Claire could find them easier. Of course in this modern age Leo always carried his trusted cell phone with him. Leo figured in three hours they would be able to make it on the other side of the valley to a lake, have lunch, then go home. About thirty minutes into the trip Barb started feeling the effects of the past few days. She was starting to get pretty tired. She usually had plenty of energy on their ski trips. She loved being outside, especially in the mountains. Leo had instilled a love of sports and the outdoors in both of his kids. After another hour Barb saw a shelter coming up, so she asked Leo if they could stop for a while. Leo was sort of disappointed. "That might throw our schedule off a little, but we are here for more than just to be on a schedule, aren't we? That would be okay with me."

The shelter was a rough wooden structure with three walls, a roof and a stone fireplace on one end. They each had their own daypack with food for the trail, so they all got into their supply and found something to munch on during their break. "This is a great place to remember as a landmark in case we get separated on this outing," Leo said with a serious tone in his voice. "You never know what might happen, and those clouds out there are getting pretty thick. Even though it doesn't seem like we are very far from the cabin, we can go much faster on these skis and get farther than if we were walking in all this snow. That means we are much farther from the cabin than you might think. If something were to happen and we were separated from each other, or for some reason we can't make it back to the cabin before dark, this would be a good place to spend the night if you can get to it."

They were ready and back on the trail after about fifteen minutes. Leo was keeping an eye on the clouds but didn't say anything to the kids. He was concerned, but he had a great deal of confidence in all of their ability to get back home, and he wanted the kids to enjoy their last day of vacation in the mountains. They made it to the lake about twenty minutes later than planned, but no one felt bad about that. The water was crystal clear and the trees and mountains around the lake had a perfect mirror reflection in the glassy calm mountain lake. They cut lunch to half an hour since Leo wanted to go home a different way. He said the map showed it as a short cut, but it was on the side of a mountain that was on the south side of the valley and might be a little more treacherous. He marked it as their return route on Claire's copy and figured it would be a good experience for the kids.

It was difficult to get started after lunch. All the muscles in their legs were stiff from sitting around for the lunch break. The blood started flowing again in a few minutes and they really started getting into a rhythm. Leo decided to pull up the rear for a while and was busy trying to read the way the trail was going and keeping up with the kids. The first half of the trail going back was different from the morning until they got within a quarter of a mile of the shelter they stopped at earlier. The clouds were getting darker and Leo noticed snow starting to come down. As they were coming to a very important fork in the trail Leo saw the marker where they needed to go to the left. They made the change of direction with no problem, but the trail seemed to be far steeper than the map indicated. They found themselves doing downhill for at least two miles. Fortunately they had plenty of experience to handle this, which also made another left turn onto the side of the mountain that Leo had concerns for. The wind had started to pick up, and the snowfall was getting heavier, and the temperature seemed to be dropping faster than he expected. He figured they still had a good hour and a half before reaching home.

"Kids," Leo said as he moved forward. He noticed they were starting to slow down. "Let me get in front so I can lead on this side of the mountain and until we get home. After I get up to the front let's see about picking up the pace some. I'm getting a little concerned about this snow and want to get home to that nice warm fire place with your mom." The short cut was starting to get longer with every minute that passed. They were skiing into the wind by now and it was blowing the snow directly in their faces. The clothes they had on were fine for a normal day, but it was turning bad at a very fast pace.

The one thing that might have saved their lives was the one rule Leo always insisted on, bring a pair of gloves and a special light-weight but warm jacket in their daypacks. They stopped long enough to put these articles on then began the journey again.

The only complaints from the kids came when they were putting on the coats and Leo just listened then told them not to worry, they had plenty of daylight left, and they would be back at the cabin soon. He also reminded them of the shelter they had stopped at on their way to the lake. "There's a fireplace there, and we can build a fire and get nice and warm to help us make it the rest of the way." This seemed to lift all their spirits.

Leo remembered one reason he was glad they had come to this area was the recent snowstorm they had the week before they had come. He never thought this same snow they loved could cause the end of all their lives. By this time of the day, visibility was poor, they could only see a few feet in front of them. The snow was blowing right into their eyes now and was sticking to their clothes. They were starting to take on the appearance of snowmen sliding on top of the snow on skis. The tree line was above them anywhere from two hundred to three hundred feet and above that nothing but snow and rocks. All this time Leo was saying a prayer for God to guide and protect them. He was starting to hear some rumbling from above them and was starting to get concerned. "Kids." He stopped. He had to yell above the roar of wind and snow so the kids could hear him. "We need to go faster so we can get away from this side of the mountain and back on the main part of the trail. Remember, if we get split up, your mother has a map showing our route she will get people to come out to look for us and help."

As they all started again there was a tremendous roar from above the tree line. They all looked up to a wall of snow that was rolling down the side of the mountain toward them. It was as if they couldn't believe what they were seeing and went into a momentary shock. The ground under them shook and the trees above them tumbled under the moving wall as if they were being eaten by snow. Leo finally yelled for the kids to "Move it, this way. Come on, kids, let's go!" They each called on every ounce of strength they had to get out of the way of this wall of snow, trees and ice. By now it was like a locomotive chugging down the side of the mountain right toward them. When they came to the side of a small cliff, Leo stopped and turned to the kids he loved. He reached for each of them and threw himself over them against the side of the cliff. He yelled, "It's no use, we can't get out of the way. We have to pray God for help and hold onto each other. This cliff might save us. After this is over us…if you can…dig up and out. Get yourselves…" From this point no one could have heard Leo, they were now under the white wall and it was if the lights went out for all three of our players. Just a few moments later Willie was the first to come to after being covered alive in what could have been a snowy grave.

The time it took for the wall of snow to roll over the Bertelli family as it roared down the entire side of the mountain seemed to take an eternity, but it was just a few seconds. On the surface everything became calm with white powder puffing up as smoke into the air over a cold and snowy grave for our three players. Under the surface, in the snow just beyond the small cliff that was now completely covered, laid three twisted bodies. They held onto each other until everything turned dark causing the muscles in their hands to involuntarily release each other. Their bodies loosely rolled, tumbled and intertwined with each other, then Leo was carried away from the children he loved and was silently buried with his face pointed downward and his body turned as a cork screw. When the snow locomotive did come to a final and haunting stop, Barb had landed bent with her legs under Willie and her torso on top of his mid section. Her right arm was pointed upward with her left following her side.

Willie was on his left side. His left arm was straight out and under his left ear with his index finger stretched out as if to point the way they needed to go. His right arm was bent at the elbow and his hand by his face and part of a large tree branch was sticking him in the left side. The force of the snow pulled the skis off Barb and Willie.

Suddenly Willie's face twitched, then his body went into a convulsion and he blew snow out of both nostrils. His eyes opened along with his mouth as he gasped for air. For an instant he didn't remember what had happened or where he was and didn't know if he were facing up or down. It was difficult to move any part of his body, but the movement of his head caused a cavity within the snow and he found enough air to breathe. With this he screamed, "Dad, Barb…Dad." Nothing came back. He started feeling his arms and the position they were in, then he felt the rest of his body. The weight of the snow was almost too much as it pressed on his chest causing him to struggle for every breath. It was a gigantic effort to move any part of his body, but he forced his right hand into a digging motion toward what appeared to be light.

As he dug, the snow seemed to be melting around him and light began filling the opening that he was creating. Soon he was able to raise his upper body a few inches, then a foot. Within a few more seconds he was able to move his legs and felt something on top and below him. At first he thought it was just another tree branch, but he kept digging upward to make room to be able to sit up, then he started attacking the snow around his legs. In a few more seconds he reached Barb. Nearly exhausted with his chest pumping and gasping for air, he kept digging harder and faster. As he uncovered her face he started rubbing her cheeks and her entire head with his fingers as he quietly, then frantically yelled, "Barb! Don't leave me, stay with me. Wake up!"

Barb's face was turning a shade of blue, and for some reason Willie remembered the Heimlich maneuver and punched Barb in the stomach the best he could. He wasn't sure what he was doing, but the force made her mouth open and she coughed, then snow blew out her nose and mouth. Gasping for air, her eyes opened, then shut, then opened again as she struggled for air. She went through this same process a few more times before she realized Willie was there. "Willie…what happened?" she asked as she gasped and choked. "Where are we?"

"Barb, we're on the side of the mountain and under the snow that came down on top of us. Are you okay? Can you feel your legs?"

"Where's Dad? Where's Dad?" Barb cried.

"I don't know. I just came to and was able to dig and found you. You have to help me dig. We have to dig our way out. Can you do it?"

Barb was still gasping for air. "I don't know. Help me free my legs." They both dug and freed both her legs. "Yeah, I think I can dig now. I'll dig, but which way?"

"This way." Willie started digging in the direction that he hoped was up. Barb followed. They had no idea how deep they were and after a few seconds of digging they both started feeling the heat being drained from their bodies. They knew they had to reach the surface quickly. They moved as tunneling moles, pushing the snow to their backs, maintaining their momentum upward. In a few more seconds Barb's left hand pierced the top of the snow and made a hole when she pulled it back letting sunlight shine on her face. "Willie, there it is. Keep digging, we'll make it." They kept on till they were both on top breathing heavily. The wind was still blowing the snow hard. "Willie, we've got to find Dad. Where is he? How are we going to do it?" She started to frantically yell out, "Dad…Dad."

Barb was looking everywhere on the surface and looked at Willie. "He must be down close to where we were. We need to go back down. You dig on one side and I'll dig on the other." Willie was agreeing with her, but then he caught a glimpse of something that gave him a twinge of hope. He saw what looked like the back end of a cross-country ski that was the same color of his dad's ski. It was at least twenty-five feet on down the slope. "Barb, don't go back down there, you might not come up again. Hurry! Look over there. Down on the slope. Isn't that Dad's ski?"

She looked in the direction Willie was pointing at. "It is, it's Dad. Come on, we've got to dig him out before he suffocates!"

They both tried running, but the snow came up over their waists, so they both dove toward the ski and did a combination of swimming and crawling motion. They didn't stop to look at the ski but started digging. Only about eight inches of the backend of the ski was above the surface of the snow. They both came to their father's left foot at the same time. It was still locked into the ski. They looked at each other with a mixed exposure of excitement and horror.

Willie started digging again with Barb following as fast as she could. They found the right leg about a foot deeper and the started following the legs up the side of their father's body. Willie decided Barb needed to stay on the surface in case they found their worst nightmare. "Barb, you need to move back up on top and help me. As I move the snow up you can spread it out on top better." She agreed and moved out of his way. As Willie made it to his father's head he found it pointing downward with his mouth opened and full of snow. He stuck two fingers of his right hand into his father's mouth and dug the snow out. Leo's color was turning blue, so Willie knew he had to move fast in order to help his dad. While he frantically rubbed his father's face, neck and back he was praying, "Lord, help my dad and help me to know what to do." At that time snow shot out of Leo's nose and he gasped for air. "Dad, Dad! Barb, he's awake!"

Leo looked up at his kids and realized what had happened. He tried moving. "Oh," he moaned. Willie was trying to move his dad. "Don't, Willie. Don't move me. I think my right arm is broken. It's twisted and I think it is broke."

Willie bent over his arm and started gently feeling it. Leo let out a yell, then said, "Willie, Barb, unlock the ski from my boot. I don't think the ski is still on my other foot." They did as he said. "Now both of you carefully turn me over." After they turned him and laid him back down he gave further instructions. "One of you see if you can find something to make a splint out of. Thank God I still have my pack. Look inside and you'll find leather lacing." Barb was able to find some small branches and made it back to them. Willie followed his dad's instructions and set the arm the best he could; then with help from Barb they made a splint around it.

"Okay, Dad. We've got that done. Now what do we do? Can you get up and walk?" Willie asked.

"I think I can. My legs seem to be okay. Help me up and we'll see."

Both kids got under their father's arms and helped to lift him to his feet. He was able to stand, but the problem was the depth of the snow and the pain he was in from his arm. They were starting to lose sunlight fast, so they decided the only choice they had would be to try and walk out of this and make it back to the shelter they stopped at earlier that day. They could at least rest, build a fire and stay warm till they had enough strength to make it back to the cabin. By now the snow had slacked off but was still coming down. Their biggest challenge was the fact they were all soaked because of being buried under the snow, and with the sun going down the temperature would drop dramatically. As they started on their journey, Leo told both kids they needed to give thanks to God for surviving the avalanche. He couldn't believe it had happened, but even with a broken arm and being soaked he was still thankful for what he said God had done for them.

Claire had been worried about her husband and two kids since they left. She didn't really want them to go, and she grew more concerned as she watched the clouds grow darker all afternoon. When the time for her family to return came and went she immediately called the ranger's office for the park. A rescue team arrived at the cabin within a few minutes to find out the route Leo and the kids took. Claire gave them the map Leo had left with the route charted, and they left on skis to look for the missing players.

It had been much easier to go over the top of the snow on skis than walking in the deep powder. Every muscle in their body struggled as they moved in more of a lunging movement through the snow. Leo was in great pain, but he did not want the kids to know how bad it was so he decided they should start singing. The kids always thought the songs their dad liked were corny but now they were hearing them differently and looking at their dad as the hero he really was.

The air became colder as the sun went down, as they knew it would. Frost started forming all over them, including their faces. Their hair froze, their joints and muscles hurt with every movement. Leo knew the colder it got the more difficult it would become for them to make it to the shelter. The other challenge before them was maintaining the correct direction at night. Leo knew only God could pull them through this. He kept on praying and hoping and talking with his kids. He asked them questions about their child hood memories. They remembered birthdays, Christmas holidays and special times during summer vacations including other ski trips while they kept on lunging through the snow in the dark.

Leo figured they had been walking for at least three hours now. Fortunately the snow had stopped falling but the clouds started moving out. This meant colder temperatures and Leo had been feeling warmth in his body slowly leave him for the last hour and a half. He figured they were probably half way to the shelter by now. That would mean they would have another three hours to walk. He was cold, frozen and exhausted, but his faith was strong. He would pray for God to send His angels to help them. Suddenly Leo remembered that night so many years ago when he first met Claire and the miracle in the building where he was blown out onto the street. He always believed God had sent an angel to intervene on his behalf that night, and He could do it again. Leo and Claire had told the kids about that special miracle many times, but it was one memory they had not spoken about on this night.

"Kids," Leo started to talk again. By now it was very difficult for them to talk, but Leo knew they had to keep it up. "You remember the story about the night your mother and I met, don't you?"

They both remembered the story and had even become bored with it, but tonight they would be thrilled to hear about the miracle. As Leo started talking about that emotional and thrilling night all of them seemed to be able to walk easier and breathe lighter. It was still cold and they were still frozen, but they were all trying to concentrate on the story and not their current condition. As they came to the part where Leo decided he had to go into the building to find the source of the scream for help, they saw a flickering light down the trail. They couldn't tell how far it was but they could tell it was moving toward them. He stopped telling the story and yelled, "Kids, there's a light. Look, there's a light down there." He pointed in the direction the light was coming from. They all began to scream and yell for help in the direction of the light. They began to smile again and felt they would be home soon.

The next day Leo and the kids woke up in the local hospital where they had been carried by their rescuers. They were there for observation and treatment for bruises, scrapes and over exposure. He and Claire decided they should stay at the cabin a few more days to rest, talk and enjoy their kids. The next Saturday evening after they arrived back home, the Bertellis were at their church worshiping the Lord that saved their lives. Claire and Leo took time to re-evaluate their lives and priorities. Maybe holding onto tradition for tradition's sake was not the way to go. One thing Leo and Claire talked about was the verse found at Mark 2:27: Jesus said to them, "The Sabbath was made for man, and not man for the Sabbath."

EXTREME REFLECTIONS

"Honor your father and your mother."
Ex. 20:12

Five

Light from the moon came through the canopy of trees causing the night to have a mysterious feel throughout the forest. The warm campfire caused shadows to appear on the tents and trees surrounding the small campsite. All eight campers were enjoying the results of a day of hiking, rock climbing and catching their dinner from the mountain streams. They were having the experience of exhaustion and euphoria that occurs after a day that started with a 6 a.m. wake-up call. The group of teenage campers had no idea they would feel this way three long weeks ago when they first arrived. The camp leaders, Robert, Laverne and Manual, were also amazed with their progress. When the eight campers arrived at the Extreme Youth Adventures headquarters they were typical of the youth that walk through the doors every day. The couple that started EYA, Frank and Sonya Grant, always hoped each young person that walked out of their office after four weeks living in the Colorado wilderness would be changed for the better. They started EYA five years ago to help troubled teens from Denver. Soon juvenile court judges from across the country filled their camping adventures with at-risk teens that seemed to be hopeless.

It was about 9:00 on a Friday morning when some teenage problem kids walked into the EYA office in Estes Park, Colorado. They didn't know it, but this would be a turning point, not only in their lives, but for the staff members who were about to work with them as well. They had caught a red-eye flight out of Chicago and landed at the Denver airport. From the airport they all had ridden to Estes Park on the same van. They were divided into two groups based on the city gang they belonged to and they did not even touch one another. Kyle, Jeremy, Lawanna and Danielle belonged to the Blades, a gang that was signified by a small tattoo of a bowie knife placed on the upper part of the right arm. Ricardo, Seth, Britney and Roth belonged to the Legions. Ricardo thought of the name one Sunday when his parents forced him to attend church. The Pastor read a passage about Jesus casting out demons from a man, and when he asked for the demon's name it said, "Legions." Ricardo thought a name connected with Satan should be shocking enough. Some of the eight came from broken homes and all of them had very wealthy parents. They all had experienced more of life by the age of seventeen than many adults at the age of fifty.

The office for EYA was a one-hundred-year-old brick building with large glass windows and doors. The interior walls had large upbeat and colorful posters of the Rockies and teens engaged in outdoor winter and summer sports. Kyle was the first of the Blades to walk in the front door. He was clad in very large and faded blue jeans that were pulled down several inches below his waist displaying the tops of his printed boxer shorts. He wore a large, black leather jacket that looked like it had been cut in several different places and the Blades insignia was painted on the back. His hair was cut several different lengths all over his head with no real style. Earphones were around the top of his head, and Deborah, a volunteer worker, could hear the music from the back of the office. The other Blades followed close behind and had the same basic look and attitude, but there was no doubt that Kyle was their leader. Each of the Blades wore the same style leather coat with the painted insignia on the back.

A few seconds later Ricardo came in and went directly to the front window on the opposite side of the room from the Blades, pulled out a cigarette from his shirt pocket and stuck it in his mouth. He then produced a cigarette lighter from his jacket and proceeded to light up while the other Legions came in around him. They were all typical "at-risk" kids and you had to wonder if they ever had parents, and if they did, where were they now? In spite of the cold air of the Rockies, each of the Blades had short sleeve t-shirts that had very strange and violent pictures printed on them. Each member had their left nostril pierced with a silver ring through it and the guys had a star tattooed to their upper right arms that Deborah thought was connected with some kind of occult. The one girl had this image tattooed to her right calf.

None of the eight said a word, just stared at the wall, each other or out the window. Nothing about these kids shocked Deborah since she was a former troubled teen herself. Her life had been changed when she was forced to come to Extreme Youth Adventures just two years before. She broke the silence with, "Hello, my name is Deborah. We have all your paper work but there are some questions that we still need answered. I'll let Alex know you're here, then I'll show you around and get you to the next area where you'll meet your leaders for the month."

There was silence and no movement for the next several seconds. Kyle finally exclaimed with a low voice, "What do you mean for the next month? Don't worry about showing me around. I'm not staying." The others looked at him with fear in their eyes. "I'm leaving and Jeremy and the other Blades are leaving with me. We didn't volunteer to come here and we won't stay."

Deborah took a deep breath. "You won't leave unless a local judge says you can after you complete the program."

"We don't care about your program," Kyle snapped back. The rest of the teens started talking more between themselves. The air was getting pretty tense.

"Look," Deborah decided to get Alex before going any further, "no one leave this room. I'm going to get Alex and some others. They will be able to take over from here."

Upon her return to the front room with Alex and a couple of other young men, they found the room empty. They all ran out the front door to find the group had separated with the Blades going south and the Legions to the north. They were just about half a block away, so the leaders split with Alex and one of the leaders going after the Blades, the other leader and Deborah going after the Legions. Alex reached the Blades first and got in front of them and stopped. "Who is Kyle?" he asked.

Danielle spoke up, "Who cares, we aren't stayin'." They all started walking again.

Alex put his hands out and reminded them, "You are all here by court order." Kyle stopped and gave him a cold look and started reaching into his front coat pocket. "You forgot your knife was taken before you saw the judge. The only other alternative for all of you will be for me to go back to the office and call the local police. When they find all of you they will take you back to the Denver airport and put you on the next plane with an armed escort. After you get back home police will meet you at the airport and take you back before the judge that sent you here. From there you will be taken to jail for the next six months. I don't think you really want that. If you come back with me you will be here for three weeks and I promise you will experience what our name says, Extreme Adventure, and you might just get yourselves a better life for it at the same time."

After saying this, Alex became silent knowing the next person to say something would be the one giving in. Jeremy, Lawanna and Danielle looked at Kyle as if they would do whatever he said. Smoke gracefully flowed out from between Kyle's partially opened lips and floated into Alex's face. The cigarette loosely hung from the left corner of his mouth. The smoke burned Alex's eyes, but he didn't dare flinch. After several seconds of this stand off, Kyle moved back a step and asked, "Will the girl be coming with us?"

Alex knew this was his way of saying that he understood and would go back but needed a graceful way of going back. "No, she won't. Why? Do you like her? Did she catch your attention?"

Kyle gave a quick look back to the office. "I don't like anyone. I was just wondering." He looked at the others as he said, "I guess we can see what this is all about before we leave. Come on, guys, let's go."

They noticed the Legions walking back to the office. Jeremy looked at Kyle. "I won't go back if those jerks are part of this. They shot my brother and I promised him they would pay."

Alex heard this and broke in, "There will not be any violence while you are here. Any action like that and you'll go back to the judge, and I understand he is not very fond of any of you."

They all turned and went back to the office. After everyone was back in the office Alex asked Deborah to get Robert and the other leaders that would be working with the eight for the next month. The other leaders stayed to give a hand in maintaining order and making sure the group stayed. When the rest of the leaders walked into the room Alex started talking to all of them. "Robert is your group leader. We use some ideas from the military around here and Robert's title is Camp Captain. You will listen and do exactly as he says each and every day that you are here. Laverne and Manual will be co-workers with Robert and will carry out orders Robert gives them. You will also listen and do as they say every day that you are here with us. I know none of you trust anyone, but you will learn to trust these people. I would trust them with my own life and I am trusting your lives with them also."

Ricardo looked up at Alex and asked, "What will we be doing, and how long will we be here?"

"We have different programs that run anywhere from just a week to four. Judge Miles signed you up for the three weeks and I think he would have made it longer if he could. The only thing that kept him from doing it was the fact that your parents are paying for this as their part. Has anyone told you what we do here?"

Most of them shook their heads to show they didn't know anything. Alex sighed and went on. "That is pretty typical. We have several objectives. The first week you will stay in tents at our base camp and we will teach you basic camping and outdoor skills along with some hiking and climbing. The second week gets more interesting with climbing, repelling and other surprises depending on how all of you do up to that point."

Ricardo gave a strange laugh and spoke up, "Man, that sounds like something you do with parents as a kid. We don't need this and we don't need to know anything about outdoor skills."

Kyle asked, "What will we do, be good little Boy and Girl Scouts and earn merit badges?"

Alex continued as if he hadn't heard any of what Ricardo or Kyle said. "Each week you are here the challenges will be greater and greater. One other thing, each of you will be issued a Bible and you will be expected to read from it every day. We will give you reading assignments and will spend part of each day in a Bible study. One more thing, I'm not sure where your parents fit in your lives right now, but our biggest challenge will be to place them back into your lives and in the right way."

This little announcement caused a small riot with the kids with everyone ready to walk at that very moment. Alex finally broke in with, "Remember, you have been ordered to be here, and the judge knows all about us and what we do here. You will be involved with all this. Just give us time, and since you don't have a choice you might as well relax and stick around."

Lawanna broke in, "One thing I don't do is cook. My mother doesn't cook, so why should I?"

"We will teach you, and each of you will eat what you cook or you won't eat." He looked at the girl. "What is your name?"

"Lawanna."

"Lawanna, believe me, with our method, you will all start cooking today. Anyway, we do have a main objective for all of you, and no one will be excluded. The last several days you are with us you will climb and repel cliffs and live on what you carry on your backs. If you run out of food you will need to rely on the survival skills we teach you. I don't mean stealing from your fellow camper's supplies either."

The group of unwilling adventurers were groaning and murmuring by now as if planning a rebellion. They were all sitting on the floor and whatever chairs they could find. Alex moved to the front door to continue. "Now you will be faced with some basic choices while you are with us. You can choose to obey Robert, myself, the other leaders and cooperate with us, or you can choose not to. You can choose to use your heads to pool your resources and help each other when the need comes or you can choose not to. You will learn whatever choice you decide will have some type of result, some good and some bad. Now I'm sure all of you truly believe you have never made a bad decision in your entire and lengthy lives, but I will go on record as saying you probably have. The fact that you are here today is proof of that. I think the decision Judge Miles made to send you here is the best thing that ever happened to you. If you don't stay the judge will have an alternative where you won't have the same scenery as we have around here. So, after all this you are now faced with your first choice. Who will stay and who will leave?"

Each teenager either stared at the floor or straight in front and there was silence again for several seconds. Ricardo finally broke the silence with, "I'm not scared of you or what you say. I just want to see what else you have around here. We'll stay." He looked at the other Legions and shook his head as to include them all in his decision. Kyle came next with a nod of his head to the others indicating they would be staying also.

"Good, I'm glad that's settled." Alex was being a little sarcastic, but he was also relieved no one actually left. "We need to get your paperwork completed, but since we are behind schedule now, I think we will do that later. You will see me from time to time checking on how things are going, but you must remember Robert, Laverne and Manual will be your direct leaders. They will be your mama, your papa, your teacher and your counselor for the next month. They will show you where you will be staying for this week, which is out back. You need to go out to the van, get your stuff and follow your new mama and papa to your home away from home. Now, young gentlemen and ladies, before we part from each other, I want to finish with one final thought. You will be taught a great deal while you are with us, and your first lesson begins at the end of this talk. I want to teach you two simple words, and if you remember these while you are here, you will make great progress. The words are obedience and cooperation. I'll see you all later. Robert, take charge of these, well, students."

"Yes sir," Robert bellowed out as if he were a private in the army saluting his general. He turned and began to give orders in a kind sort of way. "Just like Alex said, everyone needs to go back out to the van and pull out your bags and follow Manual, Laverne and myself to your tents."

"Tents?" went up in unison from each Blade and Legion as they gave Robert a disgusted look.

All three leaders came back in unison, "Yes, tents!"

Robert continued, "Now go on, get your stuff and come back up to the front of the building. We will be leaving in exactly three minutes. GO!"

Each of the Legions and Blades slowly got up and out to the van. They had been instructed to bring only one bag for this trip. Each of them had either a large duffel bag or a large suitcase to carry. When they got back to the front of the office Robert looked at them and said simply, "Let's go." As they were walking around to the back of the building he continued, "Oh, there is one minor detail Alex wasn't clear on. You will be staying out back of this building, but not directly in back. You see, there is another office building back there so you couldn't stay there. We will be walking a short distance to our base camp where the tents are already set up and waiting for your first night."

"How far will we have to walk?" asked Danielle; this was her first time to say anything since their arrival.

"Only three miles," Manual replied.

"Three miles!" exclaimed all eight in unison.

"Three miles!" repeated the three leaders right back in unison.

Several hours later eight exhausted campers staggered into their base camp along with the three leaders. About half way the Legions had to stop and pull jackets out from their bags and put them on. They were already learning about cold weather in the Rocky Mountains. Robert stopped next to his tent and turned to talk to the others. "Here we are, this will be your new home in the mountains for the next week while we teach you basic skills. Laverne and Manual will show you the tents you will be using. Since this is your first day with us, we have some volunteers bringing us lunch and supper. They should be here any minute so get your stuff stored and we'll hang out till they get here."

While Robert was busy in his tent, he heard some of the guys yelling outside, so he dropped everything and ran out to see what was going on. He found all eight yelling about the tent assignments. Alex wanted the groups mixed with all three girls in the same tent. Manual and Laverne were doing their best, but things were starting to get out of control. Robert shouted, "What's going on here?"

Danielle shouted back, "I'm not going to sleep in the same tent as her." She was pointing at Brittney.

Brittney shouted back, "Well, I'm not spending one night in any tent with you or her," pointing to Lawanna.

Robert was getting worried the guys were about ready to pull out guns, knives or chains and get after it. "Okay, listen up, everybody." Robert exclaimed but no one was paying attention. "Be quiet," he shouted at the top of his lungs. They all stopped and looked at him. "Now that I have your attention, let me remind you of the words Alex tried to teach you before we left the office which were obedience and cooperation. None of you have learned anything about either of those words yet." He reached into his coat pocket and pulled out a cell phone and held it up. "You are about to learn of a possible consequence to your continued lack of cooperation. All I have to do is give Alex a call and he will call the judge and all of you will be going back to whatever the judge has for you. Now I will tell you one more thing, I don't want to do that and I will not unless you force me to. The last thing you need to know is that I will do it if you do not start showing that you are cooperating. Do we have an understanding now?" No one said anything. "Look, each of you will sleep in the tents that we have assigned to you, and you will learn about each other this week, like it or not."

Each of them calmed down, grabbed their bags and turned to go to their tents. Each of them threw their bags in their tents and crawled in. A few minutes later Roth and Jeremy were fighting in their tent causing it to collapse on top of them. Manual went over and lifted the front tent opening. "Well, boys, looks like you will now have your first lesson on setting up a tent. Now get out and get it done, now!"

They both growled at him and each other and grudgingly got up and fumbled with the tent poles. Neither of them had ever camped a night of their lives and didn't know the first thing about setting up a tent. Fifteen minutes later the workers with lunch showed up. Robert yelled for everyone to come to the shelter they had set up for cooking and eating. Roth and Jeremy were still trying to figure out their tent and making rude comments to each other. Occasionally when no leaders were looking they would throw a punch at each other. Hunger finally got the best of them and they threw down the tent parts they had in their hands and walked very fast to the food shelter. It was hot dogs and chips and they ate all of it in a matter of seconds. Something about the mountain air, altitude or something caused them to eat faster than ever.

The food shelter was a pavilion with no exterior walls. After lunch everybody was sitting or lying around under the shelter or just outside of it. They started noticing the scenery around them that Alex was talking about. "Man, look at how big these mountains are," Roth said. "They're taller than any of the buildings in Chicago."

"I have never seen anything like this in my life." Danielle was starting to get into the scenes.

Robert walked up and said, "I'm glad you are starting to gain an appreciation for the area. You will be here in the middle of it for quite a while. I have good news for you. We will be starting cooking lessons over a fire in twenty minutes. You have that long to take care of whatever you need to and get back here for your first cooking lesson."

"Cooking!" all eight campers said in unison.

"I figured that would excite all of you. Laverne and Manual will be your teachers this afternoon, and you will be here and listen and participate."

Twenty minutes later each gang member slowly walked back to the shelter, but they were not ready to learn how to cook over a campfire. When Kyle walked up he said, "Why don't you make the girls learn how to do this? The guys don't need to learn how to cook."

With these great words of wisdom all the girls turned around and walked to Kyle and quickly started slugging him and pushed him down to the ground. Laverne and Manual broke them up and set the record straight for everyone. "Listen, what you'll be learning today will be very important to your survival. Now shape up and we'll get started."

Just like everything else that day, the cooking lessons got off to a shaky start. No one understood what Manual was doing when he brought out a funny looking little stove and set it up on the ground. "What's that?" Danielle asked.

"This is a portable stove that we'll be starting with. Each of you will be carrying one in your packs and you will be cooking on them tonight." Manual explained.

"What happened to building fire with wood?" Asked Ricardo.

"We try not to burn wood while on the trail unless you run out of fuel or need a fire for warmth in extreme cold conditions. We are trying to be responsible with the environment out here and burn as little as possible."

What the cooking lesson consisted of was heating up water and preparing packages of dehydrated food. "Uh, Manual," Ricardo said as he picked up a small package of beef stew. "I don't think this will work. How will we all eat this stuff?"

"Manual, you will be surprised at how delicious this is. From now on you will have three meals a day from packages just like this."

"Hey look," Jeremy said. "We can't have stew for every meal."

Laverne responded to this. "You will have bacon and eggs for breakfast and a large assortment for all the other meals. We promise none of you will starve."

The Bibles were handed out after the cooking lesson. "This is the most important part of your gear for this week." Robert kept talking as he handed out the books. "Open the front cover and you'll find a daily reading schedule. You will be expected to stick to this reading every morning first thing after breakfast here at base camp and when we're hiking on the trail. We'll spend the next thirty minutes each day discussing what you read. I have a couple of other things to let you know about. On our way up here I noticed at different times your language was pretty colorful. There will not be any swearing while you are here, and the last thing is about smoking. Several of you have lit up since being here. The air up at this altitude is pretty thin which makes it difficult enough to breathe. Smoking makes it even harder. How many of you brought cigarettes with you?" Several gestured that they had brought packs of cigarettes with them. "We realize it would be difficult for any of you to quit cold turkey, so we will be limiting you to no more than two smokes a day. Look at it as rationing to help your supply last through this ordeal." All the smokers kept quiet knowing a protest would only end up with Robert calling Alex and they would be in front of the judge again in a few days.

Kyle started voicing what most of the others were thinking. "We will do what you want, but we won't read this book. I refuse to do it. There is separation of church and state, you know. We'll report you to, well, I don't know who, but I'll report you guys to someone."

Manual spoke up. "Sorry, there aren't any phones out here, so how will you do your reporting? I'll tell you what, if you still feel this way in three weeks, I'll give you the name and phone number of someone you can report us to. How's that?" They all seemed to calm down with this challenge. Most of the kids felt like they could read it, but they weren't going to believe any of it.

The rest of that first week went fast with only a few snags from time to time. They did learn how to build a fire, set up tents along with what should go into a backpack and how to pack one. The leaders kept the campers busy with hikes and climbing lessons each morning and afternoon to get used to the thin air in the higher altitude. The morning Bible reading and discussions went fairly well. As the days went on most of the kids started loosening up and talking more. Most of the kids were worn out by the evening meal and would go to bed afterward. The leaders would stay with the others by the fire and let them talk about anything they wanted to in order to find out more about them. Kyle and Ricardo would usually stay up but were the only ones not talking much.

While on one of the afternoon hikes up in the mountains, they came across a cave that had a sign over the entrance that read, "Cave of Reflections." Seth asked, "What does that sign mean?"

Robert explained, "There are some strange stories about this cave. I've heard some, but I don't believe any of them."

"What are the stories?" Seth wanted to know.

"Oh, not sure where they came from. Some people say they started with the Indians that used to live in this area. I don't think any of the stories are true. They say if a person is inside the cave at the right time they see visions or something."

"Visions?" Kyle started to get interested in the cave now.

"Well," Robert kept talking. "I guess they are visions. One of the stories was about a businessman that was an avid hiker that just happened across the cave one day and decided to explore it. While he was inside a strange warm wind came from the back of the cave and he started hearing voices. Next he saw a light that seemed to come from the same direction as the wind and voices. He went toward the light and found himself in a large, natural room that had several lanterns along the cave walls and three people were sitting on rocks talking. The strange thing about all this is that he knew all three people. Of course he was shocked and didn't know what to do. You see, each of the people had two things in common. The first was that he stopped talking to each of the people because of a disagreement over something that caused them to have a big fight. The second thing they had in common was that all three were dead and had been dead for many years."

"This is a stupid story, do you think we should believe this?" Kyle interrupted.

Robert kept on with the story. "I was asked about this, so you will listen until I am finished. Where was I? I think it was when he walked toward the light and voices and found himself in a large natural room with three men from his past that were all supposed to be dead. His father looked over to him and began talking as if his son had been a part of the conversation from the first. The men were talking about the problems in their relationship with the hiker. The hiker was drawn into the conversation and started talking about these problems for the first time in his life. You might say he was able to 'reflect' on the problems with the others.

"As the story goes the hiker was able to deal with the problems for the first time in his life. The time he spent in the room seemed like hours to him but it was just a few minutes. It's said this hiker is the person that made the sign and put it over the cave's entrance. Some people say he comes back to the cave every chance he gets hoping to see the three men again. Of course I don't believe any of this, I just wanted to answer Seth's question. That is one story and there are lots of others but they're all about the same. The main point that does make a lot of sense is this seems to be a pretty good place to reflect on your life. To see if you have been going down the right path and to think on the relationships you have had. Well, let's get going, we need to be back at camp in another hour." They made their way to camp and nothing else was said about the cave from anyone.

The next day they were all on a climb up a very high and steep mountain. The path was narrow and close to the edge. They had to do a lot of hand-over-hand climbing, but Robert had promised the group their efforts would certainly be worth the effort. He warned them to stay close to the mountain and not hang over the edge. As they were almost to the top, Robert was giving more instructions to the group, but Ricardo and Jeremy weren't listening. Instead, they were clowning around and slapping each other and playing chicken by seeing how far they could to on the edge. Suddenly Jeremy's feet slipped, he screamed and desperately grabbed for something or someone. Ricardo reached for his arm, then a hand, but missed every time. Jeremy was over the edge and out of grasp in just a few seconds. Everybody started screaming for help and for Jeremy to give an answer. Robert and the other leaders made their way to the spot pushing everybody else to the side and behind them. Robert finally told everyone to be quiet so they could hear and think.

As he carefully looked over the edge, Robert could see Jeremy hanging onto a tree that was growing out of the side of the mountain. "Jeremy," Robert yelled. "I'm going to throw a rope down to you. It will have a large loop in it. Try to put it around your waist and we'll pull you up." Robert took the pack off his back, pulled out a rope, tied the loop in it and threw it down to Jeremy. "You'll need to use one hand to do this, but you can do it, Jeremy. I know you have the strength to do it. You'll have to help us by using some of those climbing skills we taught you. Tell us when you are ready and we'll start pulling." Robert put the rope around his back and he had Ricardo and Manual to hold onto him and help with the rope.

Jeremy's weight was too much for the small tree and when he reached for the rope it started to break with a loud cracking sound at the roots. As Jeremy used his right hand to pull the rope around him the tree gave another cracking sound. In another second the tree was falling to the bottom of the mountain, but Jeremy was swinging at the end of the rope. He yelled up to the others, "Start pulling. Go, I'm ready." He grabbed for any place to hold onto with his hands and feet.

The others were struggling to hold onto the rope above him and not go over the edge also. After a while the rope started getting tighter and cutting into Jeremy's middle. He gave it all he had to pull himself up and cling to the rocky side. After several minutes he was just a few feet from the trail when both his feet slipped causing him to slide back down the mountainside. Fortunately, Robert had gloves on that protected his hands from being burned by the sliding rope. With the help of the others, Robert was able to stop the slide, but now the rope was so tight around Jeremy's waist he was unable to breathe and could no longer do any of the climbing. Robert and the others had to pull Jeremy up the rest of the way without his help. They had him up and safe in a few minutes, but they were all exhausted. They quickly loosened the rope from around Jeremy so he could breathe again. As he caught his breath Jeremy looked at Robert and said, "Man, now that was extreme teen adventure. Can I go home now?"

Robert had gotten down to Jeremy's side checking for any broken bones and other injuries. "Sorry, but it is farther to get down than to the top so we have to go on. Besides, I think everyone will like the way we have to get down once we reach the top. You seem to be okay, nothing seems to be broken, just bruises. You might even be able to take the fast way down with everyone else. I won't lecture you for now, but this is a good subject lesson on obeying the rules. We'll rest for a few minutes, but we need to keep going." Robert placed the rope back in his pack and moved to his place in line, then gave the order to move out.

They were at the top within thirty minutes to find several others were already there before them. There were enough parachutes for each of the campers and leaders. Robert looked at Jeremy and said, "Now this will be an extreme teen adventure." All of the kids knew what was going on and none of them wanted to do it. They were all willing to take the climb back down instead. It took Robert and the other leaders several minutes to convince the kids this was safe. They had never lost a teen camper since starting this part of the program. Laverne explained everyone in the group had worked very hard and had come a long way and this was a method of rewarding them. Besides, it took them three hours to climb to the top and they almost lost one member in the process. How could this be any worse?

For the next hour the campers were given lessons on how to get into the parachute harness, how to jump off the edge of the cliff with the chute fully open and ride the air currents down to the bottom of the valley. They were warned about the sudden change in the wind causing the chute to flatten which would mean whoever was under it could fall to their deaths or be severely injured. The teachers checked Jeremy and gave him the option of walking back down with one of them or taking the chute down. He chose to take the chute and was the first to make the jump. As he took that last step off the edge he felt the gentle pull of the wind filling his chute and carrying him into mid air. He started to relax a few seconds into the flight while he trusted the harness with his weight. He first looked down to see where he was going. He had cleared the side of the mountain and was being carried down in a spiraling effect. He heard one of the instructors yelling down to him, "Remember to pull the lines." He reached and pulled first to the right, then to the left until he started to get the feel of it. This was far better than flying in an airplane. He saw the terrain moving closer with every second, but he wanted to stay up longer. The air was warm and he loved looking up at the colorful chute that had ballooned out above him. He started hearing the others yelling as they took off into their air journey.

Jeremy performed a perfect landing but his legs were pretty shaky more from excitement than anything. He fell to the ground, got out of his harness, and while laying on his back watched the sky that seemed to be filled with one parachute after another. He was hearing all of their yelling and screaming. Some quickly figured out how to ride the currents longer than others. They reminded Jeremy of seeing eagles soaring around on the invisible currents of power. Suddenly Jeremy started thinking about other things, spiritual things. He thought about God and Jesus and what had just happened to him above on the side of the mountain as he nearly fell to his death. He wasn't sure how he ended up hanging by a small tree that was shooting out from the side of the mountain. Memories of home and his parents came to him. Things he had said to them and how he almost lost all chances to make it all up to them just a few minutes ago. After Robert landed he walked over to him and said, "I need to talk. This has been extreme, man." Tears started forming in his eyes. Robert got out of his harness and stood there with Jeremy as he listened. "While I was laying watching you guys come down lots of stuff started to come to my mind. I wasn't sure why at first, but now I know. What you and the other leaders have said makes sense to me now."

Robert looked at him with anticipation. "What have we said, Jeremy, that has made so much sense to you?"

"Well, about Jesus being the Son of God and how we all need him and need a relationship with him. I mean after almost losing it all today I saw it all clear. I need Jesus and I want to ask to accept him right now. I don't want to wait, I mean, no telling what might happen next. You know what I mean?"

Robert looked at him for a moment, he was taken a little off guard after just landing from that terrific parachute ride. "Well, Jeremy, I'm glad you have this idea. Are you sure you want to do it right here in front of everybody and out in this field?"

"Sure, after all you have taught us God created the earth, so why can't we do it here? I don't care if everybody sees or hears us. Let's just do it!"

"Okay, let's talk for a while so you have a clear picture of it all…." For the next several minutes Robert went over what it means to be saved by asking Jesus into his life. Jeremy was still convinced he wanted to say the prayer to ask Jesus into his heart. Right there in the middle of a valley deep in the Rockies they knelt and prayed together as all the others watched. Kyle and Ricardo made it a point to look the other way when this was going on and to find something else that interested them. Jeremy displayed a new attitude and outlook on life immediately. Robert and the other leaders knew this was a turning point for the whole group.

The campers and leaders took the rest of the afternoon to hike back to base camp. They talked all the way back about the events of the afternoon. Jeremy had Roth and Lawanna praying to ask Jesus into their hearts before they were back to the tents. Manual, Lavern and Robert were amazed at how quickly the Holy Spirit was working. Bible study from that point on took on a new life with the three new Christians taking an active roll now.

A few days later Alex walked into camp just after breakfast. Alex had called Robert on the cell phone to let him know that he would be coming up to camp and why. He shared this with the other leaders but they were not to tell anyone else. Alex went up and asked Kyle to go for a walk, he had something to tell him. Neither of them talked until they were out of the camp area, then Alex began. "Kyle, I have something to talk to you about. I have never had to do this before so please understand that it will take me a few seconds to get everything out."

Kyle was maintaining his usual objective self, but inside he was wondering what this was all about. Alex continued as they walked along a rugged wooded trail by a running stream of pure, cold water. "This isn't easy for me, but it will be very tough for you, Kyle. I'm not sure how your relationship with your parents has been. I think that I can just come out and say that I have some unpleasant news about your parents. Kyle, they had an accident yesterday while driving on a highway close to Chicago."

Kyle's face started to change as Alex kept talking. "I don't have all the details, but they were out late last night and some driver crossed over into their lane and hit them head on. They were both going fast and when the impact occurred both of your parents were killed instantly." Kyle's eyes started to glaze over as he struggled to maintain control. Even though his relationship with his parents wasn't very good, his emotions began taking over. Tears started to come down his cheeks as his face turned red.

"I don't believe you. How do I know you are telling me the truth? Maybe you have it mixed up and you should be telling somebody else all this?"

"No, Kyle. I need to tell you. Your parents were in a wreck and they were killed."

"Well, do you think I care if they're dead? I've told them many times that I wished they were dead. I always used to imagine what life would be without them." They sat by the stream and spent the next several minutes talking about Kyle and his parents. His father was not home very much of the time because of his business, so he and Kyle never developed much of a relationship. He had two older sisters who were home when the accident occurred. Alex explained that his sisters had arranged for Kyle to go home immediately so they could make arrangements for their parents' funeral and to figure out what they need to do next. Alex walked Kyle back to his tent and helped him with his things. Kyle went to the area where the others just finished with that morning's Bible study. He told Ricardo and several others what had happened and that he was leaving. Alex helped Kyle load everything in his Jeep and drove directly to the Denver airport. From there Kyle caught the next flight out to Chicago. His days at the camp had come to an end for now.

Kyle's unfortunate situation was the main topic for the last week of camp for the others. It led to discussions about life and how death can come suddenly. All of the kids talked tough about death and even killing others, but when it was brought close to home it made them stop and think like anyone else. Jeremy talked about his close call with an early death while on the side of the mountain. That last week two others, Danielle and Seth, decided they needed Jesus in their lives. Out of the eight that began this journey five had become born-again Christians by the end. Ricardo and Brittney refused to admit they needed anything other than themselves to make it through life. When the time was over five campers went home with a new life and the others had a great deal to think about.

One year after the Legions and Blades had left Estes Park for Chicago, Kyle made a return trip. He had dropped out of the gang during that year as he tried to get himself together after the tragic news of his parents. He came to the mountains by himself this time and went back to the same area where the base camp was located the year before. Alex had made a decision to move the camp so nothing was at the old site. He brought a tent along with him, so he set up his own campsite as he was taught just a year earlier. He had carefully built a fire to warm himself as his thoughts went back to those two weeks from the previous summer. The day they were hiking and came across the cave with the sign above the entrance and the story Robert had told had been coming back to him for the last several months.

He woke up with the sunrise and fixed his breakfast complete with bacon, eggs and coffee. A short while later he was hiking along the trail leading up to the mysterious cave. He found the sign with the words "Cave of Reflections" on it behind some bushes, so he knew he was in the right place. While he was clearing brush from the entrance, something quickly caught his attention. A faint aroma of a fragrance that seemed familiar came from inside the cave, but he couldn't nail it down.

It was dark inside, so he pulled a flashlight out from his daypack and shined it inside. There was nothing special about the cave on the inside. A few minutes into his exploration he stumbled over a large rock causing him to fall and to lose his only light when his flashlight broke. Kyle was in a dark cave with his right knee and both hands bleeding. He didn't really know what to do, so he sat for a while and gave it some thought. He finally decided he needed to move toward the entrance and leave. As he stumbled over the cave floor, he fell again and hit his head on another sharp rock creating a shallow gash to his left temple. This caused him to become dizzy and his site was slightly blurred. The blood from the gash to his temple began to run down into his left eye causing it to sting. His pulse began to race and he started to panic. He was breathing and sweating heavily by now. He tried getting up again, and that familiar fragrance came back. He thought he could tell where it was coming from, so he decided to follow it. He was feeling his way through the cave's corridor when he felt what he thought was a hand on his right shoulder. Startled he shouted, "Who's there?"

"It's me, Kyle," a female voice answered.

Kyle jumped backward and shouted again, "Who are you?"

"Kyle, let me help you." A hand touched him on the same shoulder, then to his arm and helped him up to his feet. It was a female's hand and voice, and as she helped him a light shown on her face. Kyle looked up at her with shock, then grabbed her by the waist.

"Mother, are you really here?"

"Yes, I am here for you."

"That smell, that's your perfume, isn't it?"

"Yes, remember it was a gift that you bought for my birthday three years ago. This reminds me of when you were a little boy. There were many times when I had to pick you up and clean and dress your wounds. You were always skinning your knees, especially when you played baseball. Do you remember that?"

"Yes, I remember all that. I started thinking you were following me everywhere I went just to make sure I didn't hurt myself." They both laughed. A deeper voice came from over to their right.

"Oh, there's your father. He is here for you too."

"Dad," Kyle said in a whisper as if he didn't believe it. "Are you really here?"

"Yes, son. I am here." He reached out and started patting Kyle on the shoulder; then as he came closer he gave him a big, manly hug.

"Oh, you're hurt," his father said as he noticed the gash in Kyle's head. "You need to let your mother take a look at that. She works miracles with cuts you know."

Kyle's mother took him by the hand and said, "Follow us. We want to talk with you." The room started filling with a pleasant glow, but Kyle couldn't tell where it came from. They walked over to a large multi-colored couch and sat down with Kyle between his parents. His mother brought out a first aid kit so she could clean and dress each cut.

"You always liked this couch, didn't you?" she asked.

"Well, I did a lot of serious sleeping on it," Kyle replied.

His father said, "I failed you, Kyle. I paid more attention to the business than to you, and I'm sorry about that."

"Dad!"

"No, you don't have to say anything, son. I love you and I wanted to provide everything you ever needed or wanted. I wanted to do it for you, your sisters and your mother. Most of all, I'm afraid I wanted to be the big successful man."

This broke the ice between them, and Kyle started confessing feelings he had held inside for years. All three sat and talked for what seemed to be hours. Kyle told them all about Extreme Youth Adventures. All the people he had met and how the leaders really seem to care about each of the kids. He apologized for not being a more obedient son. He wished he could take back many things he had said and had done. Finally their time was coming to an end, and his parents' time began to fade. They had looked back, reflecting on the past. They laughed at the good and cried over the bad. Kyle realized this was what he had needed for the last year.

Kyle found himself on the cave floor again with his flashlight in his lap turned on, but his parents were gone. The light was shining toward the opening and he could see daylight. He sat as if in a daze for a few minutes and finally pulled himself up and slowly moved toward the light of the day. He felt like he had been in the cave for hours. While he was walking, he noticed his knee wasn't hurting any more. The bandage on his temple was gone also and his hands didn't have any scrapes or cuts anymore either.

When he came out into the daylight, he sat down next to the stream that was a few yards away. He felt all the wind go out from his lungs as he began to sob for the first time in his life. Then came a sound that he couldn't make out. He thought it was just the wind at first, but then he thought he heard his name being spoken. He couldn't tell where the voice was coming from and he couldn't see anyone around. There was a different feel to the air around him, but he didn't know why. When he made it back to his camp, he went to his tent and pulled out the Bible Robert had given him a year ago. He opened it to the passages he had been studying for the last year. He remembered the prayer that others of his group said the previous summer. Kyle sat there outside his tent and repeated the same words. In a few seconds Kyle was filled with peace that he had never felt before. He felt whole and clean for the first time.

The next day Deborah was working at the front desk of Extreme Teen Adventures when she looked up and saw a young man open the glass door and walk in. He looked familiar but she couldn't place him. She thought there was something special in his face, especially in his eyes. As Kyle walked up to her desk he began to speak. "Hello, Deborah. I doubt if you will remember me, but I was here for a short time last year. I came by to see if there is a way a former troubled teen could be a part of this place permanently."

PRAIRIE SUNRISE

"You shall not murder."
Ex. 20:13

Six

It was late in the day, hot and windy on the rolling western Kansas prairie. Out in these lonely plains Jesse was laying on his belly behind a horse that was stretched out on his side hidden in the tall grass. The horse wasn't much for breeding, but Jesse had trained this powerful animal to be the best partner he could ever have. As he looked past the sights of his mighty Hawkins onto another animal, Jesse squeezed the trigger, and with a loud crack hot lead was released to cut through the air to its target. As the bullet struck the giant buffalo straight through the heart it dropped instantly.

The horse didn't flinch until Jesse said, "Horse, get on up." Horse was all Jesse ever called the animal, and he responded to the words as an obedient child. Jesse straddled the saddle riding Horse as he came up to a standing position. In one swift move Jesse placed his rifle in its scabbard and pulled his mighty Bowie knife out from the sheath that was at his waist belt ready to go to work.

After standing still beside the beast for a moment partly to give respect and partly making sure it was dead, Jesse started in with surgical precision cutting down into the animal's groin. Jesse had lost track of the number he had killed through the years since starting in this business. He didn't even take time to eat any of the parts that used to be so enjoyable while completing what many would consider to be a gruesome job. He did have a respect for the buffalo uncommon for other white men of the day. This was his livelihood, and he was good at it, but that didn't mean he was a butcher like so many others. He finished about three hours later, just before dark, and loaded everything on an Indian style litter being pulled by Horse.

After getting into camp, Jesse took the skin and buffalo head, complete with horns, off the litter and hung it out to begin the tanning process. Then he got the fire going and threw some of the freshly cut meat into his skillet and got fixens going for coffee. The rest of the work on the skin would have to wait till the next day. For now he was whipped and ready to lie by the fire and listen to the steak. Horse never had to be tied up. He and Jesse had been together for so long, all that had to be done was to remove the saddle and give him a bag of oats. They camped by a creek that was running pretty low as usual for this time of year, but Horse could still get plenty of water from it.

Now being stretched out by the fire, Jesse measured an average height for his day, about 5 feet 5, wearing buckskin softened more by use than design. He had let his beard grow for the last several days on a face that was baked to a dark brown by the sun. Jesse was a perfect specimen of a man of the Kansas prairie. His Colt side arm was sticking in his groin some, so he took the waist belt off and laid it on the ground next to him. He was starting to relax next to the crackling fire while listening to the buffalo steak sizzling in the skillet and taking in the aroma of the coffee. It had been a long day, and the sun was gone with stars shining on the best roof Jesse ever knew, the sky itself. There wasn't a cloud in that night sky, the moon was full and the wind had finally died. It was a perfect night to sleep out on the grasslands.

He began thinking about how the last few years had been pretty rough, but things seemed to be turning around for him lately. Didn't know how old he was exactly, twenty-five maybe. The Kansas prairie was about all he had ever known. Never found a woman he wanted to marry but wasn't about to give up. He was born in St. Louis, but early on his Pa decided to go west, so they joined a wagon train and headed for California. When the rear axle of their wagon broke at a small cow settlement at a fork of the Arkansas River, his Pa decided that was far enough west for him. They settled right there and had the rest of the family, three brothers and a sister while farming the land. As a boy, Jesse never cared for farming much, so instead of plowing he would usually go hunting, fishing or swimming in the nearby creeks. Ma could read some and enjoyed reading to the family from the only book they ever had, the Bible. Several evenings each week, after the work had been done, they would all gather around the fireplace, light some extra candles and listen to Ma read from her favorite passages. Even though she couldn't read very good, Ma made sure each of her children could do it at least as well as she could and even write some. As Jesse grew up, the small settlement became a thriving and at times a violent cow town known as Wichita.

After finishing his steak and half the pot of coffee, Jesse laid back and fell fast asleep while being warmed by the fire. He woke up with the sunrise, but he had to lie there for a while to give his joints time to be able to move. He was a young man, but his life was hard and his body had been witness to it all. When he was finally able to move around he got up, placed the coffee pot back on the fire and went down to the creek where he knelt down and splashed cold water on his face to help the early morning waking process. After his morning coffee he spent several hours scraping and working on yesterday's kill. This was a good skin to add to his stock. He found a good market for buffalo heads so people could hang them on their walls and make up stories about the hunt they were never on. To Jesse this was a way of life, but to most of the others it was a sport and all they were after were trophies. Because of his attitude of respect for the beasts, the land and the skill he possessed in his craft Jesse had gained a great deal of respect from most of the Indians of the area and they never bothered him. Overall Jesse was a peaceful man and he was at peace with himself and his God.

About a week later Jesse decided he had enough stock and loaded his wagon, hooked up his other horses to pull it, tied Horse to the back and went to conduct his trading. Through the years Nehemiah, the owner of the trading post, had become a friend to Jesse. He was an honest and fair enough man and Jesse was getting a little anxious to see him again. This was the only trading post for a hundred miles in any direction and was pretty typical for the 1870s. About anything you needed for survival on the prairie could be found there, and if you couldn't find it then you must not have needed it. By the time he arrived to the settlement, it was too late to do any good trading, so he got a room at the Phillipses' boarding house just down the road from the trading post. He even spent fifty cents on a bath that night.

Jesse made it to the post early the next morning where he pursued his trading that just took a few minutes. He sold about half the skins and preserved buffalo heads for cash, then traded the other half for supplies. He could have gotten a better price for the skins in Wichita, but it was further to go, and besides, Nehemiah would usually throw in a few extra pounds of coffee for him. Most of the men that lived out on the plains at that time would tell you they would rather drink whiskey than water but Jesse loved his coffee much more. It was one of the few things he took real pleasure in and would start and even finish every day with several cups of the dark brew. The only time Jesse would partake of whiskey was after he finished with all his trading. Nehemiah would always want to seal the deal with a drink. This time they had finished the chore earlier than usual, so Jesse promised to come back later that day to conclude the trade officially.

With all the trading out of the way, Jesse had most of the day ahead of him. Any other time he would load up and head back to his cabin, but for some reason he decided to stay in town for a while. Leaving the wagon at the post, Jesse climbed on the back of Horse and thought for a moment on where he wanted to go. What used to be a small farm settlement was turning into a real town complete with the trading post and a barbershop next to it. There was a saloon down the road and a blacksmith shop and livery stable across from that. The town's sheriff had an office with rooms that had real bars as doors to lock up law breakers next to the blacksmith shop. In the middle of the main street was the largest sign that civilization had come to this area of the country. A few months before Jesse came to town, a church was built with a large and you might even say perfect steeple with a cross at the top and a bell inside. Around all this were about one hundred houses placed in neat rows running the length of the town. Some of them were log cabins with others built from milled lumber brought in from Wichita. Some of the houses had a coat of whitewash over the exterior, and some even had real glass in the windows.

Jesse, while on top of Horse, rode up and down the main street several times looking around and deciding what they wanted to do. Through the years he had gotten to know some of the town people, and whenever they saw each other it was usually a pretty cordial meeting. On their second time down the street, he noticed an old friend that lived out of town on a farm.

"Hey Tom," he shouted. "How are you doing nowadays? What are you doing in town? You should be out plowin' up the grass to plant the next wheat crop."

Tom ignored most of what Jesse said. "It's good to see you, too, Jesse. See you still wearin' that buckskin instead of civilized clothes. Plowin' is why I'm here. Was plowin' in a new area and hit a large rock, which is pretty strange for these parts, and it caused my blade to break. Brought it to the blacksmith to get fixed. Just thought I would walk down to the boarding house and get something to eat."

"Think I'll join you if that's okay," Jesse said.

"Sure, glad to have such good company as you." He climbed up on his horse and they rode to the boarding house together, went in and ordered lunch. As they were eating, Tom asked Jesse, "Don't you think you ought to be lookin' for something else to do besides shooting buffalo?"

"Why? Still a lot of buffalo out there and don't see any reason to make a change yet," he replied.

"Jesse, you know there aren't near as many buffalo as there were even a year ago. More of those easterners are comin' all the time and just killing them for sport, leaving most of the animals on the prairie to rot. You know what they're doing. Pretty soon there won't be enough for any of the Indians to live on, and what will you do then? A man's gotta make a living, you know, and what about getting a wife and settling down?"

Jesse gave Tom a disgusted look, then came back with, "What's goin' on here, Tom? Why are you so worried about me? We see each other about three, maybe four, times a year at the most. Truth is, I figured on getting married a long time ago but just never met a woman I wanted to get tied to for the rest of my life. Might come some day, but not gonna worry about it. As far as making a livin' goes, well, it don't cost me much to live, and I've got a good amount saved. Got my eye on a place south of here a ways. Never cared about farmin' so been thinking about cattle. With the drives coming up from Texas into Wichita, figure I'll have what I need in a few months. Hope to keep a few buffalo to make sure they will be around a little longer. So how's that for you, ole Tom? Reckon if the good Lord keeps watchin' over me it will all be okay. Been pretty much a loner since I left my folks, but that same good Lord might even bring that woman to make me a good wife." The two friends finished their meal and visit, then parted ways.

Jesse decided he needed to go back to the trading post to complete his business with Nehemiah as promised. As he rode up to the post, he noticed several other horses tied outside but didn't think anything about it. The post was built of logs roughly cut by hand with a couple of windows in front. To help bring in needed light there was an extra wide entrance that had double swinging doors usually associated with saloons. When Jesse got close to the opening, he started hearing voices belonging to other men. The sun was bright that day, and it was taking a few seconds for his eyes to adjust to the dark room he was entering. He could make out what appeared to be three men in front of the counter with Nehemiah behind it. All were dressed rough and smelled as if they had been out on the trail for weeks. The biggest of them waved his gun toward the door and said, "If you're coming in, mister, you better throw that side piece on the floor and get over here."

"Jesse," Nehemiah blurted out. "Better do it, Jesse. There are four of them, one is over in the corner carrying a shot gun with both barrels pointed at you."

Taken off guard, Jesse removed his gun belt and dropped it where he was and came in closer to the others. "Nehemiah, what's going on here?"

"Well, most people would see what's going on here. It's a hold up! These guys were proceeding to take all the money I have in the store when you walked in."

"Okay, mister," the leader said. "Just back off a few steps and we'll leave peaceful like."

Jesse backed over to his left a couple steps, and naturally put his hands up in the air to show he was not trying to do anything. The man standing by the counter was the one with the money and had put it in a cloth bag. He threw the bag over to the leader and came around so he could walk out with the others as they backed out in a straight line. There were about three feet between each man, and Jesse put his right foot out to trip the one in the middle. As he went down his head hit the leader, and his foot kicked the third man making him fall. Nehemiah jumped over his counter and there was a brawl for the next several minutes. Finally Jesse was able to reach for the middle man's six shooter, shot the gun out of the leader's hands and turned it on the third who stopped in his tracks. He told Nehemiah to go get the sheriff. Nehemiah ran out the door and returned a few minutes later with the sheriff and deputy to help take the three thieves to jail.

After the men were taken away, Nehemiah was excited but a little upset. His smile turned to a frown and he looked at Jesse. "Look at that hole in my roof. Now I've got to get up there and fix it before it rains again."

Jesse looked a little bewildered as he said, "I like the way you show appreciation to the man that saved your life and your money. Besides, it'll be weeks before it rains again around here."

Nehemiah smiled again as he replied, "Jesse, I appreciate what you did, no problem. I'm glad you came back when you did. Guess you came in to get that drink?"

"Yeah," Jesse answered, "that's it."

"Jesse, I owe you more than that. I'm going to give you the best whiskey I've got in the place and then throw in more of that coffee you like so much. How's that for you?"

As Nehemiah was getting the whiskey another deputy came in and informed him, "The sheriff needs you now, something to do with the new prisoners."

Nehemiah looked disappointed and told the deputy, "Go back and tell the sheriff I'll be there in a short while."

"No sir, the sheriff told me to bring you to him now," the deputy said impatiently. Jesse, not really wanting the whiskey anyway, told him to go on and they could seal the trade before he left town. Jesse left the post with the others and pulled his wagon over to the boarding house and tied the horses to the rail out front. After spending a quiet night in town he got up early the next morning and decided he had enough of civilization for a while. He did take time for one more civilized breakfast at the café, however, then tied Horse to the wagon and road back toward home. Traveling was slow since the wagon was so heavy with supplies. There was no way Jesse would make it home by dark so he pulled up in a grove of trees by a small stream and camped for the night. He let Horse roam the area while tying the other horses where they could drink from the stream. Jesse noticed a few clouds that looked like they had rain in them and heard thunder in the distance. Rain was always needed in these parts this time of the year, but Jesse hoped it would hold off till he got home.

Night came quickly while Jesse was building the fire and heating up a pot of beans for his supper and, of course, he fixed a pot of coffee. While he was eating, there was a crackle out in the dark that wasn't Horse, and Jesse turned and looked in the direction it came from. Didn't see anything, so he relaxed again and kept eating his beans and corn bread. A little later on he heard a crack again from the same direction, followed by the squeaks of someone moving in a leather saddle. Horse perked his head up on this and whinnied some. Jesse dropped the plate, turned and started to stand up while going for his shooter. "Stop right there! Don't move another step." He still couldn't see anything, but the voice sounded a little familiar. In a few seconds Jesse could see a man on a horse move into the firelight. Another two horses with men on them came from behind. Jesse had frozen with his right hand at the ready over his gun. His eyes followed the lead rider, and as they all got closer to the fire Jesse recognized them. "You're the men that were robbing Nehemiah back in town yesterday."

The leader hadn't moved his eyes from Jesse and said, "Boy, you're real good, ain't you? Yeah, you've got it right, and the way we figure you owe us, mister."

Jesse felt a little shocked but hoped it didn't show and asked, "What do you mean by that? How did you get out of jail and how did you find me here?"

"I'll just tell you how we got out of jail. You thought there were only three of us, but Ned here has a brother that was waiting on us back at our camp. When we didn't get back Chester got a little worried and came in town, did some lookin' around and found us in the jailhouse. The sheriff, being the humane person he was, let Chester come in and visit for a while, so we told him what happened. He did some poking around and found out where you were and saw you leave town today. That sheriff sleeps pretty heavy, and

Chester came in late this afternoon and fixed it so the sheriff can sleep from now on. He broke us out and we picked up on your trail, been following you ever since. It was nice of you to fix super for us, wasn't it, boys?"

He looked at the others and they both said at the same time, "It sure is."

Ned said, "Ridin' all afternoon makes a man real hungry." He walked over to the fire. "What are we having?" He took the top off the skillet. "Beans! Surely a buffalo killer like you can have something better than beans."

"Go ahead and help yourself, that's all there is," Jesse said with a low voice. He didn't know what to do, never been in this kind of situation before.

They all sat around the fire and ate heartily. Only thing they would let Jesse do is to put more beans and coffee on to cook. The three would talk and call each other by name and Jesse listened closely. They called the leader Jim, he already knew who Ned was, but the other was called Butler. Once they were finished Jesse asked, "What did you mean when you said that you thought I owed you?"

Still chewing on his food, Jim, the leader, looked at him and gave an answer that gave Jesse chills. "Don't you get it, mister? You stopped us on that job. Kept us from getting what we wanted from your friend's store. Chester had poked around and found out that you were a big buffalo hunter and had just come in town and traded your kill, so we figured this would be a good time to collect what we think you owe."

Jesse didn't say anything for a few seconds, then finally, "All I've got is what is on my wagon in supplies."

Jim was quick with, "That's a good start. We know you sold half your skins for money, so we'll take that too. Oh, and Chester was visiting with a friend of yours back in town and found out you've been figuring on buying a place. You've got to have a big stash somewhere and you're going to take us to it and we will finish collecting what you owe us then."

Jesse was afraid that Chester had found Tom and he was more afraid he had done something to him. "I don't know what you're talkin' about. I just have a small cabin by the river, my horses and that wagon."

"That's not what Chester told us," Ned jumped into the talking. "He ran into your friend, you know, Tom. Just talkin' to different people about who you were." Ned picked up on a worried look that came on Jesse's face. "Don't worry, all they did was talk. That's all. Chester didn't do anything to your friend."

Jesse was wondering where Chester was, why he wasn't with these three. "Where is Chester?" he asked.

Jim answered, "He got interested in a sweet little something back in town and decided to stay for the night. He promised to pick up on our trail in the morning and meet up with us. Believe me, he's a blood hound of a tracker, ain't he, Ned?"

"He'll be up with us tomorrow like he said," Ned answered, "you can count on it."

Jim decided he needed to know where the other money was, so he started poking Jesse in the left shoulder with a stick and demanding, "Where is the other money? It's at your cabin, isn't it? Or is it in a bank? No, no, a loner buffalo hunter like you wouldn't keep money in a bank. A man like you probably has it in a box, buried under a rock. Now where is it?" He had gotten himself worked up bad and had pulled his gun out and was swinging it around. Jesse looked at him and was trying to think about what to do. He was alone out here; from what these guys said no one in town knows about them coming out here. Whatever he decided to do, he had better do it before there are four of them. "I got a little saved up, and no, it's not in a bank. I got it hid."

"That's more like it," Jim said as he put his gun away. "You're right, you will take us to it first thing in the morning. Now, get some sleep. Ned, tie that horse of his up on the other side of the wagon. Butler, you can tie our host here up. Keep him by the fire and get the fire going real good so we can see him all night. We'll take turns keeping watch. I'll take the first then wake you, Butler, to take the second."

They carried out their duties and settled down for the night. Jesse got down by the fire but not like he was before. He was thinking about what to do in the morning. He will need to come up with a plan. Jesse had never harmed another person before. Looks like he might have to now. He had killed many a buffalo, but could he kill a man if he had to?

The men got up with the sun. Ned wanted to wait a while for Chester, but Jim pushed to move instead. Chester would just have to find them on his own. Breakfast was jerky, and they ate it while riding on the trail. Jesse was in the wagon with his hands tied behind his back. Ned was handling the reins with both their horses tied to the back. Jim was riding in front, and Butler was behind. Jesse decided to take them to his place, but he kept to his story about not having much there. He was taking the longest way, trying to buy himself some time to think. Jim already took all the money Jesse had on himself. Clouds were still building from the day before. They were getting darker and thicker. Jesse was starting to think a storm might be the best thing for him. It would wash out their tracks and Chester wouldn't be able to find them. Nothing on earth is quite like a Kansas thunderstorm. He had seen cows being carried away in flash floods and the wind could blow so hard people would be blown away.

As the morning hours passed into early afternoon, the possibility of a storm grew even more evident. They were still a good five miles from the cabin when the rain started and Jesse directed them to cross a stream. They had to go down a ways to find an area flat and shallow enough to cross it. The rain was getting harder, and the wind started picking up.

"I hate these storms out here," Ned grumbled. When the wagon was in the middle of the stream, lightning suddenly struck a tree on the other side several feet away. This caused the tree to fall toward Jim, spooking his horse and causing him to bolt. Jim was startled, almost came out of the saddle and was having trouble getting the horse under control. Ned and Butler didn't seem to realize what was going on, so the wagon was stopped in the middle of the stream. Jesse saw a glimmer of hope and hit Ned with his left shoulder knocking him off the wagon and into the stream. Butler was trying to gain control of his animal while groping for the reins he lost hold of.

Jesse, not really knowing what to do next, and still with his hands tied behind his back, started to reach for the reins Ned had dropped and yelled at his horses to go at the same time. The horses were so familiar with Jesse's voice they obeyed and took off. Jesse was struggling to stay on the wagon turning with his back to the horses and feeling for the reins. Finding the reins with his left hand he swung down and moved his right leg over the reins so they were under him to give better control. He was hearing shouts, "Get him. Don't let him get away. Let's go after him." Jim was finally able to get his horse under control so he could pull his shooter out of the holster and fire in the air. Pointing it at Jesse he yelled, "Stop, where do you think you're going!" Then he squeezed off a shot that purposely hit just to the left of Jesse making a hole in the wooden seat. Jesse awkwardly pulled the reins and yelled for the horses to stop.

"Ned," Jim yelled again. "Get back up on that wagon and make sure that don't happen again."

Bruised and soaked from rain and the creek, Ned made his way to the wagon and climbed back on. As he got on he gave Jesse a shove and growled, "Try that again and I'll kill ya."

After getting back on the right trail they made it to Jesse's place in a couple hours. Chester had not caught up to them yet, so Jesse felt like he still had a chance to get out of this. The rain stopped as quickly as it came up and the clouds gave way to an incredible hot sun as typical for Kansas. They stopped in front of the cabin, then Jim rode his horse over and got as close to Jesse as he could. "We're here, and now you need to either tell us or show us where all this money is, or that will be it for you." He grabbed Jesse's shirt and pulled him even closer. "You understand me, buffalo killer?"

Jesse kept a stone face and replied, "Guess I better tell ya now that I do have a big stash and you were right, I have it buried, but not out here. I have it out back behind my cabin. It's under a rock, but walking to it would be easier than ridin'."

Jim gave the order for everyone to get down, then he asked Jesse, "Where's your shovel?"

Jesse answered, "I need my hands untied. I can't do anything like this, and you know I can't do anything with the three of you hanging over me."

Jim pulled out his knife and reached to cut the rope that had been around Jesse's wrists for almost twenty-four hours. Rubbing both wrists, he pushed opened the barn door and got his shovel.

Jesse then told Jim, "We'll need that rope over there," pointing with his head over to a rope hanging on the left wall. "I've got this stash in a pretty large box and it's buried deep. You might need that to haul it up with."

Jim got the rope and looked at Butler then said, "Stay here and look out for Chester, he might be catching up with us anytime now. Ned, you pull your gun out and keep it on the buffalo hunter here till we finish this. Okay, show us this place where you got the money."

They walked behind the cabin with Jesse in front, Jim carrying the shovel to make sure nothing happened and Ned with his gun looking at Jesse's backside. They walked about a quarter of a mile behind the cabin and found a large round rock; it was more like a boulder near a small grove of trees. Jim thought this was a little odd to have anything valuable buried so far from the cabin. Jim gave the shovel back to Jesse and said, "Get after it. Do whatever you have to, but get the hole dug."

Jesse took the shovel and placed the blade under the rock and moved the rock over about five or six feet. He pushed the shovel's blade into the fertile ground with his right foot and pushed down on the handle. He took his time and dug a few shovels of dirt and placed them a couple of feet to his right.

Jim was getting a little impatient. "How far down is it? Go faster!"

Jesse looked up. Jim had moved to the right spot; now if Ned would come around to his left a few more steps. Jesse backed up some and slung the shovel in a way that made Ned move to just the right spot, then put the shovel back into the dirt and said with a strained voice, "That's it." He pulled the shovel out quickly, slung it to his right to throw dirt in Jim's face. Jim screamed and automatically tried to get the dirt out of his eyes with his hands causing further damage. Jesse took one step backward just as Ned fired a shot and hit Jim in the right shoulder. Jesse had shifted his hands on the handle of the shovel in order to use it like it was an ax and swung it at Ned, hitting him to the ground. Jim was moaning and trying to get his shooter, so Jim slung the shovel one more time knocking him out too. After dragging Jim and Ned into the trees Jesse tied both men with the rope so they couldn't get out. He picked up both guns from the ground hoping he didn't have to use them. While leaning against a tree, he stopped for just a second to consider his next step.

With the two taken care of, he needed to concentrate on Butler. Sitting on his knees now, he didn't know how he would get across the clearing without being seen, but he had to. All of a sudden he thought of his mother reading her Bible to him and his brothers and sister. He was sweating nervously, but with this thought he started to calm down. He took a quick look up to the sky and whispered a short prayer, "Never harmed nobody. Never wanted to. Lord, just give me a way." With this, Jesse took a six-shooter in each hand and made a desperate run across the field to the back of the cabin. When he was just about twelve feet from the cabin a shot rang out and the dirt just in front of Jesse flew up. Jesse stopped for just a second then started running again. Then another shot went off and Jesse heard the bullet zing past his right ear. He didn't flinch but ran faster and dove behind his cabin for shelter from the flying lead. With his back against the cabin he slowly walked to the edge. He turned as if he were going to crawl up. After taking a deep breath and holding it in, he carefully looked around the corner. Butler fired one more time but hit about a foot above Jesse's head. "Butler, you're a poor shot," Jesse shouted.

Butler ignored his remark and instead asked, "What happened with the others?"

"They're back in the trees and sleeping pretty sound I might say." Jesse checked the guns for bullets. The one in his left hand had four shots, and the other had five. There was about ten feet from the back of the house to the back of the outhouse and that was between the house and the barn. He took one more look; couldn't tell where Butler was but thought he was just in front of the barn. Taking a leap, he ran toward the outhouse and made it among three poorly fired shots. Jesse thanked heaven for Butler being such a poor shot as he ducked behind the small building. After a few seconds he heard some voices out front. Chester had found them. He figured the rain would have washed out any sign of their tracks but he must have been wrong. With one more to worry about, what would he need to do now?

Jesse yelled out, "Hey, is that Chester I hear out there?"

Butler answered back, "Yep. Say hello to the buffalo killer, Chester."

"Hey, I guess you think you can take all of us?" Chester was hoping Jesse would stick his head up. "We'll just see about that now. I'm a better shot than Butler here."

"How did you find us?" Jesse asked. "Didn't that rain wash our tracks out?"

Chester answered, "Lost them a mile or two on the other side of the creek but kept going in the same direction and picked them back up a few hundred yards this side of the creek. Mostly cause that wagon of yours cut deep into the dirt. Too much in it I guess. You must be figurin' on livin for a long time, buffalo killer."

Jesse started to move slowly to a back door of the barn while he answered Chester with, "I guess I'll live till I die, whenever that might be." If he could make it there he could climb up in the hayloft and might be able to make his way to the front without the others knowing it. As he was walking he kept talking. "Either one of you ever read the good book?"

Butler replied, "Good book? I always figured that was something for weaklin's, people that couldn't live like they really wanted to."

By this time Jesse had made it across the distance to the door in the back of the barn. As he pulled it open he yelled one more time, "The good book tells us a lot of things about living this life." At this time he ducked into the barn and ran to the ladder and climbed up to the loft. He heard gunshots outside as the others were hoping to hit Jesse just by shooting blindly. Jesse slowly made his way to the front of the loft. There was the opening they would throw bales of hay through in the front of the barn.

While Jesse was carefully moving to the front of the loft, he heard the other two outside. "Where is he?" one voice said.

"I don't know, didn't see him leave from behind the out house."

By now Jesse was up front and was able to peer out from the side of the opening. He saw Butler just below him and to his right at the corner of the barn. The man that had to be Chester was in front of the cabin on his porch. He could easily draw down on Butler and take him out; then Chester would probably run to the back of the barn or house. His mind was racing while trying to come up with an alternative plan. He finally decided the only way was to attempt to wound Butler, then worry about Chester afterward. Even though Jesse had never shot a man, that didn't mean he couldn't. A life on the plains made Jesse develop many talents, even being accurate with a handgun. He only had seven shots left, so he had to make every one count for something. Jesse moved to the opening again and leaned out just enough to be able to aim the gun at Butler. He had practiced shooting left handed but never thought he would have to actually shoot this way in a time like this. Quietly taking aim at Butler's right calf, Jesse squeezed off a shot, and as the gun fired the bullet made its way to the target. The bullet cut through the flesh, tearing away a large chunk as it passed out the other side causing agonizing pain. He fell to the ground and grabbed his leg in shock of what happened. As he fell his gun went off into the air. This caused Chester to look up toward Jesse, but he had ducked back. Instead of running toward the back of the cabin, Chester steadily backed up on the front porch out of Jesse's sight.

Butler had dropped his gun and was holding his wounded leg trying to get the bleeding to stop. There was a pulley on a wooden brace over the opening of the loft with the rope Jesse used to haul hay up for storage. He had to get down fast, so he decided to jump, grabbed the rope and slid down not knowing where Chester was. Fortunately, the other end was tied to a bale of hay that hadn't been hoisted up yet. As he came down, Butler reached for his gun, but Jesse ran over and swung the butt of his pistol to the left side of Butler's head knocking him out cold.

Chester had been watching all this from the other end of the porch and squeezed off a shot that glanced off Jesse's left temple. The shock caused him to fall back for a second, but he quickly recovered and got up finding Chester was gone. He needed to find out where he went, so Jesse moved to the end of his porch and climbed on top from the corner post. From there he crawled very quietly to the top of the roof to see Chester making his way along the backside of the house. Jesse carefully crawled down to the back edge as quiet as a cat, not wanting to make noise to give his position away. Below, Chester was getting close to being directly under him. Jesse patiently waited, then at the right moment jumped, knocking Chester to the ground. Pulling Chester's gun out of his holster, Jesse brought the fighting to an abrupt end. Chester staggered to his feet as he was directed inside the barn to be tied up against a post. After that was done, Jesse went out and drug Butler inside the barn and tied him to another post across from Chester. Two were taken care of and he was still alive and so were they. He breathed a sigh of relief.

After securing Chester and Butler, he went back to get the other two. When he made it to the trees, Ned and Jim were waking up. He pulled them to their feet and jabbed them with the six-shooter toward the barn. Once inside Jesse tied them to separate posts with his best and strongest knots. Still out of it from being hit on the head, no one said anything until Jim asked, "What are you going to do with us?"

Jesse answered, "Don't know yet. Gotta think on it for a while. Don't any of you boys go anywhere now, I'll be back later."

With all four secured in the barn, Jesse felt safe enough to leave them and go inside the cabin. When he got in his cabin, he threw the guns down on the table and went to a washbasin where he splashed water on his face. What will his next step be? After giving it some thought, he started unloading the wagon. It was starting to get dark, so he pushed his tired body to finish before the sun went down on him. When the chore was finished, he went back into the barn to make sure his knots were still tight around the four. They were all awake by now, and Butler was really moaning because of the pain from his leg. Jesse brought some bandages and wrapped it the best he could. Jim asked the same question as before and he answered, "Gonna take you back to the sheriff." All of them started laughing at this.

When Jim calmed down he looked at Jesse. "How do you think you'll do that?"

Jesse, aggravated by all the questioning, finally said, "You'll see in the morning. Now get some sleep, you'll need it." He walked out of the barn confident that none of the four could get away but not really confident of how he was going to do what he just said.

Sleep was rough for all that night. The men in the barn kept thinking how they blew it that day and how they had to turn it around the next day. Jesse tossed most of the night trying to figure out how to do this impossible task that had been pushed onto him. There was still that one question plaguing his mind and heart, could he actually kill a man if it came down to it? Jesse was up before light and offered up a short prayer, "Lord, would ya watch over me today and give me strength." He fixed a large breakfast for himself and quickly consumed it all. Then he took jerky and some hard tack along with water to the men in the barn. He untied one at a time and let him eat and drink for a few minutes, then tied him up. This was repeated for each man, and when the last finished, he pulled and pushed him into the wagon, then tied his hands behind his back and his feet together. After all four were placed in the wagon and secured, he took a long rope and wrapped it around each man twice and tied it onto the frame of the wagon under the seat where he would ride.

Provisions were placed under the seat, along with a rifle and extra ammunition. He climbed on board, turned around to the four men and with a stern voice explained, "I'm going to take all of you back into town and turn you over to the sheriff. Your horses and other belongings will be here and will be taken care of until the sheriff decides what needs to be done with them. You need to understand that we will make it to town today, and I will turn you into the sheriff." Jim had to ask how he expected to get there in one day after taking so long to get out to Jesse's place in the first place. "Well," he said with a smile, "I'll be going the right way this time." As they pulled out from the barn into a clear sunny morning, Jesse thought to himself, a prairie sunrise is like no other.

It was a long and hot trip, but they did make it to town as Jesse said and delivered the four to the new sheriff. He then went to the trading post and found his friend, Nehemiah. After telling him all about the events of the past two days, Nehemiah insisted on having that drink they were unable to have earlier. Jesse thought it over and agreed but insisted that his would be cold apple cider. While he was enjoying the pleasure of the moment, Jesse found a great peace in knowing that he made it without having to pull that trigger to kill a man. His mind went back to his mother and what she taught him when he was a child and never forgot.

BROKEN PROMISES

"You shall not commit adultery."
Ex. 20:14

Seven

The alarm went off at 7:00 a.m. as it did every Sunday in the Spiegel household. With one large sweeping motion, Alan reached for the alarm button then turned and shoved Linda to make sure she knew it was time to get up.

"Honey," he moaned. "Honey, it's time to get up. I'll let you take the first shower."

Linda pushed her dark black hair out of her face with a hand then said, "Thank you, dear. You always let me take the first shower. It lets you sleep longer. I know what's going on here."

Alan was still half asleep but managed to give a rebuttal. "I do sleep a little longer, but I am just giving you the extra time to get ready. I'll get up and wake the kids in a minute so you don't have to worry about it."

Linda was slowly moving out of bed and toward the shower when she said, "That's very nice of you, Alan. You're going to spoil me with all this kindness." With this Alan rolled over and went back to sleep as fast as he woke up.

The kids got up and were ready in time for a fast breakfast before leaving for church in the family van. Linda was interested in the lesson Alan would be teaching in their adult class this morning. "Are you ready for this morning, Alan?"

"Well, I don't know," Alan was hesitant to say.

"Didn't you prepare this week?" Alice asked.

"Oh, I studied the lesson and even prayed about it all week. Stayed up late last night going over all of it. Being ready isn't the problem, it's the content."

Linda understood where he was coming from. "Yeah, I know what you mean. Just teaching on relationships would be easy, but teaching what the Bible has to say about divorce and purity in marriage is really a bad one to get stuck with. How did this happen anyway?"

Alan answered with a disappointed tone, "Tom and I are co-teaching this class, and as you know we put all the topics for the next several months on pieces of paper and we drew for what we would teach."

Linda knew what happened; she just liked to go over it and hit Alan with, "Oh, that sounds like a very spiritual way of seeking what God would want to be taught in our class."

"Don't worry about it." Alan had a slightly harsh edge to his voice by now. "It'll work. I know there are some members in the class that are on their second and even third marriage, but what I think we need to do is focus on where each person is today with the spouse they have now and get away from the past."

Linda was surprised with these words. "That's a good take on it. I'm looking forward to this."

As they turned into the church parking lot, both of the kids, Shirley and Jeff, were making a lot of noise in the back and Linda turned and yelled, "Okay, back there, shut it up!" just as Rev. Morris was walking by them on his way to his office. Linda caught a confused look on his face, but she turned quickly and looked straight ahead till they got the van parked.

After the adult class was over several people came up to him and complimented Alan on how he handled such a difficult topic. A co-worker from Alan's job and fellow church member, Jerry Blake, came up to him. "That was a good lesson, Alan. It makes you stop and think, doesn't it?"

Alan answered, "I guess it would if you don't have your marriage going in the right direction."

Jerry looked a little down. "How's work going for you, Alan?"

"I guess it's okay. What's on your mind, Jerry?"

"Oh, nothing, really, I guess. Well, there is something." Jerry started to cough nervously and Alan stood waiting. "I was hoping we could meet tomorrow for lunch. I'll even pay, we can go anywhere you want."

Alan felt a little relieved. "That sounds good. Don't think I have anything going. What time?"

"How about 11:30, we can beat some of the lunch crowd." Alan agreed and suggested that Jerry should come by his desk about 11:15 in the morning, and they can walk down the street to a new place, Casa Rosita, Mexican food was his favorite.

On the way home from church Linda started bragging on Alan's teaching. "You did great this morning, honey. I thought everybody in the class got something out of it."

Alan responded a little doubtful, "Are you sure? I thought most were either bored or offended."

"Oh no." Linda was surprised Alan would think that. "Most of the people had some kind of input or questions, and that doesn't happen very often. No, I think it was very good. I got something out of it."

"What do you think you got from the lesson?" Alan asked her.

"I'm going to check our history on the computer for the sites everybody goes to on the Internet. You know me, my knowledge of the computer and the Internet is about the same as what I know about how the space shuttle works. I just never thought about bad stuff coming into our house over the computer. I mean, friends and I talk about some of the sites that we read or hear about, so I'm not stupid or naïve. I'm aware of the sort of things that are out there, but just to think it could come into our house really, well, in our old teenage language, it really freaks me out, man."

Alan didn't want to talk about this, but he knew Linda did, so he kept going with it. "What do you mean about all this with the Internet and computer? Where did you get that from our lesson anyway?"

Linda answered, "You remember what Gary brought up, don't you? He was saying with the technology of computers and the Internet there is a new type of adultery entering into relationships." She kept on, "It's similar to a man thinking about another woman or looking at pictures from *Playboy* or some other magazine. You know what I mean, don't you?"

Alan got a little on edge. "Are you sure we ought to talk about this in front of the kids?" As teenagers do, both Jeff and Shirley homed in on this last remark and perked their ears up as they moved to the seat just behind their parents so they could hear every word up front.

"Thanks, Alan. We will pick this conversation up later at home." Linda turned around to look straight ahead and did not say another word till they pulled into their drive. Things got busy that afternoon with dinner, clean up, and then Alan decided to take Shirley and Jeff and go hiking down at a local state park for the afternoon. Linda wasn't able to continue the conversation or to get Alan to show her what to do to look up the history for what sites come up from the Internet onto their computer.

Monday came quickly and Alan was at his desk hard at work when Jerry came by and tapped him on his shoulder. "Oh, Jerry, what are you up to today?"

Jerry answered, "Don't you remember our appointment for lunch?"

Alan was a little caught up in his morning so he had to think for a second. "Sure, I remember. Just busy, that's all."

Jerry asked, "Did you know it started raining?"

"No," Alan replied, "I didn't notice. Let me get my jacket and we can go. Guess we will have to drive down instead of walk."

They ran out to Alan's car from the side exit of their building and made it to the restaurant without getting too wet. Once they were seated, the discussion was about the latest rumors at work and some of the changes they have both been through in their different departments. They went over the last high school basketball game as they ate chips and dip. About half way through the lunchtime, Alan finally asked Jerry what he wanted to talk to him about. Jerry suddenly got quiet as if he didn't want to say anything. He finally started, "Alan, you did really good yesterday leading our Bible study at church. Logan and I talked about it for a long time during lunch and even after."

Alan smiled. "Thanks for the vote of confidence. Is that why we met for lunch today?"

Jerry stuttered a little then finally said, "No, that's not the only reason. You see, the lesson yesterday really said something to me. It made me think about my own life and what's been going on with me. I mean with me and Logan."

"Been having some problems at home, Jerry?" Alan said with a concerned voice.

"Oh, things haven't been the best. Seems like yesterday was the most Logan has said to me all at one time in months. I guess that's part of what I want to say, but not all of it."

Alan was eating more chips along with his Mexican sample platter "Okay, Alan. I'll tell you. I, well, you know you are about the best friend I have had in years, don't you?"

Alan was getting real confused. "No, I didn't know that, but that's great. If you want to know the truth I feel the same toward you. Jerry, I don't mind words of affection, but I have a feeling that is not why we are here."

Jerry became calm suddenly. "You're right. Just wanted to let you know the lesson yesterday along with our friendship convinced me you were the one to tell."

Alan interrupted, "Tell me what, Jerry?"

"Don't interrupt, man, this is hard enough. I'm trying to say it, but it's getting difficult. Maybe we should go and I'll just forget it."

Alan calmed down. "No, Jerry, let's start all over. I'll keep my mouth shut and let you talk."

Jerry took a deep breath, then finally said, "Okay, Alan I appreciate that.

I'll just come out and say it. I'm having an affair."

Alan stopped chewing mid mouthful of a chip and dip. "You're what?" Alan's voice cracked.

"I know, Alan. I know. Just hold it for a little while."

"Jerry," Alan continued. "You must be joking. Aren't you?"

"No, I'm not, Alan. I've been seeing another woman for the last four or five months, and it has started to get to me."

"What do you mean by that? How could anything like that even get started?" Alan was starting to act like he never heard of this before.

"Alan, don't you remember your lesson yesterday? It all started here in the office."

"You've been seeing another woman who works in our office?" Alan asked excitedly.

"Well, yes, she was someone in another department. Alan, she's a supervisor."

"How did this get started?" Alan asked.

"We were at a meeting between the Marketing and Real Estate Departments. From that time on when we saw each other in the hallway or anywhere else we would talk, you know, just innocent friend stuff. We were just getting to know each other. She started coming to my desk and talking during her breaks. Alan, I know it sounds like some movie or a story of some kind, but I guess we just became interested in each other. Maybe I was looking for someone at that time. Logan and I haven't been getting along that great. Afraid we have been changing and finding other interests."

Alan thought this was a pretty classic situation and he was wondering why Jerry was confiding in him on all this. "Jerry, I need to ask you why you are telling me about this? I'm glad you have enough trust in me, but why?"

"It's that lesson you taught yesterday at church." Jerry went on, "Don't think there was any one thing, just the whole lesson. Things have been sort of bothering me lately. I'm not sure what to do about all this. One question I want to ask you is what do you think I should do?"

This shocked Alan; to him Jerry should cut it off with this other woman, tell his wife, beg her forgiveness and hope she doesn't go out, file for divorce and take him to the cleaners. After pausing and thinking for a second, he decided to take a different approach. "What do you think you should do? Are you still seeing this other woman? I guess you aren't going to tell me who she is?"

Jerry got a little tense with all these questions, but he tried to answer them all. "I hope I can remember all the answers I'll need. First, I've been considering telling Logan, then getting a divorce and marrying the other woman. The only problem is I don't want to do that, but I don't want to give up seeing, well, I don't want to quit seeing Angela." Alan looked a little puzzled as he tried to figure out who Angela was. Jerry continued, "It's Angela Wilkes, Alan. You remember her, don't you?"

"I guess I do, but that's besides the point. You are telling me you don't want to stop seeing her, but you don't want to tell Logan. You want both like you've got a harem?" Alan was getting impatient with this as he kept on going. "Is this what I was talking about yesterday in church?"

Jerry answered while playing nervously with his glass, "I don't know to be honest with you, Alan. I don't think it was, and in fact what you and the others in the class were saying convinced me that I needed to do something, and I guess this is it. I would like to ask you to pray for me so that I will be able to figure this out."

Alan really didn't have to think much on Jerry's last request. "I'll certainly pray for all of you, Logan and even Angela. The only thing is it all seems pretty simple to me, Jerry. You need to come clean with Logan and break it off with Angela. You also need to hope Logan doesn't skin you alive and take everything you have. I also want you to know that I am glad you felt enough confidence and faith in me to tell me all this. The only other questions that I have for you are why did it take you so long to come to me, and why didn't I notice any of this going on?"

"Well," Jerry came up with his answers, "I didn't want you to be burdened with any of this, and I guess we kept it all pretty hushed all this time. The only other thing I need to ask you, Alan, is not to tell your wife or anyone else. I understand what you said about ending this and telling Logan, but I'm not sure if that is what I need or want to do. I'll take your prayers, and if we can meet more and talk about it that might help a lot."

Alan was determined to make another point. "To be honest, I can't keep this from Linda. She knows of this meeting and she will ask me what it was about. You have to understand that she is the person that prays with me and for me. She will be the best prayer warrior there is for you and everyone in this situation. I will agree to meet with you as often as you want whenever I can, but this bargain has to be two sided. I have a requirement for you. While you are trying to figure this out, you have to tell Angela you can not see her at least while you are going through all this with me. I mean, you need to tell her today that you will not be able to see or even talk to her, understand?"

This caught Jerry off guard, but he was sincere about needing Alan's help with this, so he agreed to tell Angela when they got back to the office. He did ask why, so Alan explained, "I think you need to be able to think with your head as clear as you can, so you need to get away from the temptation as much as you can. I would prefer one of you take a leave from work till you work through this, but that is impossible." With this their lunch hour was over and they drove back to the office in another downpour of rain that started just before they left the restaurant.

That evening back home Linda did ask Alan about lunch with Jerry as he first walked in the door. "I'll tell you all about it after dinner when the kids are doing their homework and we have some privacy." Linda didn't really like it, so she got dinner ready in record time and after they were finished she incorporated the kids to help. The kids were upstairs doing homework and Alan and Linda had the living room to themselves. Alan was on the couch watching their favorite evening TV game show when Linda came in and sat down beside him.

"Well," she started, "dinner is over, everything is cleaned up and the kids are upstairs doing homework. Are you going to tell me all about this meeting with Jerry today?"

"Honey," he said, hoping to put it off, "I will, but I was watching our show now."

Linda persisted a little further, "Alan." She reached up to his face that was toward the TV and moved it with her hand to look at her. "Start talking, buddy. I care more about our friends than I do this TV show. I'm listening."

With a deep sigh Alan started. Like he promised Jerry, he told her everything except who the other person was. Linda was upset about it, but Alan didn't think she was really surprised or shocked as he was, so he asked her about this.

She wouldn't say much at first until she finally caved in. "Well, I have been wondering about Logan and Jerry for a while. I just didn't see what I used to in their relationship. Whenever they've been here, or remember when we went out together a couple weeks ago? There was something about Jerry and how he was treating her. I just didn't think things were going smooth for them. What I want to know is what is he going to do now?"

Alan explained, "He's asked that we pray for him to be able to figure that out and…"

Linda interrupted him on this line. "What do you mean pray so he will be able to figure out what to do? Didn't you tell him he needed to break it off with this other woman and beg Logan's forgiveness?"

Alan tried to reason with her. "Of course I did, but with everything that's going on, I think Jerry is confused. He wants to do the right thing and he did promise not to see this other woman during this process."

Linda gave a sarcastic sigh of relief then said, "Well, that is mighty big of him, isn't it? I'll say one more thing, Jerry is a pig, and if he told me I would have jumped on him and kicked his behind all the way to his house and made him tell Angela; then I would probably help her kick him out of the house."

Alan ducked as Linda threw a pillow his way. "Maybe that's why Jerry didn't ask about meeting with you today? I guess I'll watch myself real good. No mercy from you?"

She looked right in Alan's eyes and gave him a very firm, "NO! Now, you have to tell me who the other woman is so I can effectively pray for her like everyone else."

"I promised not to tell you that. He didn't want me to tell you, but I convinced him that would be okay." Alan attempted to hold his ground. Linda would not give up, and she kept after Alan all night about this one point. When they were in bed she stopped what many would call nagging and Alan succumbed to Linda's female charm that she is very well endowed with and told her the name he was supposed to have guarded from her. Now he only hoped Jerry never found out about this.

The rest of the week went as good as it could, nothing great or bad happened. Jerry and Alan agreed to meet on Mondays and Fridays at lunch and if Jerry needed he could call Alan at home any evening. They had been meeting for a couple of weeks and had agreed on studying what the Bible had to say about marriage, wives, husbands and extramarital affairs.

About three weeks later, Alan was at home in bed and wide awake at 1:30 in the morning. He wasn't sure what woke him, but he couldn't go back to sleep. Linda was sound asleep on the other side of the bed, and Alan knew nothing would ever wake her, so he slipped out of bed and through the door. He closed the bedroom door behind him slowly and softly, then turned and quietly walked up the stairs that led to the room where they kept the computer. After gently closing the door, Alan sat down in front of the computer and clicked a connection to the Internet. The familiar beeps, bongs and static came up as the modem did its work.

Since Alan couldn't sleep, he thought he would check his e-mail and some sites for his 401K and other stock accounts he had. While he was doing all this, he started thinking about Jerry having this affair with Angela. There were other sites he had been to in the past, but he never saved their addresses. He knew all he had to do was a search and he could find all he wanted. He was a little torn inside, thinking about what Gary had said that one Sunday when he talked about adultery with the Internet. He decided to glaze over that and went ahead and pulled up a site that promised x-rated pictures and indulged his late night fantasies.

It was about 2:30 that same morning and Linda had rolled over toward Alan's side of the bed with her arm moving onto his pillow. She was half awake and noticed Alan's head wasn't on his pillow. She thought he might have gotten up for several different reasons. She waited for Alan to come back for a few minutes. When he didn't return she decided to go find him. She went into the bathroom first, then the kitchen downstairs with no luck, so she went upstairs and was hearing music from the room with the computer. Realizing this is where Alan was, she went to each of the kid's rooms to check on them. Hearing a door open out in the hallway, Alan quickly got out of the site he was on and pulled up a more innocent one on lawn and garden problems that he had been looking at for a few days. After making sure both kids were okay, Linda went into see what Alan was up to.

As she walked in she saw Alan sitting at the computer. "What are you doing this time of night, honey?"

He looked at her a little red in the face and finally replied, "Oh, I woke up and couldn't get back to sleep, so I decided to come up and check on my stock and 401K accounts, then start planning for what I want to do with some of the gardens this year."

She believed Alan because she trusted him, but she thought since they were both awake and up this would be a good time to learn how to check the Internet history. "You know since we are up, why don't you show me how to look up the history on the computer?"

Alan couldn't do that tonight or she would know exactly where he had been not only this night but also many others in the recent past. "Why do you think you need to do that, honey?"

Linda said half asleep, "Mostly to be able to tell the kids that I know how as a way of scaring them into not going to sites they shouldn't."

Alan had to think quickly. "I was starting to get sleepy again and wanted to come back to bed. Couldn't I show you this some other time?"

Linda was pretty sleepy herself and would rather be in bed, but she pressed a little more. "You know I was speaking with Denita from church the other day about this, and she told me how to do it. I might be able to remember what she said by just looking at the screen."

Alan was getting a little nervous but thought Linda wouldn't be able to figure it out and go back to bed. The only problem is that after a few tries she did figure it out. "Look, Alan, I think it's working. Something is coming up."

As the addresses came up Linda read the short descriptions that came up with them. "Alan, look at these. If I want to go to any of these sites, do I just click on them?" Alan was feeling a little sick by now, and all he could do was to shake his head for the yes. Linda double clicked onto one address and kept her eyes glued to the screen till the entire page came up complete with woman completely undressed and in very compromising positions. Completely awake by now, Linda looked at Alan with her eyes wide and her mouth opened. "What is this, Alan? I mean for a second I thought Jeff might have found this, but it was for tonight wasn't it, Alan?" She was keeping her voice down because of the kids, but she was getting very anxious and worried.

"Honey, I don't know how this got there. You know sometimes site addresses come up on e-mails so maybe that's what happened. Look." He went to the history screen again and showed her the other sites he had been to. Then Linda noticed the other addresses for pornographic sites.

"Alan, what about these other addresses, there are three others for tonight. Look, Alan, there are others here for last week. Who's been doing this? Would Jeff or Shirley do this? I hope they wouldn't. What's going one here, Alan? You've been going to these sites, haven't you?" Alan looked down to the floor. Linda repeated her question, "You've been going to these sites, haven't you?"

"Yes, yes I have. I've been going to them, but I have never bought anything from them."

This made Linda get even hotter. "Does that make it okay that you haven't bought anything from these? Who are you? Are you the man that I've been married to for the last eighteen years? How long have you really been doing this?" She started crying. "I know you can clear out the history. I don't know why you didn't clear it out from the last several weeks." She started scrolling up and down the screen looking at previous weeks where the x-rated site addresses started to mount up.

Alan tried to get to the keyboard so he could clear the histories, but Linda wouldn't let him. "I don't want any of these taken off, and I don't want anyone touching this computer."

Alan figured this was it, she was going to file for a divorce. "What are you going to do?"

"I don't know, Alan, but get out of this stuff on the computer and shut it off and don't do anything to lose any of this."

He did exactly what she said and they both walked down the stairs to the bedroom. Linda was careful to muffle the crying until they got behind closed doors downstairs. Once there Linda let it rip and she tore into Alan as she never had before. Alan silently sat on the edge of the bed and placed his head in his hands. After about fifteen minutes of listening to Linda, tears started coming down Alan's cheeks. Linda noticed this but would not let this soften her attitude.

"Don't think crying will change my mind on this."

"I'm not thinking that at all, I'm just sorry this happened."

Linda looked at him. "Do you mean you're sorry you were caught or sorry you did this?"

"Honey."

She interrupted him. "I don't think I want you to call me that right now."

He changed his approach. "I'll go to the living room and sleep the rest of the night on the couch. I think we both need to calm down and talk more later." Linda agreed this was probably the best thing to do, so she let him leave the room.

The next morning was a work and school day. Alan woke up before the kids and went back into his bedroom where Linda was starting to wake up to the alarm clock. She looked up at him and said, "I'm not going to work today, and I'm not going to get the kids off to school either. You'll have to do it."

Alan had decided not to go to work either. "I'm going to call in sick today and don't worry about the kids. I'll get them to school."

He did all this, and when he came back home from taking the kids to school he found Linda in the kitchen fixing breakfast. As he walked into the kitchen the air was heavy and thick with tension. Linda would not look up, she just kept working on breakfast and did not say a word. Alan finally broke the silence with, "Let me help you with that." He got a coffee cup out from the cabinet and started pouring and getting plates down for the table. They both ate very slowly and did not look at each other. Alan thought this was going to be a very long morning. After they finished Linda quietly said, "Don't worry about the dishes. We can clean them up later, maybe after lunch." Linda would always rush to take care of the dishes, pots and pans immediately after each meal. Alan let Linda lead and control everything that morning. Taking the kids to school gave him time to think, and he had decided to take the advice he tried giving Jerry and was going to tell Linda everything and beg her to forgive him. He knew he would have to let her take charge of everything that morning and he would need to do whatever she wanted him to do.

After breakfast they both went into the living room and Linda began with her ideas of the situation. "Alan." She had to fight tears back. "I didn't sleep much after our little discovery early this morning. The longer I thought about it the more upset I became. Do you really understand what you've done?"

Alan looked down and thought for a moment. "I think I am realizing the magnitude of what I've done."

"Alan." Linda didn't let him say anything else. "You are as guilty as your friend, Jerry, of committing adultery with that other woman at your office. You weren't going to those Web sites and reading articles, were you? You were going there and having fantasies about those women, weren't you?"

"I don't know, I mean, I don't think I was doing that." Alan's voice was shaky.

"Then you tell me, Alan, why you were doing it. Don't you get it? The message I am getting from this is that I have failed and am not good enough for you. You have to go to other women on the Internet to get satisfied. You have broken your promises to me. I should kick you out of the house and file for a divorce today."

Alan finally started breaking down emotionally. "No, don't divorce me. I'm sorry. I love you. I'm sorry. I won't do it again. I promise. Don't kick me out, what about the kids?"

Linda, failing at holding the tears back, said, "Alan, you don't understand the promise you broke to me. It was our marriage vow. You promised to keep yourself for me only and you promised I would be for you only. How do I know you will keep another promise to stay off those sites if you have already broken your first promise to me? Alan, I have to know if you have ever gone out with any other woman since we've been married. I mean, I've been wondering this morning if the reason why Jerry came to you is because he knew you've been there, done that."

Alan jumped in on this with everything he had. "I know I have blown your trust." Alan was starting to get a grip on himself. "Your trust is something that I have always cherished. I realize I have betrayed that, and no, I have never gone out with another woman. I mean I have not gone out with another woman ever since we first met. I love you and have never loved another and don't plan on doing it in the future. I want another chance."

The conversation was starting to change more toward discussing the problem and not so much accusing and yelling. They spent the next couple of hours talking about what Alan did and all the reasons. It came down to a basic male need to fulfill a sexual drive that Alan had, and as Linda told him during their discussion, it was a sin. Linda let him clear the history from the Internet and she would work with him to clean this part of his life up and get it straight. She loved him and could not imagine life without him, but her trust in him had been diminished. She now knew why Alan was so hesitant to teach that lesson in church a few weeks earlier.

Lunch was much less tense than breakfast until Linda brought up Jerry and asked Alan what he would do about their meetings now. "Why can't I still meet with Jerry? Do you really think I have to tell him or anyone else? Why can't this just be between us? I mean, this is embarrassing enough with you finding out, but do I have to tell others?"

Now Linda knew she was fighting an evil that had a grip on Alan. She needed to get him to admit to others what he had been doing. If he did not do this, then she knew he wouldn't change. He needed someone to be held accountable to other than just her. "Yes, you have to tell someone else besides me. Alan, you don't have to tell everybody, but I want you to get into a group of men from church that meet once a week, and I want you to tell them you need their prayers and their help to be held accountable on this. That is what I want. If you choose to tell Jerry or not is up to you."

Alan knew of a group of men he could get with and thought that would be an idea he could go along with. "Okay, I'll do that, and I will think about telling Jerry."

It was about 2:30 and they would need to pick the kids up from school in a few minutes but Linda had one more thing to say to Alan. "I don't want the kids to know about any of this, and I will check the Internet history daily for a while and then go to weekly. I think it would be best for you to stay off the Internet completely. Do you have access at work?"

"I do, but I have never and will never go to those sites at work. Too many people around to see," Alan replied. This gave Linda a little better feeling. They hugged after all this, but Linda wouldn't let Alan kiss her. He asked about praying, but Linda couldn't bring herself to do this either.

The next week went okay with Alan and Linda. Alan tried to act as if nothing ever happened. Linda would act as she always did when she was with the kids or anyone else, but when she and Alan were by themselves she would not talk very much and would not return any affection. Alan was willing to take it slow, and he was determined to win over this problem and win his wife back. That Friday Jerry and his wife were supposed to come over for dinner and to watch basketball on TV. Alan didn't have a problem with it, but Linda was not comfortable with this idea, and on Thursday evening she let him know it. "Alan, I'm not sure about this idea of Jerry and Logan coming over tomorrow night. Has he told her about Angela yet?"

Alan had been meeting and praying with Jerry for several weeks now and nothing had been decided, and he had to tell Linda. "No, he hasn't. I've been warning him that she will be finding out from someone else if he doesn't hurry up and tell her. There might have been someone else that saw them together and put two and two together and might talk to Logan before he has a chance."

"Well," Linda looked at him, "they're both our friends. I don't want to do anything to hurt either one of them. I'll be okay, but I just don't want anything to come out while they are here."

"Nothing will happen except pizza and basketball the whole time they are here, okay?" Alan was able to put his arms around Linda as he said this, and she gave him a smile and said, "Okay, I'll hold you to it." He gave her a small kiss on the forehead as she said this and then bent down and placed his lips on her for a few seconds before she pulled away but with less conviction than a few days ago.

The next night Jerry and his family had come over, several pizzas were delivered and the Bulls versus the Lakers were on TV. Everybody seemed to be enjoying themselves from the kids to adults. At one point toward the end of the first period of play, during a commercial, Alan and Jerry went to the kitchen to get more pizza. Jerry asked Alan, "I know you told Linda about our sessions. Has she been that prayer warrior you told me about?"

Alan told him with a smile, "You know it, man. She is faithfully praying for the whole deal every day. Now, buddy, let me ask you something. When are you going to know what you are going to do? We've been meeting and going over this for several weeks now. I think you should be getting pretty close to a decision."

Jerry put a serious look on his face and explained, "I've decided to tell Logan everything and as you said, beg her forgiveness and hope she doesn't kill me. You know, your faithfulness to me has been great. It was a good idea to tell Angela that we couldn't see each other during this time. I've decided what I have with Logan is worth keeping and working at. I figure on telling her this weekend."

Alan was happy but also nervous for his friend. "I'm glad you're going to do this. I know it will be hard, but I agree that what you and Logan have is worth fighting for. Just look in that living room at those kids of yours. Leave it like it is, brother."

CHOOSING YOUR PRICE

"You shall not steal."
Ex. 20:15

Eight

It was a Friday evening at the Blue Creek Mall, the biggest night of the week for business and the largest crowd. It was like a river of people of all types flowing along the walkway. The trees, bushes and exotic foliage that had been painstakingly planted and cared for along with the low lights created a park like setting. Teenagers had been brought to the mall by their parents and dropped off just to hang out. There were young couples out for a movie, a walk around to shop and eat at the food court. There were families taking advantage of back to school sales for the lowest prices in months. Everyone was taking advantage of the mall air conditioning since this was one of the hottest summers on record.

The parking lot was humming with people coming and going. There had been a dramatic rise in drug trafficking in this quiet town during the last five years, but there was a determination to defeat this growing problem. Security employees were driving in their SUVs attempting to keep a check on the area. There was a great effort made to light up the entire lot to help guarantee everyone's safety at night.

In spite of stepped-up efforts, officials knew the trafficking was actually on the rise from all the arrests they were making. As security measures increased the traffickers and buyers somehow developed a method of completing their transactions that was deceiving most law enforcement officers. That night in the middle of the crowded mall, the ones who craved the illegal substance knew who their suppliers were and got what they wanted.

Kevin was in need that night and arranged to meet with his supplier in an area behind the mall where the lighting had been neglected. Kevin called his supplier Mason, but he knew this wasn't has real name. Kevin never understood this but didn't worry about it. There was only one thing he was worried about, getting what he needed. It was pitch black in this area and it took a few seconds for both Kevin and the illegal retailer to be able to detect each other's presence. Kevin greeted the dark figure. "Am I glad to see you.

I've been waiting for over thirty minutes. Was afraid you weren't going to make it."

"Well, security around here is pretty tight any more, and I had to come a different way. I'm sticking my neck out to help you, man. This will be fifty bucks. Where is it?"

A nervous smile came across Kevin's face. "Could we work something out? I don't have any money tonight. I'm broke."

This didn't make the supplier very happy. "What do you mean you don't have any money? What is this, a joke? I risked being caught coming here for you. You didn't tell me you wouldn't have any money."

Kevin held up his hands and tried to work out a deal. "I know I didn't tell you, but you wouldn't have come if I told you I didn't have any money. Look, I've always been good for what I got from you. I've always paid you up front. I was just hoping we could work out a deal tonight."

"What kind of deal? This is a cash business, so what do you mean?"

Kevin thought he had this planned but felt like it was falling apart. "I was hoping because of my record with you guys that we could work out a loan and you could give me the stuff tonight and I would pay you next week."

Mason turned to walk away. "I don't think so. Like I said, this is a cash business only. Now I have another appointment so I can make. Kevin, you're a waste of my time."

"Wait." Kevin sounded desperate. "Isn't there anything we can do where both of us walk with what we need or want out of this? I didn't want this to be a waste of your time."

"No, man, all I want from you is cash. $50.00 a bag is the going price for this stuff tonight." He stopped and turned back toward Kevin. "There is something." He had an evil look on his face.

"Won't you just let me pay you later?"

"No, I told you that wouldn't work. However, if you just take a look around you will see opportunity for you to make good on our little transaction tonight. You just need to go in the mall and pick some items up and bring them to me in a different meeting place and we will finish this."

"I told you I don't have any money. If I did I would just pay you, get the stuff and leave."

"I don't care how you get what I want. Just get it and meet me down at the river in back of that old barn down below the city water tower. I've got to be there for another business deal in thirty minutes. If you're not there before I finish that deal, I won't stay and you won't get your stuff. You know I am the only supplier you can go to tonight, so you better be there."

Kevin walked back into the mall to think this over. While he was watching the crowd he started thinking he might be able to pull this off by taking advantage of the large crowds. The shops Mason wanted him to go to were packed. The sales people were so busy trying to keep tabs on everything he could pick everything out, stuff it under his jacket and walk on out without being caught. Little over thirty minutes later he was down at the river where he had been instructed. Mason was finishing up with one other guy and a girl as Kevin walked up.

Mason looked at Kevin. "Finished shopping?"

Kevin reached in the inside pocket of his jacket and pulled out a handful of CDs and handed them to Mason. "Good, let's look at them." He held them up to the moonlight as he focused on each cover. "Looks like you did a good job. You got my whole order. All those drugs that you've been taking haven't affected you memory yet." He reached down into his briefcase that was propped open on a park bench, pulled out one bag filled with a white powder and handed it to Kevin. "Here you go, man. This should fix you up for a while. Next time have the money and everything will go a lot easier for you."

The last two customers had come back and began to argue with Mason about something being wrong with what they just bought. The brief case was just a few inches from Kevin's right hand so he quickly reached in and snatched another bag, turned and walked away. He thought Mason was too busy with the others to notice what he had done. Unfortunately this was not a correct assumption on Kevin's part.

Kevin's phone started ringing at 9:00 the next morning. He was in such a deep sleep it took him several seconds to figure out what the sound of the ring was. Kevin used to think having a private phone line in his basement bedroom was a good idea, but he was having seconds thoughts now. After finding the phone he grabbed the receiver. "Yeah," he grumbled. "Who is this?"

"Hey, Kevin. It's me. You know, Mason. The guy you took the stuff from last night."

These words quickly got Kevin's attention as his eyes opened wide. "What do you mean and who is this?"

"You know who this is. Why did you do it? You little creep."

Recognizing the voice, Kevin kept denying the accusation. "I don't know what you're talking about. All I did was take what you gave me after I risked taking those CDs for you. How did you get my phone number anyway? I've never given it to you."

"I know where you live, Kevin. If I have to I will come there and get my money or my merchandise, but if I do the price you pay will be more than you can afford."

"No, don't come here. okay, I took one more bag. When those other guys came up, I just got it and left. I'll pay you for it. I'm getting some money later on today for something I'm doing for my dad. I can call you when I get it and we can meet."

"Oh no. It's not that easy. It was more like three bags that you grabbed and you made me come up short. Yow owe me interest, and if you don't have the extra money I have another way that you can pay it. Since you proved your abilities so well last night, I have some other ideas for you."

Kevin's stomach was starting to cramp when he heard these words. "What do you mean? Last night was a onetime deal. I can't do that again. Look, I'll pay you for whatever I took, but I can't do anything else."

"You'll do whatever I ask. You owe me big time now. I hear you have a pretty sister. How old is she, sixteen or seventeen?"

"Leave her out of this, man."

"I knew you would see the light. Meet me this afternoon at 2:00 in the back of River Park and have my money with you."

Kevin just sat on the edge of his bed shaking while his brain was working overtime to figure out what to do next. He was only seventeen and was in big trouble with a drug pusher. He had no one else to blame but himself, and he had to get himself out of it. Kevin was able to get out of his house by telling his parents he was meeting his best friend Jerry at the mall. Instead he went to Jerry's house to see if he could borrow the money. Jerry was very good about saving his money, so he knew his friend would have it. His best friend refused to get involved, but Kevin walked away with the money in his pocket after promising to get treatment that next week. The promise Kevin made to his best friend turned out to be the most important one of his life. Jerry was a believer and began to pray for Kevin to be able to be placed in a position where he would have to get that treatment.

Kevin made it to the park a few minutes early and found the site where they were to meet. He sat there on a bench nervous and wanting to get this over with. The one thing that scared him the most was the idea of his parents finding out what he had been doing. He had to ask himself why he was doing this and he couldn't really answer the question. All of this started out at a party where some friends dared him to try what they were doing. He couldn't remember why, but he caved under the pressure. Now he was hooked on the stuff and needed it daily. He had been lucky about keeping it from his parents and sister, but he wasn't sure how much longer he could do it.

Two twenty and he was still not there. Kevin wanted to go, but knew he better stay and wait. A few minutes later he heard leaves rustling behind him. He turned and the same man from the night before was walking toward him. He sat next to Kevin but stared straight ahead for what seemed to be several minutes. He finally interrupted the silence. "Got the money?"

Kevin nervously said, "Yes, I have it." He started pulling it out from his coat pocket. "Here, take it."

"No. Not like that. Wait till we get up and slowly pull it out from your pocket as you turn toward me and then bump me with that hand. I'll take it from you. Got it?"

"Yes, I think so."

He turned his head toward Kevin as he started to give him instructions. "Like I said, there is interest on this transaction."

"What do you mean anyway?"

"I mean you have to do something for me and I'll count it towards that interest."

"Look, I admitted I took the stuff and I just paid you the money. I don't understand any of this. I haven't used any of the three bags and could have just brought it all back. What do you want from me?" His voice started to shake and go off the scale.

"Hold it, man. All you need to do is one job and the debt will be paid. I've always wanted a Rolex watch. The only thing is all the stores around here are too cheap to handle them. Sherwood's has about the best knockoff around. It's a small jewelry shop and the mall has about killed their business, so most of the time they only have one salesman now, even on Saturdays."

Kevin knew this wasn't a good idea. Mr. and Mrs. Sherwood were friends of his parents and they see each other a lot at their church. "I can't go there. Isn't there something else I could do? Can't you find something else at another store?"

"No, they have the watch I want. It's the only one with gold trim around the face and the price tag is $2,500.00. The cabinet is locked so you'll have to get the salesman to unlock the case and show the watch to you. You'll need to distract him somehow and then run with it."

"I can't do that. The owners know my parents. We go to the same church."

"Church? So you're a drug addict that goes to church?" His tone was sarcastic. "Oh, are you a little sheep that has lost its way?" He placed his hand on Kevin's shoulder and pressed hard. "Go and get that watch, and when you have it don't come back here. You'll need to meet me over at the back entrance of the mall. If you don't deliver on this one, there will be another till you do deliver."

Thinking he had no choice he slowly got up and walked through the park and down the street. When he saw the jewelry store, his palms started sweating and his knees shook so bad he almost fell over. When he made it to the front door he looked at his reflection in the glass and couldn't believe what he saw. The drugs were just beginning to make their mark on his appearance. He decided after this he would go to his parents and tell them what has happened and ask for help. They've helped other kids, surely they would do something for one of their own kids.

A bell announced Kevin's arrival as he pushed the heavy glass front door open to step inside. Elevator music was coming from two speakers at the back of the store. Low glass display cases lined three sides of the small store. There were several rotating racks with different types of inexpensive necklaces and earrings hanging from them. The salesman was in the back room and watched Kevin for a few seconds before coming out. He realized a teenage boy in his store was not a good thing. He walked out to the first glass case and greeted Kevin. "Hello, my name is Burt. How are you today?"

Kevin looked down toward the base of the case and replied, "I'm okay."

"Are you looking for anything particular today? Anything I can show you?"

Kevin had to think for a second then said, "I'm looking for something for my dad. It's his birthday."

The salesman had moved out toward Kevin by now. "Do you have any idea of what you want for him?"

"I'm not sure."

"Well, could I suggest, unless your father has pierced ears, that you move from the earrings."

Kevin laughed nervously. "No, his ears aren't pierced. I think I might want to look at a watch."

"A watch is a good choice, but could I ask how much money you have to spend on this gift?"

"Oh, not very much really. I just came in to get an idea of what you have, then work on saving for it. Well, you see, my dad's birthday isn't until November so I have lots of time to get the money together." He walked around the store looking down into the display cases.

Burt directed him to the case with the watches. "These are the more expensive watches that we have. We also have some on those two racks over there that are under fifty dollars."

Kevin looked at him and said, "I would like to look at the ones in the case. He has always had those cheap things and I would like to get him something special this year."

He looked around inside the case to see if he could find the one that he was told to get. "Dad has always said he would like a Rolex, but there is no way anyone in our family could afford one. I've heard about copies that look just as good but don't cost very much. Do you have any of those?"

The salesman was starting to believe Kevin by now. "I have these over here. There are three that are just like Rolex, but they are still very expensive."

"Well, I have a job and I could save a lot between now and November. Could I take a closer look at those?"

Burt figured since they were the only ones in the shop he could control the situation okay and went ahead and unlocked the case. He pulled one of the three out and laid it on top. Kevin picked the case up that contained the watch but sat it down and asked to see one of the others. The salesman pulled the other of the three out and Kevin saw the $2,500.00 tag and there was gold trim around the face. He took his time and looked at it closely. He sat it down on the counter and looked over to another case but kept his hand on it and asked, "Do you have any watches in the other cases?"

Burt told him "no" and began to pick the one up from the top of the case. Kevin kept his hand on it and said, "Wait, I really like this one and need to look at it outside the case." He started taking it out when the salesman told him that wasn't allowed. Kevin knew it would take the salesman a few seconds to get around the display case and he could be out the door by then. He pulled the watch and case out of the Burt's hands, turned and ran. As he reached the door it opened and a middle-aged man and woman began to walk in.

Burt yelled, "Stop him."

The man reached out with both hands and grabbed Kevin by the shoulders, turned him around and tried to control him. Fortunately the jacket Kevin had on was big and bulky. He pulled both arms out of the sleeves, but he dropped the watch in the process. The only thing he wanted to do was to get out of there. Burt saw the watch drop to the floor but kept running to the door. He opened it and yelled at Kevin, "Don't ever come back here again. If you do I will call the police."

Kevin ran harder than he ever ran in his life. He wasn't sure where to go, he just wanted to get away from that jewelry store. Of all the luck to have more customers come in just as he was trying to get away. He started laughing as he thought they were probably the only other customers Burt would have all day. Now he had to go and face Mason. This has not been a very good Saturday.

The mall was a good half hour walk from the park; he figured the salesman suspected something because he was wearing a coat on a hot day. He found the meeting place and walked up to Mason and decided to just come out and say, "No, I don't have it."

The man had a look on his face as if he expected this result. "What did you do, chicken out? Did you even go into the store?"

"Yeah," he sat down on a bench. "I went in and got the salesman to show me the watch. Just as I was running to the door another customer walked in and stopped me. He grabbed my coat and the only thing I could do was to drop the watch and slide my arms out and run. Now I can never go back in that store again and I hope my parents never find out about this."

"Well." Mason looked at him. "Your debt is still not paid, you know. I'm disappointed. I wanted that watch. I just have to think of something else now. There is this big mall with all these shops and stuff to choose from."

Kevin jumped up. "No, I'm not going to do any more. This is it. I can't help what happened and I am not going to go into this mall and take another item."

"That's okay, pay for it if you want. You owe me and you'll pay me."

"Okay, what is it you want?" He decided if he got the list then he would get into the mall and make his way to the front and leave. He would go home and finally tell his parents what he had been doing and ask them to help him. He was going to get out of this, but it wouldn't be easy.

After getting the list he carried out his new plan and left the mall through the main front entrance area and made it to his neighborhood in record time. When he got home no one was there and he didn't have a key. Fortunately there was a back door he could open by a little trick. Once in his basement bedroom he felt safe again. He turned his stereo on and fell back in his bed listening to the heavy sounds and beats of rock.

About thirty minutes later he heard someone ringing the doorbell at the front. He was able to go to a window upstairs and look out to see an older man standing at their front door waiting. The thing that caught Kevin's attention was what the man had in his left hand. It was his jacket. This was Mr. Sherwood and somehow he figured out that was his jacket. Kevin just stood there and watched and waited. Finally Mr. Sherwood turned and left. He was going to tell his parents about all this and now he has to do it before Mr. Sherwood comes back.

It was several hours before his parents and brother and sister made it back. His dad walked down to the basement to find Kevin sacked out in bed, but the music was blasting away through his oversized speakers. He walked over to the system and turned it off. That woke Kevin up causing him to turn over from his side. "What happened?"

His dad said, "Kevin, where did you make off to this morning? We went out for lunch then to the movies and wanted you to go with us, but we couldn't figure out where you went to."

"Dad, I need to tell you about all that."

"What is it, Kevin?" His dad looked at his eyes and saw a hollow look. For the first time he noticed that Kevin had been sweating and looked pale. Before Kevin could say anything else his dad started talking, "I know I've been very busy lately and haven't been able to give you and the others the attention I should. There's been lots of stuff going on, but that's squared away now. I will be home more and we will be doing more things together as a family."

"Dad, I haven't had a problem with you working lots. That's not my problem right now. You asked me where I've been. That's what I need to talk to you about."

Before he could get another word out the doorbell rang. A few seconds later Kevin's mother walked down into the basement and told his father Mr. Sherwood was there and wanted to talk with him. Knowing it was hopeless, Kevin gave it one last try. "Dad, that's what I want to talk to you about."

"Okay, son, I'll be right back. I wonder what Mr. Sherwood wants. I haven't seen him for a while and he has never been over before. Don't worry, Kevin, I'll be back and we can talk all you want."

Kevin sank into his bed as deep as he could get. He knew what was coming next. Several minutes later both his dad and mother slowly walked down the stairs. They walked over to Kevin's bed and stood there looking down at the floor, then his father explained why Mr. Sherwood had come. "I was getting ready to tell Mr. Sherwood he was crazy and to kick him out of my house but then he pulled this out from behind him." He showed Kevin the jacket. "What do you have to say, Kevin?"

His heart was pounding. "That was what I was trying to tell you about before Mr. Sherwood came. He wasn't even there this morning. How did he know it was me?"

His mother stepped forward and explained, "After you ran out the salesman called Mr. Sherwood and he came down to the store. He searched the pockets and found a school paper that was crammed in the inside pocket. It was from last year so you must have forgotten it was there. He remembered we had a son named Kevin and from Burt's description he thought it might be you."

"What does he want to do now?" Kevin asked. "Did he call the police?"

His dad answered this one. "He thought about it but decided that since we were friends and you didn't get anything, he would talk to us before deciding what he wanted to do. You know if you got out of the store with something that cost as much as a watch you would be in big trouble. Mr. Sherwood thought there must have been a reason for what you did. So why did you do it?"

"There was a reason for it. There was somebody that made me do it." Kevin painfully began at telling about his weekend starting with Friday night. He told them about the drugs and the party where he started getting into them.

His mother had been crying ever since Mr. Sherwood's accusations, but she was really crying now. His father tried to console her then finally said, "Help me understand all this. You said we didn't do anything to cause this. You just happened to go to this party and these, uh, so-called friends pulled you into using drugs. Is that right?"

"I guess that's it." He paused and no one said anything for several seconds. "Now what? What am I going to do?"

His father looked at him. "It's not what you are going to do. It's what are we going to do? Kevin, I'm not going to give you any corny stuff right now, but I will say we will figure this out together. The first thing is for you to tell your mother and me where this stuff is that you have been fooling with. After that I'm going to call a couple friends. One is a doctor that I hope will help us make it through the weekend till we can get you to in to see him Monday. The other friend is an attorney. We need to see where we are legally. Your supplier will probably try to get in touch with you since you ran out on him today. We had all better stay in the house for the rest of the weekend. After that, I'm not sure. There will be some kind of punishment, but we won't worry about that now."

The supplier, Manson, did call later that day and he was hot because of

Kevin running out on him. He tried to get Kevin to meet him again on Sunday. Kevin refused but did get Mason to agree on meeting Tuesday night at the same place in the park. Kevin and his parents did meet with the attorney on Monday morning. The managers of the stores in the mall were informed of what Kevin had done and charges were filed against him. Even Mr. Sherwood decided to press charges against him. Of course buying and using illegal substances made matters worse. The attorney decided to see if he could work out something with the prosecuting attorney.

They did come up with a plan that Kevin and his parents would have to agree to. Kevin would play a key role in an attempt to catch his supplier and possibly get to the main source for the drugs he was selling. There were no guarantees, but Kevin might be able to get a lighter sentence by helping. Kevin was willing immediately, but it took a while to convince his parents.

When Tuesday night came Kevin felt like he was in an action cop movie. They had him wired with a special electronic microphone and miniature camera. There were several law officials in a van parked a block away and ready to come in if needed. The night of the meeting was dark, cold and windy. He drove up to the agreed site in his dad's car and walked up to Manson. Kevin was wearing the same jacket that he had on Saturday and Mason realized it right off.

He asked, "How did you get your jacket back?"

Kevin replied, "Mr. Sherwood found a school paper in a pocket that had my name on it. He brought it over to my house and told my parents all about what happened."

"You didn't tell them anything about me or what we have going, did you?"

"Hey, do you think I'm nuts? Anyway, what do you want from me now?"

"What I want is for you not to screw this job up like the last two. If you do there will not be another chance. You need to go over to Electric City tomorrow night. There's a guy that works there that will help you with this one. He owes me like you. Here's a shopping list for you. Get everything and take it to checkout number three at exactly 8:45. The guy that will be checking you out will give you a receipt and you will hand him a twenty-dollar bill. He'll even give you change. You'll walk out and bring everything to me Thursday night on the other side of town at the old railroad station."

Kevin tried to steer the conversation to get information on how the supplier got the drugs he sold but he didn't fall for anything. This man was good at what he did, but he would soon be in for a downturn in his business. Kevin got into his dad's car and drove off for a few blocks. Then he turned around and went to the van where the law officials were. They told him to go through with the plan and they would go talk with the manager of the store and get them to go along with it all.

When he walked into Electric City the next evening he didn't really know how this would work. He had been on edge all day but he knew he was trapped and had to go through with it. He tried to look as normal as possible by walking around a lot and taking his time to look at all the areas he needed. When it was 8:40 he decided to look for register three. He made it through the checkout process without a hitch. Of course the store manager knew about what was going on so they wouldn't interfere.

Kevin was not ready for the next step, but his parents were very encouraging, which made it easier for him. The plan now would be to grab the supplier that night and see if they could get any information out of him. There would be five officers close by in the background of the park waiting. Kevin was able to drive up to the meeting area that was in an open area of the park. There weren't any trees or bushes at all. He started to worry about how the police were going to sneak up to the area without being seen. To make matters worse, the moon was full that night. It was almost as light as a football field with the lights turned on. He got out of the car and stood by the door as the supplier got out of his car and walked toward him.

"Looks like you finally came through for me. I heard everything went fine."

"Yeah, it went okay. I made it." The signal for the police to come was when Kevin opened his trunk. Unfortunately when he did this no one came and he was getting worried. He started helping load the boxes and packages into the other car. Just before they loaded the last box Kevin caught some movement a few feet on the other side of his car. He looked over in the direction and saw one of the policemen crawling along the ground toward them. They kept loading and Kevin couldn't wait till this would be over. Finally he heard a voice calmly say, "This is the police. Stop what you are doing and put your hands up in the air."

In a split second Mason ducked down, reached in his coat pocket pulling out a shiny magnum 44, jumped up and grabbed Kevin holding the gun to his throat. "I'm getting in this car and getting out of here or else I'll shoot this kid," he shouted.

One of the officers, remaining calm, tried to be reassuring to both Kevin and the supplier. "There's no reason for this. If you do anything crazy we'll open fire and that will be it for you. Is that what you really want?"

At this same time an officer from behind fired a shot that just grazed the supplier's left shoulder causing him to drop the gun and fall to the ground. In a few more seconds there were five police officers surrounding and holding Mason down on the ground. He was holding his shoulder and looked confused and angry. Two of the officers lifted him up and pushed him against the car, searched him and led him away for questioning and to spend the night in the local jail until he could be brought before a judge.

Mason told the officers to stop when they got in front of Kevin and he grabbed his shirt. "Do you think this is over? You'll hear from me sometime. There will be a payment due for this."

Kevin took Mason's wrist and pulled his hand away, but he couldn't respond with anything.

The next five years rolled by as Kevin worked to get his life in order. Part of the price he paid for his past was six months in a juvenile detention center, one year reporting to a juvenile parole officer and treatment for drug abuse. This was not an easy price to pay, but with the support of his parents he learned to take one day at a time and began to build a life for himself. The fortunate part of Kevin's story was that he was a minor during those wild days. By state law when he turned eighteen his criminal record was completely cleared. It was as if nothing had happened. He was able to enter City University and work toward a degree in communications. He hoped to get into radio and TV news broadcasting. By the time he entered his last year of school he was juggling a full load of classes while working as an intern at a local television station and there was Amanda, his full-time girlfriend. Things were looking up until the day Mason came back to collect on that debt he believed Kevin owed him.

Kevin and Amanda had just finished their last class for the day at the university. They went to Amanda's car as usual and kissed goodbye as they each went off to their afternoon jobs. As Kevin was going over to his car he noticed a figure out of the corner of his right eye that didn't seem to fit the university campus. He didn't think too much of it and walked onto his car. While he was unlocking his door, he heard a voice in his left ear and he felt something sticking him in the middle of his back. "Kevin, remember me, Mason?"

Kevin jerked trying to free himself, but Mason stuck the object further into his back and held his right arm tightly. "What are you doing here?"

"Remember what I told you the last night we saw each other five years ago? I said you would pay, and I don't forget the debts owed me. We need to finish our deal. People are coming out from their classes and we need to go where we can talk. Get in the car, now."

They got into the car, and with Kevin driving they pulled out into the street. Kevin could only listen as his captor gave the instructions. "Let's go to our old meeting place at the park. I want to take you back in time for a while."

Kevin became overwhelmed with old feelings that had taken years to clean up. He was trying to control his fears and think clearly of how he could get out of this. Punching 911 on his cell phone and letting it stay open hoping the person on the other end will hear what was going on might work. The only problem with this was that the phone was in his jacket pocket and that was in his back seat. He could drive by the police station and yell out the window for help, but he figured he would be blasted away before the window was rolled down. He finally decided making conversation might help provide an opportunity.

"You said something about owing you. I have paid for those mistakes. I realize you went to a prison and had a hard time of it there. I went to a juvenile detention center for six months, was on probation for a year and had to go through treatment for drugs. You've forgotten I was the one on the stuff. All you did was sell it, you weren't hooked. I might not have had to go to jail like you, but I did have a rough time of it and still do because of the habit."

This didn't seem to faze Mason. "You don't have any idea of what has been going on with me. You don't know. I intend to do real damage this afternoon. You know I never told them about my boss or anything about how the operation worked. That's loyalty, which is something you will never understand. Even though you might be getting educated, you still will not understand loyalty."

By now Kevin was starting to give up hope. They were getting close to the park and he hadn't come up with any ideas, and his assailant sounded very intent on doing something he was afraid to think about. As they came to a stop light at the corner of Washington and Main, something Kevin didn't expect occurred. A long time friend, Miles, was walking on the sidewalk and saw him. Kevin looked over to the sidewalk but did not wave or talk back to him. Miles thought that was strange and he didn't recognize the man that was in the front seat with him. Miles and Kevin went through high school together and he was aware of Kevin's past. After giving a few seconds' thought, Miles went into the nearest business that had a phone and called the police. He had read Kevin's license plate. He gave the police a description of Kevin's car and the street and direction they were going. Miles knew something was wrong, so he asked if an officer in the area could follow the car for a while to see if Kevin was in trouble. The police agreed to do this and called an officer that was in his squad car close to the area.

Kevin and Mason passed the building that used to be Sherwood Jewelry. "Do you remember that place, Kevin?" Mason asked.

"Yeah, it took me years to regain Mr. Sherwood's confidence after that stupid thing you made me do. Competition from stores in the mall finally drove him out of business."

"You know I never got myself a Rolex watch or a cheap copy. Too bad they aren't open any more. You could go and get me one today. Well, I told you I wouldn't give you any more chances anyway. I meant it too."

"I remember."

"I always follow through with what I say and I intend on keeping up my reputation. Now let's go to the park."

After a few more blocks Kevin noticed a police car about a block behind them in his rear view mirror. No matter what he did he couldn't come up with any way to get help. When they turned the final corner before their old meeting place, Kevin said a brief prayer under his breath, "Lord, I know you have forgiven me for my past sins. Please help me today."

"Okay." The supplier started giving more instructions. "This is good enough, stop here."

Kevin pulled over to the side of the street. Not much had changed in all those years.

"Now get out." Mason's voice was real stern and strained. After they got out there were more commands. "Move down to the river. I want to show you something."

His assailant was tucking the gun into the pocket jacket as he said, "There are some trees over there to your right. Move to them where we can get out of sight."

After getting into the trees they began talking about that night and everything that led up to it. Kevin tried talking about what he had gone through after that night and the help he was able to get. The longer they talked the more Kevin could sense the man was getting more intent on carrying out his mission. No amount of reasoning was going to change the man's mind. Kevin could tell he was working himself up to carry out his mission. Kevin was desperately looking for a way out when suddenly something told him to stop trembling and start praying. Kevin, being the fast learner that he is, began to follow what he was sensing. Finally the time came and his former drug supplier began to pull out the weapon from his coat pocket. Kevin noticed there was nothing on the gun to keep it quiet when fired.

"You know if you shoot me people will hear it. Don't you think the police will come and figure out what happened and come looking for you?"

"I don't care about that any more. I figure I'm heading in the wrong direction no matter what. Might as well get there now as later."

This sent chills down Kevin's back. He knew unless God intervened, this would be it for him. He thought he had paid his price for the stupid mistakes he had made in his past, but it looked like they were haunting him all over again. It was at this point they heard a voice that was similar to the one they heard five years before say, "Stop, this is the police. Throw your weapon down or I will have to shoot."

The man looked at the policeman then at Kevin and said, "Like I said. I'm heading in the wrong direction. Might as well get there now as later." With this he turned and fired on the police officer. The policeman was more accurate and deadly when he returned the fire and the former drug supplier fell backward hitting the ground with an awful thud. Kevin ran over and kicked the gun out of his hand and bent over the man trying to see if he were dead or alive. The officer was running toward them in the background. His former supplier slowly opened his eyes and Kevin could only look at him. His eyes became hollow and lifeless a few seconds later. Mason had paid the price that he had chosen.

A STAGECOACH MYSTERY

"You shall not bear false witness."
Ex. 20:16

Nine

There was only one advantage in riding a stagecoach across central Kansas on a fall day instead of a day in a hot summer. The hard blowing wind is cooler, but everything else is the same. Those same winds bent the few trees all in one direction that dot the flat landscape.

The Santa Fe Trail was just as rough and unforgiving regardless of the season. Drivers and messengers were hard and colorful men willing to risk their lives to transport people and cargo in exchange for little pay. Jack Slade was no different from any other driver of the times. A man with a reputation of being talkative and as cordial as any cultured gentleman while sober but mean enough to kill when he was in a state of intoxication. Most that knew him figured the temperament was the result of fighting for the South during the recent civil war.

Henry Hughes wore Union blues during the same conflict and seemed to have been able to preserve his quiet attitude through it all. He didn't mind riding as a messenger but wished Jack would stop telling his stories of the way it was while fighting with General Johnston in Georgia. The worst part was the singing Henry suffered through. "Dixie" and "The Bonnie Blue Flag" were the limit of what Jack knew by memory. Henry knew this was Jack's way of making him suffer for the North winning the way they did.

After a few hours on the trail Jack started his fourth round of Dixie. "I wish I was in De Land ob cotton, old times dar am not forgotten; look away, look away, look away, Dixie Land. In Dixie Land whar I was born in, early on one frosty mornin', look away, look away, look away, Dixie Land."

"Do ya have to keep singin those old songs?" Henry asked as he was holding onto the seat of the stagecoach. "If you gotta sing, can't you come up with something different?"

Jack switched to "We are a band of brothers, and native to the soil, fighting for the property…"

"That's the third time for 'Bonnie Blue Flag' today. Why don't you just shut up!" Henry exclaimed.

"I might be able to come up with some new ones and it might be a good idea. I'll tell you what, when we get to Fort Dodge, I'll get with some of my old friends down at Ham Bell's and learn myself a new song or two. How's that for ya? The only problem is I gotta have something to sing between here and there and these are all I know. Besides, I couldn't say I'm ashamed of what I did during those days when we were repelling the invasion of all you Yankees."

This little comment got Henry every time. "Wait a minute. We've gone over this before. We weren't invading you. We were just trying to get all you arrogant rebs back into the Union. Look, the war has been over for almost seven years, can't you do like everyone else and forgive and forget. I didn't want to fight, but I knew something had to be done. I don't want to relive the war every day that I'm riding up here. The ride and this seat are rough enough, but when your attitude is thrown in it's almost too much."

"Well, Henry, I'm certainly sorry if the history of the glorious South and its undefeated fighting men offends you."

"UNDEFEATED!? Haven't you heard? Lee surrendered. Your side lost. You lost. The South lost and the Confederacy does not exist anymore. Old Jeff Davis was arrested and thrown in prison and I'm beginning to think that's where all you rebs should be."

Jack turned to Henry with a shocked look as his mouth slowly started to drop open as if he were looking at an insane fanatic. "Man, you really need to just simmer down there. Old Jeff Davis as you called him was and is the greatest man ever made President in the history of this or any other nation on earth. Oh, and by the way, he was unjustly placed in prison as a political prisoner by the aggressive Northern government but was released."

Before Henry could say anything else they both heard another and much loader argument going on between some of the passengers. Thomas Stuart, a businessman that had gotten on at Fort Larned, was trying to defend himself against accusations from Preston and Virginia Dale.

"Sir," Mr. Stuart said, "I know you both are upset at the results of what appeared to be a good investment but these things can go either good or bad. Unfortunately this one turned out bad."

Preston angrily replied, "Yah, it turned out bad because you didn't handle it correctly. We came on this trip because we thought it would be a good time to talk to you. We know you deal with the army back in Abilene and Fort Larned and you have a partner at Fort Dodge. The drive wasn't managed right and you know it. In fact we've heard some things we need to talk to you about in private. Virginia and I want to meet with you tomorrow morning. We lost our shirts and almost lost our farm on that deal and it was your fault."

Virginia sided with her husband. "We have two children to think of and we were counting on that money to help pay for their school and a lot of other things. We used our life savings to buy into that deal. Isn't there anything that can be done?"

Thomas looked at her. "I regret that you are having such a difficult time right now, but you have to understand there is nothing I can do for you now. We both lost money on that deal. I don't see how a meeting tomorrow will help and I will be very busy."

This argument was wearing on the other passengers. What was typically a long and hard ride was being made worse by this conflict. Will McKinley, a passenger that was on his way to Fort Union, attempted to change the subject. "You know I haven't lived in Kansas very long. Is this a typical fall day here? If it is, I think I will like it here tremendously." No one volunteered an answer to this.

Clara Parker, a much more sophisticated lady, picked up on what Virginia had said about having children and asked her, "How old are your children, Mrs. Dale?"

She was trying to regain control of her emotions. "John is three and Emily is four. They're staying with my parents for the next few days while we are on this trip. Do you have children?"

"I haven't had any myself," Clara replied. "I'm still working on getting the husband part."

Horace, Clara's traveling companion, perked up from an attempted nap because of the last statement. "I hope you are not thinking you can work on me for that part of your life."

Clara laughed and continued to talk with Virginia who was sitting across from her. The one thing to remember about a stagecoach is the space for people to ride in is small and cramped. No matter where a person would sit the ride would be rough and you better not want to talk about something that is supposed to be private because everyone can hear everything you say.

"Coming up to our next stop, Fort Larned," Henry yelled down to the passengers.

About fifteen minutes later they were pulling up to a small structure built of sod. Smoke was drifting out of the mud brick chimney, and you could hear the spare horses out in the corral. After climbing down the side of the coach Jack opened the door as he told the passengers about the stop. "This is our last stop before Fort Dodge. The food here isn't much for taste, but there's usually plenty of it. Better take advantage of it while you can. No more stops till we get to Fort Dodge."

It was an effort for anyone to get off a stagecoach, but it took an extra effort for a woman with a dress. When all were unloaded, they made their way inside the building to be greeted by the smells of a thick stew made with buffalo meat, potatoes and carrots. They had boarded at 5:00 that morning in Abilene and had only one other stop for lunch so they were all hungry, tired and dusty from the road. Dinner was at a long table with one large pot containing the hot mixture with platters full of a type of hard fried bread and pitchers of water. Clara had the hardest time relaxing in her fancy pink dress with all its frills. She was rather warm and considered taking her hat off but that just wasn't done in the company of people that you do not know well. Virginia was less sophisticated but just as warm and did remove her hat. She placed her hat and pin on a table that was close to the door.

While they were all dipping into the pot and passing the bread around, Horace began the next conversation. "Mr. Stuart, what type of business do you own?"

Thomas was trying to chew his first bite. "Well, I supply various things for the army. I have a sutler store here in Fort Larned and another in Fort Dodge."

Horace continued with another question. "What type of things do you supply for the army?"

Thomas swallowed then answered, "Anything they need and that I can find for them. Soldiers come to the stores and buy their personal things. You know, tobacco, anything they might need."

"I noticed your watch bob earlier. It looks like some kind of military emblem." Will McKinley joined in questioning Mr. Stuart.

"That's because it is a military emblem." He carefully reached into his vest pocket and pulled it out and held it up for everyone to see. "Umm, during the war I served with a special unit under Sherman during his march through Georgia."

This sparked Henry's attention so he probed further. "Sherman? I was with Hancock for the year and a half I was in the fight. I signed up a few months before Gettysburg. That was not a good time to remember. I'm sure you feel the same about Georgia."

Mr. Stuart had just taken a bite of buffalo and was attempting to chew the tough meat but worked an answer in. "I never held anything against any southerner. I still don't. I was young and joined mostly for the adventure and the uniform. Didn't realize we would end up...." He stopped for a second. "Well, I do not believe it is proper to discuss such things with ladies present. What we did we believed needed to be done. I am proud of being part of ending the struggle so I had my hat pin made into a watch bob after the war."

Jack had been quietly absorbing the conversation. Henry decided to warn Thomas about Jack's attitude toward the war. "You know, Jack here was with Johnston in Georgia. I'm sure we don't need to keep bringing this up any further."

Mr. Stuart looked at Jack. "Were you at Atlanta, Mr. Slade?"

Jack slowly leaned toward the table and stabbed a piece of meat with his fork and held it up in the air as he answered the question. "Yeah, I was there and we didn't back off from you Yanks. But just like my pard, Henry, here says, we should forget and forgive. I'm working on it all the time. Don't worry, the wars been over for a long time. I'm just out here in the West driving for the Sanderson's Overland Stage Company helping others to get where they want to go. That's my life now. Live in the present and not in the past, that's what I always say."

These words made Henry stop chewing in the middle of a mouthful. He almost choked but recovered quickly. A few minutes later Jack stood up and announced, "Need to keep moving, folks. Be back on board in five minutes." He turned and walked out to the team of horses to make sure they were ready to go.

Most of the passengers left what was on their plates and quickly took advantage of the other facilities and splashed water on their faces to get ready for the last leg of their long trip. Virginia hurriedly grabbed her hat to make it outside and didn't think about looking for the pin. After everyone was settled and they were traveling again, she started to put her hat on realizing she didn't have the pin. "Did anyone see my hat pin back at our stop, or maybe I dropped it on the floor?" No one really gave her an answer. "Preston, did you get my pin?" He shook his head to signify that he hadn't. "Oh well, I must have knocked it off the table when I reached for my hat. That Mr. Slade has been pushing us too hard today."

"Virginia," Preston said with an agitated sound to his voice. "Slade is just doing his job to get us to Fort Dodge on time."

Preston decided to bring up their problem with Mr. Stuart one more time before they came to their final stop. "Mr. Stuart, we need to talk more. Virginia and I came on this trip just to talk to you because it's so hard to even find you back home. I have to remind you that we have more information that we have found that just might change your mind."

Mr. Stuart thought for a moment before replying. "Okay, I am like you and don't want to bore these good people with this any more. Let's meet first thing in the morning after breakfast. Will you be staying at the Great Western Hotel?"

"Yes, we'll be there."

"Good, meet me in the lobby at 8:00 in the morning and we'll walk over to the store and maybe I can help you to understand everything better. At least we can talk in privacy there. Is that acceptable for the both of you?"

Both Mr. and Mrs. Dale agreed to this and they were quiet for the duration of the remaining part of the journey.

About a half hour into the last leg of the day's journey the coach's left wheel hit a large rock that jarred everyone riding the coach. Jack stopped and got down to inspect it. He had a spare, but it was getting dark so he didn't want to take the time to change it out. After a few minutes he felt they could make it into Fort Dodge in good shape. He could take his time with it in the morning and there would be a blacksmith shop for help.

After almost two more hours of the Santa Fe Trail they were pulling into their final destination on Front Street. Fort Dodge was a young and wild cow town that was growing like the rest of the West, fast and hard. The dirt streets were lined with saloons and brothels. Most homes were small temporary buildings put up quickly. Front Street was rapidly gaining a reputation of being the place to become known as a fast gunslinger. It was not uncommon to hear gunshots in the night and to wake up to bodies stretched out in the street.

The stagecoach stopped in front of the Great Western Hotel and all of the passengers were grateful to be going to a room with a nice soft bed. Henry was working to carry out his duties of unloading the luggage. There was also the strong box under his seat that contained any valuables the passengers would trust to him. Lloyd Walker, the hotel owner, gave everyone a warm welcome as they approached the front desk. Jack had made his way down and to the team of horses to begin their care.

Will McKinley came up to him and asked, "Now, Mr. Slade, we will be leaving first thing in the morning, won't we? I must arrive in Fort Union on time. I have very important business there."

Jack looked up. "Mr. McKinley, isn't it?" Will motioned yes with his head. "I'm going to have to take that wheel down to the blacksmith as soon as everybody is unloaded to make sure it's okay. If he has to do anything to repair it we might be starting a little late. I could use the spare, but I refuse to go all the way to Ft. Union without one. I'll know in about a half hour. I'll leave a message at the desk for you and all the other folks that will be leaving in the morning."

The wheel was damaged beyond Jack's ability to repair and he found the front axle needed work. It was something the blacksmith would have to complete and it was too late for him to do it that evening. No one would be leaving on his stagecoach any time before noon the next day. He went back to the hotel and left a message for his passengers as he promised.

The Dales were up early as was their custom at home. Mr. Stuart hadn't come down yet, so they decided to go the café next door for breakfast. They left word at the front desk that he could find them there if he came down soon. She couldn't keep from looking around bodies in the street on their way next door. There were gunshots that woke them from cowboys visiting the saloons that lined the street. To her dismay there were only a few people with their horses and they were all living and breathing. They did see Jack and Henry walking to the blacksmith's place where they hoped to resolve the problems with the stagecoach that morning.

After a hardy breakfast Preston and Virginia walked back to the hotel ready for their meeting with Thomas Stuart. They walked up to the front desk and asked the clerk if Mr. Stuart had come down yet. The clerk replied that he hadn't seen Mr. Stuart yet. They checked the time, but it was not yet 8:00, so they decided to sit for a while in the lobby and give him a few more minutes.

Pretty soon Mr. McKinley came down to ask the desk clerk about the condition of the stage coach and walked away very disappointed after finding out the stage would not be leaving right away. He saw the Dale couple and went over to explain what he had found. "Unfortunately, we won't be leaving till later today. I must get to Fort Union as soon as possible. Will you folks be going on with the trip?"

Preston replied, "No. We are heading back home on the morning stage tomorrow."

"That's right, you have the business deal you have to talk over with Mr. Stuart. Well, my room was next to his, and I think he might be sleeping in for a while longer this morning."

"Why do you say that, Mr. McKinley?" Virginia asked quickly.

"I'm a pretty light sleeper on trips like this. I really hate traveling and I hate strange hotel rooms. That's the main reason I need to get to Fort Union as quickly as I can. That's where I'm from, you see."

"Okay, Mr. McKinley," Virginia interrupted him. "I do hope you get home soon, but what about Mr. Stuart?"

"Oh, well I heard foot steps over there off and on during the night. There were voices the first time, then someone left and others came at different times. He must be a busy man to have things going on late at night. Couldn't tell what was being said or anything. I was in and out of sleep myself. I just hate hotel rooms. Well, I'm sure Mr. Stuart will be sleeping later than he said last night. I'm going to check with Mr. Slade on the condition of the stagecoach."

After Mr. McKinley left, Virginia and Preston talked and decided to wait for Mr. Stuart till 9:00. If he did not come down by then, Preston would go up to his room and see what was keeping him. Within the next few minutes Philip Rodgers, Thomas Stuart's business partner, came into the hotel lobby. He went up to the front desk and found Mr. Stuart had not been down for the day yet. He couldn't understand this because they had an appointment for that morning. After getting Mr. Stuart's room number, he went up the stairs to check on him. A few minutes later Mr. Rodgers came back to the front desk and told the clerk that Mr. Stuart did not answer when he knocked and even when he asked for him. The clerk reached for a key and led the way back up the stairs with the business partner following. Virginia and Preston overheard what was going on and also followed the two up the stairs.

After they made it to the door of Mr. Stuart's room the clerk first knocked with no response. He then yelled out, "Mr. Stuart."

Philip impatiently said to the clerk, "Don't wait any longer. Open the door. He might be hurt or something."

The clerk fumbled with the keys till he was finally able to get the door open. All four walked cautiously into the room only to find Thomas Stuart still in bed and not moving. Philip called for him as if for the first time, "Thomas? Thomas, are you okay?"

Thomas was on his side with his back to the door. Preston reached for his arm to pull him over to see if he was okay. His face had a gray lifeless tone and he was not breathing. Virginia, realizing Mr. Stuart's condition, screamed. Preston leaned over him placing his left ear on his chest to detect a beating heart. A second later he raised back up. "Well, not surprising, no heartbeat.

This man is dead."

Philip told the clerk to run and get the sheriff. He then looked Mr. Stuart over and found a bullet hole in the back. "He must have been shot while in bed. That's strange. The door was locked. How did this happen?"

Mr. McKinley walked in but didn't realize what was going on. "I've been looking for everybody. That Jack Slade hasn't even had the blacksmith look at the stage. We won't get out of here till tomorrow I'll bet." He looked up at everybody. "What's going on? What's wrong with Mr. Stuart?"

"He's dead," Philip said in a low voice.

"He's what? How did that happen?"

Preston responded, "We don't know, but the sheriff is on his way."

Everyone just stood around for several minutes not knowing what to do. Preston was comforting Virginia in his arms, then finally suggested they should go to their room. As they were leaving he told Mr. Rodgers, "If the sheriff wants to talk to us, you'll know where to find us."

A few minutes later, Sheriff Justin Stonegate walked into the hotel lobby and up the stairs to the scene of this curious death. The sheriff was a lean but commanding figure standing well over six feet tall. Dressed in a dark suit with vest, white shirt, black tie and a six-shooter strapped to his side. His black hair flowed down to his shoulders from his broad-brimmed beaver felt hat. His most defining feature was the long black handle mustache that seemed to follow the contour of his face outlining his downturned mouth. It hung to the end of a strong chin that seemed never ending. In spite of his size and demeanor, all attention went to the bright star pinned to his vest just over the heart that symbolized who this man was. He had served under an intelligence man named Pinkerton during the war and had learned a thing or two about investigating. His gate was long and slow, but his mind was quick to observe and evaluate.

"Sheriff, we found him on his side and I think he has been gone for several hours," Mr. Rodgers exclaimed to the sheriff pointing to the body.

The sheriff took his usual wide steps over to the bed and started examining the body, then said, "I had the clerk fetch Dr. Freeman. From what he told me I thought the man might still be hangin' on, but now I see he is quite dead. I'll still want the doc to tell me what he thinks." He looked over at Mr. Rodgers and asked, "Who found him and when?"

"I did," Mr. Rodgers answered. "This morning, I came up because he was supposed to be over at the store this morning at 8:00, but it was way after, so I came to check on him. When I came up I knocked on the door and yelled his name. When he didn't answer, I went for the clerk who let me and the others in and we found him like this." He pointed to Mr. Stuart.

Dr. Freeman walked into the room about this time. "Hello, Sheriff, Philip. What happened here?"

The sheriff answered, "He was killed sometime during the night and Philip found him this morning. He appears to have more than one wound, so I need your idea of which was first and which he died from."

"I'll take a look, but why don't all you go on back downstairs and I'll come down after I'm finished." The sheriff and everyone else backed out of the room and headed downstairs. Mr. McKinley went to the Dales' room and told them about the sheriff and doctor being there. They decided to go down to the lobby with everyone else.

After just a few minutes of examining the body, the doctor came downstairs to the lobby where everyone was sitting or pacing the floor. "Well, Doc?" inquired Philip.

"This is what killed him." He held out what seemed to be a simple but long hatpin.

Virginia let out a gasp of shock when she saw the hatpin was the one she thought she had lost at the last stop the night before. Clara thought she recognized the hatpin and caught Virginia's reaction and began to put things together. She didn't have a clue how it got to the hotel or who used it. She only knew she had to remain calm and quiet.

"A hatpin?" asked Philip and Mr. McKinley almost at the same time.

"A hatpin," Dr. Freeman repeated. "Of course, this was the first wound. The one causing death."

"The first wound?" asked Philip.

"Do I really have to repeat myself for you all the time, Philip? The stabbing with the hatpin was the first wound and I believe caused his death. The other wound was the bullet to the back, so he must have been on his side when this was done. Of course, there is that other stab wound that must have been with a knife."

With these revelations everyone became quiet and Clara suddenly did recall Virginia taking her hat off at the last stop and saying she had lost the pin when everyone got back on the stage. "Virginia, isn't that your hatpin? Isn't it the one you said you lost when you got back on the stagecoach last night after our last stop?"

"Oh no, that's not mine," she nervously replied. "Mine was fancier than this one. It couldn't be mine."

"But I saw it as you were taking your hat off when we went in to have our supper. Yes, I know this is the same hatpin you placed on the small table along with your hat just before we ate. Then after we all got back on the stage you were frantically looking for it and even asked if someone had seen it."

Philip Rodgers was observing what was going on between Clara and Virginia. "If this is your hatpin, Mrs. Dale, then you must have done it. You killed my business partner."

The sheriff picked up on this and took the hatpin from the doctor's hand and held it in front of Virginia. "Mrs. Dale, is this your hatpin? Now think very carefully. Is it yours?" He held it with the point up in the air. There was no blood on it because the doctor wiped it off.

Virginia was looking at her loyal and loving husband while moving anxiously clinching her teeth trying to figure what answer to give. "Yes, I think it is my pin."

The sheriff held it closer to her. "Now, Mrs. Dale, you think it is your pin?"

"Well, for one thing, the end of it is too pointed, but other than that it looks just like mine."

Sheriff Stonegate turned to Dr. Freeman and asked, "Well, Doc, how do you know the pin got him first?"

"Well," the doctor began with a touch of sarcasm, "based on my many years of higher education and professional experience in the field of medicine, I deduced the hatpin was the cause of death because it pierced the left lung traveling all the way to and through the heart. It was also the only wound that bled, leading me to believe there was no blood pressure when the other wounds were inflicted. Now the question is which of the other two came next? After thinking about this, I would have to say the stab to the other side of the chest came next and the person that inflicted this wound must have turned his body on his side. The gunshot wound must have been the last because surely the person that stabbed him last would have noticed the bullet wound as he leaned over him. The gun could have been fired from across the room and with it being dark, he or she would have probably just figured he was sleeping. Anyway, he's dead and the last question is who did it?"

"Don't you mean who did which one, Doc, and if there is more than one killer, then do I arrest all three or just the first one?" asked the sheriff.

"Well, I'll leave all those legal questions to you and all the attorneys in town. You ought to have Joe the mortician come and get the body. I'm sure he will be interested in the potential business. Anybody know where the fella is from?" The doctor looked around the room for an answer.

Philip Rodgers slowly stood from the chair he had been sitting in during this entire conversation. "I know only too well where he is from. We were business partners and he would travel here a lot from Abilene. That's where his wife June is. They have a place in town close to his business there. She'll need to know about this. She ought to come get him and take care of his services over there in Abilene I guess."

The sheriff took charge. "I'll wire the sheriff over in Abilene to find her and let her know what has happened and I'll have Joe come get the body and all his personal things. I understand now that Mr. Stuart had arrived on the stage last night. I need to talk to every person that was on that stagecoach. No one can leave town until I have had a chance to talk to them and figure this out."

When Virginia heard this she said, "Sheriff, we have two small children back home and we need to get back."

The sheriff gave her a stern look. "Seems like to me you and your husband chose to go on this trip leaving your two kids, didn't you?"

"Well, yes we did, but we left them with their grandparents."

"That's good," the sheriff replied. "I'm sure the grandparents won't mind a couple more days with their grandkids."

Hearing this, Preston became concerned. "A couple more days! Sheriff, we also have a business to take care of, we need to go home today."

This caused the sheriff to lose all patience. "Mr. and Mrs. Dale, I am placing you both under arrest for the murder of Thomas Stuart. I'm going to go wire the Sheriff in Abilene then get the mortician. I'll be back in a little while and I will start with the both of you."

They both gasped and reached for each other. Preston defended Virginia and himself by exclaiming, "You have no proof. What about the other wounds? Do you think we did all three of them?"

"I'm not sure about anything today. I do know since this is your hatpin, Mrs. Dale, that either you or your husband are suspects, and I would rather arrest you and throw you both in the same cell so I know where you are than take a chance on you running off. Besides, this way I'll have more time to think of more questions of you after talking with everyone else." With this, the sheriff led the Dales to the jail then walked to the Wells Fargo office where the telegraph office was located. Preston was loudly protesting all the way.

By now it was almost eleven o'clock and Jack Slade walked through the front door of the hotel just as the sheriff left. "I heard what happened to Mr. Stuart. Can't believe it."

Clara asked, "How did you hear about it? It's just been a couple of hours since we found him."

"This kind of news travels fast in a town like this. I came in to tell my passengers that we will not be leaving till sometime this afternoon. The stage is over at the blacksmith's with a damaged wheel and axle. It will take him a while to fix them. That rock we hit yesterday didn't do us a good deed at all."

"Jack," Mr. McKinley said. "The sheriff told us no one leaves town till he has talked to all of us. That might be a couple days."

Jack didn't like these words. "No one tells the Sanderson's Overland Stage what to do. I say when we leave. No Yankee sheriff will ever tell me how to run my stage."

The front door to the hotel opened just as Jack was making this statement and the Sheriff walked in. "I'm not sure what Yankee sheriff you're talking about, Mr. Slade, but this sheriff will tell you that no one on that stagecoach, including you and your messenger, Henry, will be leaving town till I say. I saw you coming to the hotel, so I got my prisoners to the jail and turned them over to my deputies then came back. I'm going to question each person and see if I can piece this thing together and find the killer of Mr. Stuart."

Jack jumped directly into the sheriff's path and stretched his body as tall as he could up to the sheriff's face. With his nose up to the sheriff's chin Jack yelled, "What about all those poor boys that get killed every night out there on Front Street? What are you doing to find those killers? You won't push the Sanderson's Overland Stage Company…"

Jack didn't finish this before the sheriff came up with an undercut to his chin. This caused him to fly into the air leaving him sprawled unconscious on the hotel floor. "That is the way we communicate with people like him," the sheriff informed everyone in the room. "Now everyone stay in the hotel until I can talk to each of you. You can go to your rooms if you wish, and I will find you. Don't worry, folks, I don't think this will take long."

The sheriff wanted to talk with Lloyd Walker to find out what he knew about Thomas Stuart before going any further. He found him in his office there at the hotel. While talking with him Walker brought up the fact that Mr. Stuart came to town around the same time each month and always stayed there at the Great Western Hotel. He supposedly came to check on his business partner but Walker knew there was another reason for him to come to town.

There was a certain lady Mr. Stuart would see on every visit. He happened to know her name, Varina Jackson. "She waits tables at the restaurant next door. Rumor has it they've been having an affair." He went on, "There's already talk that she killed him because he had come to town to break it off with her. He was going back to his wife and that would end things between them."

The sheriff took notes on what he said but didn't take anything too serious at this point in his investigation. "I'll go next door later and talk with Varina. You've been a big help to me, Lloyd." He walked out and since he didn't see any of the passengers from the stage he went to the desk and asked for a list of all their names and room numbers. Of course, he didn't have to worry about the Dales since they were being furnished with a room complete with bars on the windows. He wondered about what happened with Jack but figured someone carried him over the blacksmith shop.

He went up to Mr. McKinley's room after this and found him to be a passenger who's sole interest was to get home and no more. He understood Philip Rodgers was a business partner with the late Mr. Stuart, so he decided to go talk to him after stopping at the restaurant to speak with Varina, and besides, it was getting close to lunch.

On his way out of the hotel he remembered about wiring the sheriff in Abilene so he went and accomplished that task. He made his way to the Lone Prairie Restaurant and found Varina Jackson hurriedly waiting on hungry customers as the only waitress in the entire place. The sheriff sat down at an empty table taking his hat off and sitting it on top of the table. In a few moments a very friendly but rushed Varina made it to his table. "Hello, Sheriff. What can I do for you today?"

"Why don't you give me the lunch special with coffee."

"Is that all, Sheriff?"

"Well, that will do for now."

Sheriff Stonegate slowly ate his food and drank down several cups of coffee while the lunch hour rush cycled through to one or two other customers. Varina came over one more time asking if there was anything else she could get for him. He replied, "If you're not so busy now, you could sit down with me for a minute."

"Oh, I'm not allowed to do that. If you want that sort of thing the saloon is just down the road."

"Varina, that is not what I mean. I need to tell you something that you probably need to know. I am surprised with the way news like this gets around town that you haven't heard it yet."

She saw the serious look on his face so she trustingly sat down in the chair across from him. "Varina, I understand you know a Mr. Thomas Stuart. A business man from Abilene."

"Yes, that's right. He's a friend of mine."

"Well, Varina, what I have to say is not easy, and I'm not sure just how close you two were, but I have to tell you Mr. Stuart is dead."

These words stung Varina in the middle of her heart while she sank in her chair sobbing. "I'm sorry to bring this news to you here like this. Lloyd, the owner of the hotel, told me that Mr. Stuart and you saw each other every time he came into town. Is that true?"

"Yes it's true."

"Have you seen him since he came into town last night?"

"No I haven't. I was getting concerned and thought something was wrong. He usually comes into the restaurant and then we meet after I get off work."

"I need to ask what kind of relationship you and Mr. Stuart had."

Varina felt like she knew where this was going. She gathered her wits and said, "We were good friends. I knew Mr. Stuart while growing up in Abilene. We are, well, I guess I need to say we were good friends that's all. I know where you're going with this and I don't appreciate it. I not only knew Mr. Stuart, but I knew Mrs. Stuart. They helped me move here and get this job after having troubles back home. My parents refused to help so they stepped in. You can ask my boss, Mr. Edwards. He'll tell you."

"Varina, please understand Mr. Stuart did not die of natural causes. He was murdered."

"Murdered? How, why? He was a nice man. He just wanted to help me, that's all. I wonder if it, no…"

"He seems to have had quite a few enemies for such a nice guy. Looks like he was stabbed once in the chest with a very sharp hatpin that was strangely left for someone like me to see. One more time in the chest with a knife and then shot in the back. What were you wondering about there, Varina?"

"It's nothing. I shouldn't say anything."

"Your friend is dead and if you have any information that would help find his killer, or in this case killers, I need to know what it is."

She placed both hands on the tablecloth pushing down on the table as she spoke. "The last time he was here Mr. Stuart said something about having problems with his partner, Mr. Rodgers. He wasn't specific. Just said he was figuring he would be back sooner than usual because of it. Wanted to surprise Mr. Rodgers to see if his suspicions were right."

The sheriff made his mental notes and thanked Varina for her time. It had been several hours since he sent that wire to the sheriff in Abilene and he wanted to check on a reply so he walked down to the Wells Fargo office. There was a response waiting for him. The Abilene sheriff had gone to Mrs. Stuart and told her the news. She was making preparations to come to Fort Dodge herself to get her husband's body and carry it back home for a proper burial. According to the message she would arrive late the next day.

Later that day he found himself at the blacksmith's talking with Henry, the messenger for the stagecoach. While they were talking Jack cautiously strolled up. "What are you doing here, Sheriff?"

"Doing my job. I see you've learned a lesson. I'm a pretty good headmaster, aren't I? Where were you last night, Jack?"

"What do you mean? I was at Ham Bell's Saloon."

"All night?"

"Yeah, all night. They have rooms in the back and that's where I stay whenever I'm in town." Jack walked over to the forge, picked up a stick from the floor of the shop and started stirring the red-hot coals.

"I suppose you have a lady friend that can prove this?"

"Sure, more than one. Why don't you get out of here and let us do our work."

"You were in the war, weren't you, Jack?"

"Sure was."

"A Confederate Reb I would bet."

"Proud of it too. Served with Johnston in Georgia. What else do you want to know?"

"That's enough. I'll see you later, Jack. Good day, Henry."

He started walking back over to the hotel. When he got half way across the street a shot rang out from behind him. Dirt flew up a few inches from his right foot. It was as if the sheriff's body knew what to do without taking time to think. His right hand went directly for the pistol in his side holster as he spun on his left heel. Placing his right foot solidly on the ground while crouching low, he didn't see anyone behind him, and there were no other shots being fired. He was sure it was Jack but couldn't see him. Several seconds in this defensive position and he decided to holster the pistol and see if he could get across the street.

As he turned still tense another shot was fired causing dirt to fly up between the sheriff's feet. This time he spun on his right heel while drawing his pistol in one swift and flowing movement. With the precision of a professional he fired at the figure that was half hidden by the wide doorway of the blacksmith's shop. The sheriff jumped to the right hitting the ground just as another shot barely missed him. As he hit the dirt, Sheriff Justin Stonegate proved his skill as a truly great lawman. He fired and hit his target, causing the man to reel as another shot went off into the air from his rifle. The sheriff stayed on the ground watching and waiting. Deciding it was safe enough, he slowly got up and was soon standing over Jack Slade.

He looked down at Jack and commented, "With you shooting like that, it's no wonder the South lost. Now get up." The sheriff could have easily hit Jack straight through the heart but choose instead to hit him in the right arm, effectively putting him out of commission. He picked up Jack's rifle and pulled him up to his feet, then drug him to jail. Once inside, the sheriff instructed his deputy to get the doctor once again. He then escorted Jack back to a cell, opened the door for him and showed him in. Then he quietly shut the door, causing it to give that clinking sound as it shut and locked into place. "I like that sound," the sheriff said to Jack. "It sounds so permanent." Jack didn't say a word, only groaned as he held his arm.

After his deputy arrived with the doctor, Sheriff Stonegate went back to the hotel and finished his investigation for the day by speaking with Clara and Horace. He found out they were traveling together but staying in separate rooms. Clara's room was right across the hallway from Mr. Stuart's. He thought it was funny that she didn't hear the gun that fired the bullet into Mr. Stuart's back. She just said she had been raised in a town similar to Fort Dodge and gunfire didn't seem to bother her. She had been trying to escape her past ever since leaving home, which would explain her frills and fancy clothing. Horace was staying down the hall and said he didn't hear anything all night. During a moment while Clara left the room, Horace explained their destination was Denver where Horace would be exploring a business opportunity. If this worked out, he was going to ask Clara to marry him. The sheriff decided to end that day of investigation and mull over everything in the comfort of his own place that evening.

The next day went slowly for everyone, especially the guests staying in the jail. Will McKinley came by to see how Virginia and Preston were doing. He agreed to bring them their personal items and bags from the hotel. They reassured Mr. McKinley they were innocent. He agreed to send a message to a friend by wire that was also an attorney back in Abilene. The sheriff seemed to be busy all day long, making another trip to the hotel and visiting around with others staying there. He also made another visit to the Lone Prairie restaurant for lunch where he found Varina faithfully waiting on tables. There were also several trips to the Wells Fargo office on this same day.

Mrs. Stuart arrived late that afternoon from Abilene riding on a wagon being driven by a hired hand. They went to the sheriff's office when they arrived. When the sheriff and Mrs. Stuart met she was teary, but he could tell she was a strong and impressive lady. They agreed on arrangements for her to leave with her husband's body the very next day. The sheriff personally went to the mortician's office and informed him of the arrangements after directing Mrs. Stuart to the hotel for the night. The sheriff had one last visit with Mrs. Stuart before she left town with her deceased husband properly placed in a simple wooden casket and loaded in the back of the wagon she rode into town on. He asked her questions that he felt were pertinent to completing his investigation, and she agreed to come back for the trial of the murderer of her husband.

By noon that day all of the passengers were in the sheriff's office wanting answers and protesting having to stay there another day. He had come up with an idea and explained it to everyone. "I want to meet with all of you this evening in the special meeting room next to the lobby. I will be there at 8:00 tonight with Jack Slade and the Dales. I will explain everything then, and I think we will have this matter resolved." They all reluctantly agreed to wait around town for the meeting.

That day went slower than the one before, and the guests at the hotel were becoming more restless as the day went along. Finally 8:00 came and they were all in the parlor next to the hotel lobby. The sheriff sent his deputies out to every person involved and gave them a verbal invitation and warning to be sure and be there. Sheriff Stonegate walked through the double doors flanked by two deputies to assist him. In front of him were his three prisoners, Jack, Virginia and Preston. Once safely in the room with closed doors he ordered his deputies to unlock the handcuffs from the prisoners. They even had Virginia's hands cuffed behind her back.

The sheriff began this unusual meeting by greeting each one individually with a handshake then announced, "Everyone needs to sit down and become comfortable. Men," nodding to his deputies, "stand at the doors. No one is to leave this room till we take the murderer or murderers off to the jail house."

Up till now the people were basically quiet, but his orders started the group demanding that he should hurry and name who he believes to be the killer and his reasons for the accusations. "I realize I have to spill my guts for you tonight. I have inconvenienced all of you folks in one way or another and I apologize for that. What you have to understand is that I am bound to uphold the law in this town. The people of Fort Dodge elected me to do a job, and I will do it."

Philip spoke out, "Then why are there dead bodies on the streets almost every morning. What are you doing to stop the violence and unlawful murders in the streets?"

"Now, Mr. Rodgers, my office takes every one of those cases and attempts to solve them, but I might also add there are budget limitations placed on me here at Fort Dodge. We try to have enough deputies working the streets at night, but we aren't always able to. Who ever did this must have known there weren't deputies out in this area. If someone heard anything like a gunshot no one would probably come to investigate. The one thing that was not figured into the plan were other guests in the hotel that have problems sleeping at night and tend to check out noises. They also didn't count on me and my investigation skills learned from Mr. Pinkerton himself."

"Would you just get on with it and tell us what you found out!" Preston shouted.

"Okay, Mr. Dale. I will get straight to it. I need everyone's undivided attention to every detail I am about to explain. Deputies, I think you can go home. I should be able to handle things." They left the room as the sheriff continued. "Let me go back to the day you were all traveling on the Santa Fe Trail on your way here to Fort Dodge. Mr. and Mrs. Dale, you were on a stage with Mr. Stuart, a businessman whom you let talk you into a business deal concerning driving cattle up from Texas six months ago. It was reported to you most the herd was lost due to heat, draught and finally rustlers getting what was left before they made it to the Red River. You were unwilling to accept this as fact and both of you argued with Mr. Stuart while on the stagecoach. I was curious as to why you chose to bring this up in front of all these people. I would think you would want to discuss this sort of thing in private."

"We did want to," Preston interrupted. "It's just that we had tried to speak with him several times, but he seemed to be avoiding us each time. Sitting there on the stagecoach he was trapped and I got anxious and nervous. I began to think when we arrived in Fort Dodge I wouldn't see him again. I also started thinking witnesses of what he said might be a good idea."

The sheriff continued, "Oh, it was a good idea, but not for you. It was good for one of his killers, but not right away. That one person didn't think about utilizing your circumstances until yesterday when she saw your hatpin, Mrs. Dale."

Virginia looked at Preston with wide eyes then to Clara. Clara responded to this accusation, "What do you mean by insulting me like this? I still think they did it." She pointed at Preston and Virginia.

"Sorry, Clara, you are the one that admitted to me that you were raised around guns and gun shots don't bother you. There was something about your name also. I did some checking and confirm my suspicions. Your father was Pawnee Parker who came here to Kansas before the war. He built one of the largest spreads this side of the Mississippi. A few years ago he came to Mr. Stuart for financial help. He had overextended himself and made some bad decisions. Mr. Stuart was a businessman and he saw an opportunity and was able to buy most of what your father spent his life building up. He just left your father with a small remnant of what was to be your inheritance. You have always felt cheated by this."

"These are all lies, Sheriff," she exclaimed.

"Are they, Miss Parker? I have been busy the last two days going to the Wells Fargo office sending and receiving wire messages. I've been in these parts for some time and have connections throughout the state now. I checked my sources and found all this to be true."

"Okay." A calm came about her as she confronted her accuser. "If you are a great investigator and know everything, how did I do it?"

"Well, you used a small derringer that you keep in your bag. Miss Parker, you are the one that placed the bullet in the back of the man you believed to be your family's worst enemy."

"I was in my room all night. I was worn out and sleeping in my bed."

"Miss Parker, do you know you sleep walk?"

"I do not. What do you mean?"

"I mean you must have been walking in your sleep because there was a guest in a room on your floor that saw you walking toward Mr. Stuart's room very early in the morning. The guest has problems sleeping many nights and tends to check out any noise he hears. He heard footsteps in the hallway and opened the door just enough to see in the dim lighted hallway that you were walking in the direction of the room in question."

"How do you know it was a derringer that was used?" she inquired. By now the conversation was concentrated between the two. Horace couldn't even get a word in.

"I had Doc take the slug out of Mr. Stuart's back. It was for a small caliber weapon such as a derringer that would be carried by a very stylish female such as yourself. That type of weapon would be very effective at close range."

With these words Clara started reaching in the bag she kept with her at all times. Horace was standing next to her and reached for her hand and kept her from pulling it out. He used his other hand and found what she was reaching for was a small derringer pistol. "Clara, you were just using me all this time." He sadly handed the weapon to the sheriff.

"Don't worry, Clara. I'm not finished yet. You were the last of three killers."

"One last point that you haven't brought up. How did I get into his room? He would have locked the door."

The sheriff smiled. "Good question. When all of you arrived late that first night, there was confusion in the lobby. You simply took advantage of that and observed where the keys were kept. When the clerk was busy helping people, you reached over and palmed one of the passkeys and returned it the next morning much in the same way. You unlocked Mr. Stuart's door, walked in and shot what you thought to be a sleeping person. In realty he was already dead. Does that answer your question, Miss Parker?"

Clara glared at the sheriff as she replied, "You still have to prove it in court, you know."

"Oh, I know that. There is the question concerning you being held under arrest and even trying to shoot a corpse that was already dead. I just try and figure out who I need to arrest and let the judge do his job. You falsely accused Mrs. Dale of murder. I believe you owe her an apology. All this leads us to the second killer. I am walking toward that person and getting warmer and warmer," he said as he moved toward Philip Rodgers. "Mr. Rodgers, I beg your pardon, but I am also going to have to place you under arrest for the attempted murder of your business partner, Mr. Stuart."

"What are you talking about, Sheriff? This is absurd. I certainly do not believe you should run for office next election. I think I'll run against you and might win at that."

"You think so? How will you run from behind bars? You see, I had a long talk with two very nice females, Varina Jackson and Mrs. Stuart. It was interesting how you formed another partnership in order to try and get away with this."

"Explain yourself, sir," Philip said.

The sheriff continued, "You went to Lloyd Walker, the owner of this hotel. Didn't he, Mr. Walker?" He looked across the room at Mr. Walker.

"I don't know what you are talking about," Mr. Walker replied.

"I mean the day we spoke you directed me to a young lady by the name of Varina Jackson who you said was having an affair with Mr. Stuart. You said he saw her every time he came to town and that rumor had it that he was coming to town on this trip to break the relationship off."

Mr. Walker shouted, "Those were the rumors. I was only repeating what I had heard, thinking it might be helpful to you in solving this crime."

"Oh, it was helpful all right. I found Varina to be a young lady that lived in the same town as the Stuarts. The Stuarts were lifelong friends with Varina's parents. She got in a little trouble concerning a boy and her parents threw her out of their house. She needed a place to go, so Mr. and Mrs. Stuart took her in. In time they all decided it would be best for Varina to move to a different town for a fresh start. That is when she moved here. Mr. Stuart helped her get a job at the Lone Prairie restaurant. He thought this would be a good town because he had the partnership with you and he was already coming here on a regular basis on business. That would mean he could check up on Varina whenever he was in town. I checked this story out with Mrs. Stuart and found it to be absolutely true. Mr. Rodgers, you indirectly accused Varina Jackson of murdering Mr. Stuart through Mr. Walker. You made Mr. Walker an accessory to your crime."

Mr. Rodgers calmly asked, "Are you ever going to give us your theory on why you think I did this and how?"

"Forgive me, I got carried away for a moment. One of the pieces of information Mrs. Stuart and Varina both shared with me was that Mr. Stuart had expressed a concern that you were cheating him in the partnership. He was planning this trip for some time and hadn't told you that he was coming. Mr. Stuart was going to walk in on you during a usual business day and surprise you. It would have worked, too, but Mr. Walker got word to you right after Mr. Stuart went upstairs to bed. Mr. Walker gave Thomas a room that is easy to access by climbing up the outside of the building onto the balcony. The lock to the window in that room is broken, so you can open it from the outside. You simply climbed up and came in through the window.

"Once inside, you thought Mr. Stuart was in a deep sleep so you walked over to his bed and took the knife you carried with you and stabbed him in the chest two times. Afterward you checked for a pulse. Not feeling one, you believed you were successful and you left the room the same way you entered. The only question that I have pertains to how soon after the first killing took place did you come into the room and commit your crime? His body must have still been warm, otherwise you should have felt that Mr. Stuart was cold and wondered about it." He looked for a reaction from Philip and Walker both.

Philip admitted he felt for a pulse and yes he was still warm. "Mr. Rodgers," Lloyd cried out. "What are you saying? Do you know what you've just done? You idiot."

"I have to place both of you under arrest. I will have one of my deputies search your store, Mr. Rodgers, for your books, and we will look through them together if you would like."

There was a feeling of relief in the room but also anxiousness. Preston asked the sheriff, "Are you going to tell us who killed Mr. Stuart first now, or are you going to wait till tomorrow?"

"Patience, Mr. Dale. These things take time, and yes I am about to tell you who killed Mr. Stuart with your wife's hatpin." He walked over to the table where he had placed the hatpin earlier and picked it up. He walked around the room holding the pin up toward the ceiling stopping at the opposite end of the room as Jack Slade. With his back to Slade he began, "Mr. Slade. Did you tell me the other day that you served in the war between the South and the North?"

Jack was still hurting from the wound he received the day before, so he was slow to talk. "Yes, I told you that."

"Which side did you serve?"

"I told you that too. The South. I was with Johnston in Georgia."

"Mr. Slade, were you with Johnston during the battle for Atlanta?"

"Why yes I was. What does this have to do with someone murdering Mr. Stuart?"

"I have to ask you for patience now. Did you know Mr. Stuart also served during the same war?"

"I believe someone mentioned it. I think it was at our last stop while we were eating. Why?"

"Well, Mr. Slade." The sheriff was baiting the hook now. "I understand that you took the oath of allegiance to the United States government shortly after the South lost, but you have never really forgotten the past. Is that correct?"

"Sir, I did take the oath, but I disagree that I have not forgotten the past."

With this Henry Hughes stood up. "Jack, now that is just a bold face lie and I need to tell you that. You know all you talk about while we ride that stage is the 'glorious and undefeated South.' The only two songs you know are the 'Bonnie Blue Flag' and 'Dixie.'"

Jack looked pretty sad at Henry and responded to this. "Can a guy help it that he only learnt two songs in his life?"

"Jack," the sheriff continued. "While you were eating with the passengers at your last stop you had a conversation with Mr. Stuart at the table. Everyone heard this. It was about the war. Did you know that Mr. Stuart fought at Atlanta and was part of Sherman's march through Georgia?"

"He spoke of it, yes I did."

"Jack, how did you take the hatpin from where Mrs. Dale had placed it?"

"I didn't do anything like that. I am a southerner and we do not steal from ladies."

"Jack, you took the pin probably on your way out of the room after you found out Mr. Stuart had fought in Georgia. That is why you were suddenly in a hurry to leave, wasn't it, Jack?"

He didn't say anything, just looked intensely at the sheriff.

"After you got everybody off the stage coach, you did take it over to the blacksmith, and you did go over to Ham Bell's Saloon. You stayed in the back room as you said, but you slipped out of the room after you figured Thomas Stuart had gone to bed and went to sleep. You also climbed up the outside of the hotel and tried the window only to find it was easy to open. You crawled into the dark room saw Mr. Stuart in bed. At this point you would have had to place one hand over his mouth to keep him from crying out while you rapidly thrust the hatpin into his chest. You took some time while in the blacksmith's shop to use one of his files to sharpen the point of the pin to make sure you could stick it more effectively. It must have only taken a few seconds before Mr. Stuart was dead. Your hand over his mouth and nose probably assisted in his death by smothering him also. After making sure he was dead, you left and left the pin in Mr. Stuart's chest hoping there would be a connection with Mrs. Dale. Jack, you falsely accused Mrs. Dale for the murder that you committed out of revenge for a cause that died long ago."

Jack was not a man to be placed behind bars easily. No one had been holding him and his handcuffs had been removed, so he lunged at the sheriff with both fists stretched out, knocked the sheriff down and then ran toward the fireplace where a saber, a relic from the past was hanging. He grabbed the saber and began to swing it wildly as he made his way to the door leading to freedom. The sheriff did not dare to fire a gun for fear he might hit someone else in the room. When Jack made it to the doors he yanked one side open only to find both deputies had been outside all this time. They both jumped and subdued him taking the saber away.

Having solved the mystery, Sheriff Stonegate ordered his deputies to take all the guilty to jail to be held over till the circuit judge arrived in a few days. There was a sigh of relief amongst the innocent as the guilty parties were marched out of the room.

INTERSTELLAR MISSIONS

"You shall not covet."
Ex. 20:17

Ten

After being persuaded by close friends and family, I have decided to give my own account of events that took place so many years ago while on my first missionary journey. Since I was a participant of events that served to change the destiny of a planet, it is time to set the record straight and give my story for all to read and judge for themselves.

Although many years have passed, my memory is clear of those exciting times as they flow from my mind onto these pages through my pen. Fortunately, I maintained an old-fashioned handwritten personal journal that has sparked much of my thoughts. The reasons for this effort should become clear as events unfold. I realize the controversy concerning extraterrestrial beings, life on and from other planets, that has sprung up within the church and still exists even today. The question that began to haunt me concerned the verse that has become known as the Great Commission. The words Jesus said in Mark 16:15: "Go into all the world and preach the Gospel to all creation...." How should the church respond to this verse if other intelligent life is found on other planets? How would it compare to the reaction of others in our world? Would we live together as brothers or as conqueror and slave?

I was a twenty-three-year-old engineer with a promising career ahead when my fiancée decided she loved another and our engagement came to an end. I loved Roseanne with all my heart, so I tried to persuade her to come back but failed in my attempts. I had been a believing Christian for several years and thought I had found God's will in my life, but this tragedy brought about a change that led me down another path.

My prayers were full of pain from the heart and my work began to suffer, so I decided to take some time off and do a little re-evaluating. While listening to an on-fire missionary named Keith Anderson in a Sunday morning church service, I became caught up in a cause far greater than my small problems.

He was from an interdenominational group called Interplanetary Missions for Christ. Keith was reporting on the latest developments of the fantastic discovery of life on another planet in a remote area of outer space. Keith informed us of studies that had been conducted by Christian sociologists and scientists that led them to believe the inhabitants had souls and they were in need to hear of the Gospel of Jesus. The primary purpose of I.M.C. as it became known was to evangelize these souls for God's Kingdom. I would find another purpose and unknowingly play a key role during my great journey of faith and discovery. The media presentation and Keith's ability to describe the friendly natives pulled at my heart, and I responded by volunteering for a five-year commitment to work for I.M.C. on this distant planet.

The decision felt simple, but telling my family and friends was not. The next few months sped by while I prepared for the journey. The day of departure was in Earth's early summer. After our takeoff I was sitting silently with my group and had lost all track of time while watching the round and colorful ball called Earth get smaller with every passing moment from a side window.

I thought about Mom and Dad having a difficult time understanding my decision at first, but with time they came to accept it. My friends tried talking me out of going by saying it was a waste of my talents and I was just emotional after losing Roseanne. I let them know this would be the best way ever to use my talents, and I was not doing it just because of Roseanne. There were people within the church that didn't believe evangelizing the newly found planet was right because they would not accept what had been found there. For some reason the toughest people to tell were my grandparents. I guess it was because they were at the stage in life that we think of as the end. The chance of them being around when I finally come home is less than most others.

The toughest and most exciting day of my life was when I got onto the shuttle that would transport our group to the main space terminal to catch our flight out. Saying goodbye does not come out of my mouth very well. I shook and couldn't say anything for several moments, then regained control and gracefully and with love said goodbye to all that came to see me off.

I must say even the shuttle flight was much smoother than I anticipated. Take off was a bit rough because of the blast from the rockets, but beyond that I have been very pleased. Most of our thirty-five members were enjoying themselves watching movies or playing games on the personal monitors stationed in front of every seat. The same monitors could be used to communicate to people on Earth, so some were talking to friends and family they had just left. There was some low sobbing in the background along with airing of regrets for even coming along.

I became amused when some of the group came down with space sickness. Many newcomers to space travel can be effected and I've read it is similar to being sick at sea. I know it sounds cruel to laugh at someone that is sick, but I couldn't help myself. The bathrooms were to the back of the flight deck and when the symptoms came on you only had a few seconds before everything in your system came up.

The entire ship was pressurized, but being in space we didn't have gravity. When you unfastened your seat belt you would float out of your seat. You had to grab handles that were strategically placed along the luggage compartment and pull yourself to the main aisle. You would have to get enough control of your legs to pull them down toward the floor. The crew issued all of us special shoes that would trigger an electric impulse that caused an artificial gravity along the floor. Even though I am an electrical engineer by education, I couldn't begin to explain how this works. It's similar to static electricity when you rub a balloon on someone's clothing, then you can place it on their coat or whatever and it sticks. This means a person can walk to any point in the cabin, but it is a slow pace. If a person went too fast the impulse would stop and you would fly up hitting your head on the ceiling. When you see people clinching their stomachs and holding their hands over their mouths while attempting to maneuver in these circumstance to the facilities it can just strike a person as funny.

Keith Anderson, the same missionary that had come to my church and introduced us to this great mission, stood up from his seat. He made his way to the aisle and slowly walked in a very unsteady fashion to the front where a microphone was hanging on the wall. He pulled the microphone off the hook and began to speak. "I would like to welcome everybody with Interplanetary Missions for Christ to the *U.S.S. John Glenn*. Our ship has been named after the first U.S. citizen to orbit the Earth in the early 1960s. This great space ship has room for one hundred fifty passengers plus the crew that keeps it running. Out of the one hundred and two passengers currently on board, thirty-five are missionaries from many different countries on earth. Each of you that are missionaries are embarking on a journey that is just as historic as that first flight of John Glenn, and I dare say it is more historic in many ways." Clapping and some muffled cheering went up from the missionaries.

"I would also like to thank our pilots for such a smooth flight. This is my third trip like this into space and I have to say it has been the best. This is an historic journey because we are the first group of missionaries to Anthemus with long-term missionary commitments. We do have several volunteers that will be short term and will be going back home in a few months, but most of us will be staying for as long as five years before heading home. I am thrilled to be part of this expedition for our Lord Jesus Christ. Now that we are on our way we have some business matters to take care of, and everybody in our group needs to make their way down to the conference lounge that is found on the diagram of the ship that each of you have. It is on the deck just below this one. Considering that some of you are experiencing some problems and how long it takes to move around up here, let's meet in thirty minutes from now. I will see all of you in the lounge." He replaced the microphone and slowly made his way back to the area of his seat where he assisted his wife Lori to make her way to the aisle.

After listening to his announcement, I decided to get up and slowly walk to the conference lounge. There were two other seats to my left to go over and my new friends Pat and Ellen were starting to move also. As I got up I noticed a different feeling in my stomach. "Pat, Ellen, stay seated for just one moment and please let me by first." I grabbed the handholds and pulled my way across my friends. Both of them smiled at each other and gave a short laugh. "It caught up with him," Pat chuckled.

Thirty minutes later we were all comfortably seated in overstuffed leather chairs in a room to make you feel like you were back on earth complete with potted plants and modern art hanging from the walls. I was feeling much better and had found the room with no problem. Keith came up to me and said, "Curt, hope you're feeling better. Don't worry, the same thing happened to me my first time up. Give yourself some time and watch what you eat for the next several days and you will be all right. Could you hand these out to each person and then we will begin." I proceeded to pass out all the booklets that would be just the first of many we would be studying from during our long trip.

Keith began, "Thanks, everybody, for being so prompt. I know this is the first trip into space for most of you and you are very excited about being here. This orientation session will last forty-five minutes to an hour, then you will have free time for the rest of the day. Everything I will cover is in the booklet that Curt gave each of you. As you know by now, our travel time will be filled with training sessions and study time. Just think of this as a traveling university. Don't worry, there will be free time to take advantage of special areas of the ship. During our month on board the *U.S.S. John Glenn* we will be taking a survey of the history of Anthemius along with introducing you to the language and customs of the different native groups we will be working with. After we land at the terminal base on Mars, we will have a three-day layover before taking the second and final leg of our trip to our destination. That part of the trip will be six months. We will have time for in-depth classes on the topics found on page two of your booklets. Your studies will cover the history of previous missionaries; the language and culture of those you have chosen to live with; along with many other classes. Your time will be filled and you will be amazed at how fast the next several months will, well, fly by."

The group gave a big "Ugh!" after this last remark.

Keith continued, "Okay, I'll quit with the puns. Turn to page ten in your booklets and you will find the section on the ship that we are currently on. You'll find recreational areas for exercising, movie theaters, there is a library and communication center. The cabin we were just in is used for takeoff and landings as well as relaxing during the flight. Feel free to punch up any movie that is on the approved list whenever you are up there. I believe all of you understand that you can call home anytime during the first eight hours of our journey today. The bad news is this will be the last time you can call home until we arrive at Mars. Exceptions to this rule are emergencies or someone from home calls you with an unexpected problem. Curt, I need you to pass out these forms with everyone's room assignments."

He handed me a stack of cards that had everyone's name and a cabin number. "Look on page two of your booklets and you will see a diagram of the deck with the living quarters. After we finish here you will want to get settled into your rooms. I certainly hope each of you followed instructions on what you are allowed to bring on board for this next month. I understand each of you are in compliance on shipping all of your other personal items to Anthemius before leaving Earth."

After getting my luggage I started looking for my room. While going slowly down the hall I bumped into another fellow that appeared as confused as myself, so I asked him the room number that he was looking for. "Two twelve," he said.

"Looks like we're roommates. I think it's over here." I pointed to an area just down the hall. We each carried our stuff to the room and slid the door over to the right and I walked in first. The recessed ceiling light came on automatically as I walked in, and there was a friendly and very feminine "Hello, and welcome to your personal space for sleeping and lounging while you are on board the *U.S.S. John Glenn.*"

I use the term room loosely because it was more like a broom closet in size. Fortunately there were only two of us assigned to this room. Some had as many as four, but I guess those rooms were as large as a good size walk-in closet. The beds were interesting because they were suspended from each corner inside an inset within the wall. They were on top of each other similar to bunk beds with a short set of steps on one end to help the occupant of the top "bunk" to get in. The mattress was thin, but once you crawled in and got situated it was quite comfortable. The biggest problem became how to get out of bed without bumping your head on the ceiling of your nook that was only three feet above you. There were a couple of nicely upholstered chairs and a ceiling light. The room's décor was complete with the walls being painted in a sort of depressing shade of gray with no windows. After just a few moments in my "living quarters," I realized all this was designed to motivate a person to spend most of their time at other activities besides sleeping.

"Will we have to hear that voice every time we walk in through the door?" Mark asked.

"I think we can change the settings on what the computer does from this control panel." I walked over to the back wall, opened a small door and started playing around with the buttons. The monitor lead me through steps to quit the greeting and set a wakeup call for every morning and a lot of other things the on-board computer would do for us.

"I can see Central Aviation didn't spare the bucks decorating this part of the ship," Mark said very tongue to cheek.

"I guess the next several months will be a lesson in austere living. I'm sure you've read about the people on Anthemius. They say you are better off if you don't own or want anything materialistic. We can use this time to clear our minds of a materialistic nature."

By this time in the conversation Mark's eyes began to glaze over. "Yo, uh, well, that sounds good." He looked over at the beds. "Which do you want? Top or bottom?"

I looked at them. "Doesn't really matter. How about you pick what you want now and we can switch in two weeks."

"That sounds good, I'll take the top for now." He grabbed the step rail and pulled himself up toward the top bunk. He started floating after his feet came out of range of the electrical current. When he got to his bunk he asked, "I have a question about these beds. Since there's no gravity, how do you stay in these things?"

I walked over and looked at the lower nook and saw a button with instructions over the top of it that read, "push for gravity sleeping" and brought it to Mark's attention. A push of the button brought a low but pleasant hum and a feeling of gravity came over him. We also discovered straps for when a person wanted to experience sleeping without gravity.

After a few minutes I climbed out and began putting my belongings away while Mark asked, "After we get our stuff put away, you want to go up on the observation deck and check out the view?"

"Do you mean the view of the stars or the view of any young ladies that might be there?"

"Uh, if both are there we can't help it, and we might as well take advantage of the natural beauty and observe it all we can."

"How old are you, Mark?"

"What does that have to do with anything?"

"I just want to know. If you don't want to tell me then tell me how long have you been a Christian."

Mark started climbing out of his bunk. "I'm nineteen and I've been a Christian now for about a year and a half. Why?"

"Oh, I just wanted to know if I was right about at least one of those, and I was right about both. Mark, we just met and I can already see why God placed you and I together."

"Yeah!" Mark looked at me with kind of a confused look on his face. "What do you mean by that?"

"All I mean is that I can see we both have a lot to learn, and we will learn lots from each other. Let's go to the observation deck. I would like to meet more of our group."

The next day everyone began class promptly at 9:00 a.m. and began a month of learning how Doctor Ilian Isomov of the International Astronomy Society first discovered a new solar system toward the end of the twenty-first century. With the assistance of an old space telescope that could see further and clearer than any placed on earth he was able to discover various details on each of the seven planets. The most interesting details were found on the fourth. After news of his discovery became known to the world the Society, as it will be called named the entire solar system after the founder making it Isomov Seven. Until better names could be determined at a later date, each planet was given Isomov's name followed with a number beginning with the one closest to the center. This would make them Isomov One through

Isomov Seven.

Scientists concentrated their attention on the fourth planet where the details became more fantastic and exciting with every new discovery. The data was so impressive that private businesses and the U.S. government joined forces in the biggest surge of exploration that had been seen in years. They even partnered with other nations of the Earth in their efforts.

After years of research and development along with billions of dollars spent the first true interstellar spaceships were launched to explore Isomov's planet. The first explorers were not men or women but robots that had a very human-like appearance. These robots were designed to approach the inhabitants of the planet very cautiously and respectfully. They used symbols that were considered to be universal here on Earth to communicate with the inhabitants until they learned the languages. The robots were programmed to learn from what they observed.

People on Earth had been reporting things like flying saucers and contact with extra terrestrials for centuries. Now we were being the extra terrestrials attempting to make contact with beings on another planet. When the results of the first robotic explorations came back the excitement grew even more. There was definite proof of life on the fourth planet of the Isomov Seven solar system and it was intelligent. One of the most surprising discoveries was that all the inhabitants of the planet spoke the same language. Another surprise was that it was very similar to the language many believed was spoken by the ancient Romans. This made all the Latin teachers on Earth very happy, for they finally came into great demand. Because the form of Latin spoken by the inhabitants of this planet it was tagged Neo Latin.

The scientists belonging to the Society decided to christen each of the discovered planets after ancient Roman Emperors. The one we are most concerned with was named after one of the last emperors known as the "shadow emperors," Anthemius. While I was learning this I couldn't help thinking of the relationship of the Roman Empire and the early beginnings of Christianity.

All of the first explorations stirred the people of Earth like nothing else had since Columbus discovered the New World in 1492. This was another "New World" that had to be explored. The reaction from the church was mixed, but it was just a few months after the discovery was announced that a small group of Christian men and women formed Interplanetary Missions for Christ. These were believers that took the Great Commission seriously and applied it to this New World.

The first mission to go to the planet was met with controversy from those hoping to keep the church back home on Earth only. Many explorers brought up mistakes that Missionaries had made during the exploration of Earth. They didn't want Christians to have any influence on Anthemius. Although the planet's inhabitants accepted the missionaries easier than their fellow humans, few had become converted to Christianity. Many hours were spent in prayer and study of the planet's culture and religious writings. Many Biblical scholars, pastors and teachers tried to discover how to approach the Anthemius with the Gospel.

The ultimate goal was to establish churches all over the planet and to train the natives to operate them and to expand the Kingdom with a minimal amount of interference from the missionaries on Earth. This system had been working very well for the last two hundred years on Earth and everyone thought it would provide the same results on Anthemius. Unfortunately, it had not worked and many leaders within the movement were frustrated.

Those early space expeditions also disappointed most on Earth that were hoping for the facts to be more like what they had read from science fiction novels and what they saw in movies. The truth was the planet that Doctor Isomov stumbled across was very similar to our own. The atmosphere was made up of many of the same gases found on Earth and was breathable for us. The only continent was a band of land that traveled the entire middle circumference of the planet. Some areas were five hundred miles wide and other areas were more than two thousand miles across. The remaining area of the planet was covered by water not unlike our oceans and seas.

Deserts, snow-capped mountain ranges, prairies and lush green, tropical areas covered this land. There were an abundance of natural resources, such as rich mineral deposits, iron, bauxite, and many more. The soil was rich and the growing season was long, so several crops of many types of food could be grown each year.

The waters of the planet were filled with all types of creatures worthy for anyone's seafood appetite. The most disappointing news for most people on earth concerned the people of Anthemius. A more accurate description would be in order at this time. The natives of this newly discovered planet were of various heights and widths as on earth. None were less than five-foot-three and no one above six-foot-two with two distinctive features. The first was very straight and thick hair that came in the same colors as most people had on earth. The next was a very unusual skin pigmentation that seemed to be constantly fluctuating from a shade of light tan to dark tones of brown. Their skin color would never remain the same for more than approximately thirty days. A slow change would take place and sometimes would continually be in a state of fluctuation for weeks at a time. Sometimes what we would refer to as a state of depression would set in during the period of change. Scientists spent years researching this unique characteristic of Anthemian natives and they still do not have answers to their many questions.

The early explorers convinced us on Earth that we should not repeat the mistakes of past explorers. We needed to honor the language and customs of this "New World." The early explorations with the robots were friendly missions to help establish a positive relationship for the future. Word of these robots and their mission traveled fast throughout the planet and with few exceptions they were easily accepted and many are still being used in more remote areas of the planet to this day.

The cultures were behind in developing technology as compared to what we had on Earth, but our Scientists believed the planet was in the middle of its own industrial revolution. The people seemed to be very hopeful and exhibited an attitude that they could accomplish anything they put their minds to. This might be the explanation of why our missions were so readily accepted. Everything the robots observed was constantly being transmitted back to the people on Earth and passed on to everyone willing to learn of the new planet. We were told the robots would teach Anthemians of the history of Earth in an objective manner. They would learn of the bad as well as the good.

We learned Anthemius had a violent and bloody past very similar to the Dark Ages of Europe. There were warlords ruling over small provinces throughout the land. Several centuries before Dr. Isomov made his discovery, a band of men and women of every geographical region on Anthemius came together for one purpose. This small but uncommon group of patriots became known as the Peace Makers. They were able to bring all the warlords together and convince them of their plan being the best for everyone. It was agreed to divide the planet into three areas with boundaries and even a primitive form of democracy for each nation was developed. A rough translation of the names of each nation would be Comron, Aremas and Ildura.

The Peace Makers knew any plan they or anyone devised would not be perfect. Conflicts would come and war between the nations would occur, so they developed a method of peaceful resolution for those times. Their ideas and work brought the longest period of peace the planet ever knew.

They also decided each nation should select a large portion of what they considered the most valuable metals, minerals and jewels and form them into the most beautiful artwork they could. The most important artifacts representing their history and development were gathered in every nation. The nations built a highly guarded fortress to house all their shared treasure with an international police force to guard it. All this would be located in each of the national capital cities of all three nations.

As time went on each of these fabulous collections became known as the Shrines of their world. The idea was to give the treasure mystical power; fantastic legends were created about each item in the different collections. All the legends had something to do with saving one of the Peace Maker's lives while working for unity. Soon the nations of Anthemius believed they had a duty to guard the treasures for each other and as long as they did this peace would last. The treasure and the duty to protect it became the common thread that bound each nation to the ideals of the Peace Makers. This treasure is also what became the focus of the events this account is about.

Our month on board the *U.S.S. John Glenn* went fast and before we knew it we had made our landing on Mars. Since there is no breathable atmosphere on Mars, we stayed in self-contained quarters with the ability to move freely around large common areas. There were many forms of entertainment and personal fitness gyms to take advantage of. I believe everybody in our party had a good time and there were no classes or lessons for the entire three days.

After our time at the Mars terminal base, we boarded a larger spaceship called the *I.I. Isomov* after the discoverer of the solar system we were bound for. The *I.I.* stood for International Interstellar since almost every nation on earth had some degree of participation in developing and building the system of travel. The personal quarters on board this new ship were smaller than on the *Glenn*, and since Mark and I were used to each other we chose to remain roommates for this part of our trip. We were getting along well and had developed a system of survival on the *John Glenn*, so, since nothing was broke, why fix it? The next six months were spent increasing our ability with the native language, studying the Bible and how to relate its lessons to all the people from Anthemius.

The day of our arrival was busy, tense and the most exciting time of my life. Our docking station was several miles above the planet's surface. A special ship shuttled all of us to the planet so we could begin what was to be the longest, most difficult and most rewarding time of our lives. The Anthemian sun was bright and the sky was filled with dramatic white and gray clouds. Our landing pad was in the center of our destination, New Charleston, Aremas.

The city was located along the coast with rolling hills, majestically surrounding a deep, clear bay much like the one found in Charleston, South Carolina, U.S.A. The homes were built of large blocks made from red clay and painted white. The roofs were a grass thatched together to create a thick cover similar to the old homes of Ireland back on earth. When we burst through the clouds above the city, I was overwhelmed with the site. The inhabitants of the city surrounded the landing site and were bursting with excitement for the moment and filled with hope for their futures.

As we ventured out from the shuttle the natives of Aremas reached out to touch and to shake our hands while they cheered our arrival as if we were heroes coming home from a distant battle. It was there that I fell in love with the people of this far-off planet and I knew I was in my place. A man came up to Keith and welcomed him and they talked for a short while. I was close by but could not hear anything because of the crowd. We were led off the platform through the crowd and into several beautifully crafted carts that were pulled by dark colored horse-like animals. Eight carts carried us through the streets of New Charleston to one of the taller buildings along the bay I had admired from the sky.

We were taken to a large, circular room designed with seats terraced downward and surrounding a podium. After everyone sat down, a middle-aged, slim and somewhat scholarly man walked to the center podium and began to speak. His mustache was trimmed close and tight to the top of his mouth that spoke methodically and graciously.

"I want to welcome all of you to the House of Peace and Hope. I am William Long, one of a few people that came to Anthemius many years ago to begin a work for our Lord, Jesus Christ. Thank you for your enthusiasm, and I am glad you are all excited to be here to serve our Lord. You have all learned about the history of the House of Peace and Hope in your classes while traveling. We have made great progress in many ways with our work. There have been many miracles during the past five years, such as this building being given to us by one of the wealthiest families of New Charles. We have been able to renovate it to meet our needs because of the generosity of people back home on Earth. I am sure all of you have questions, and there will be time for that, but first we need to pass out some written information for all of you. As that is being accomplished I would also like to remind everyone this will be one of the last days that you will be allowed to speak English or whatever your native tongue from Earth might be. Starting tomorrow we want to encourage all of you to speak Neo Latin, as much as possible."

William Long was a modest man who did not boast of his own importance. Everyone knew that Interplanetary Missions for Christ (I.M.C.) was struggling until William landed in New Charleston. He was able to assess the situation and gather the leadership and create a plan that unified the organization for the first time. The building they had was small and inadequate for the vision William brought to the work.

All the leadership came together every day at 6:00 a.m. to pray for the people of the planet and back home on Earth. They spent time in preparation before the Lord. From this point they all would go to the government houses and meet the political leaders of the city and nation. They walked neighborhoods and found what the needs of the people were and found they would respond to someone that cared about them.

Since the Anthemian calendar was not the same as on Earth, the leaders had a difficult time figuring out when to have church services. To make things worse, the natives were used to their own religions that did not require any type of formal meetings as Christians on Earth were used to. William talked the leadership into having small, informal meetings whenever and wherever they could. After a few months, William planned a series of journeys that took him and his fellow workers to every corner of the nation of Aremas. They went to every village they could and found natives that had heard of their mission and were willing to create a network of friends as William called them. Very few of these "friends" converted to Christianity, but that would change soon. William made it a policy for all of the leadership to keep in tight communications with the network of friends in order to spread the good news. He reminded the leadership their job was to sow the seed and to let God do the watering and harvesting. They just needed to get after the task at hand.

News of William's leadership skills traveled fast throughout the other branches of I.M.C. He found the demand for his help so strong that he decided to take a year to visit each branch in the other nations. He would spend much time in prayer with the leadership and taught them what had been working so well in Aremas. Three years after his arrival, William had organized I.M.C. and conveyed a vision for their mission as no other leader had in the past. He considered many of the leaders of each of the three nations among his friends. The men and women from Earth that were in charge of establishing relations with the nations of Anthemius requested meetings with William. He would meet and pray with all of these frequently.

The next month would be our formal, hands-on orientation to the planet. We lived in the House, as we called it, where most of our time was to be spent preparing ourselves by praying and reading our Bibles. We would also do chores to help maintain the building and surrounding grounds.

There were junior staff members that had been staying and working at the House for several months. They took us to local markets and establishments called gathering houses to get a feel for the people. The staff assigned each of us to a family in the local area to live with for six months after our orientation was up.

About two weeks after our arrival we had a social function where these families were invited so we could meet each other. Some of the families had converted to Christianity, but most were just friendly to us and probably more curious to learn about people from Earth than anything else. The family they chose for me lived in what could be called a suburb of New Charleston. It was a small community about a twenty-minute ride by cart from the bay area. They were a family of four, Marcus was the husband his wife was named Rhea. They had two sons, Remus who was four years old and Decius was seven. Mark, my old roommate, chose to go to the other side of New Charleston. We would see each other throughout our stay at various meetings and a very special event that changed our lives.

On the day I moved to live with my assigned family, I was carried over to them in one of the small carts that was painted black with green wheels. My personal belongings were stacked up around me and on my lap. As we pulled up to the front of the house, the driver, a volunteer worker for the House, stopped and gave me just enough time to jump out and to pull my luggage and boxes off, then he drove away.

I walked up to the house holding a bag in each hand and one under my arm. Remus and Dicius ran up to me and grabbed my bags to carry them inside for me. I followed them to the door where Markus was standing with open arms. Instead of shaking hands, which was considered anti-social, everyone on Anthemius gave a warm and hardy hug.

There was one spare room in the back of the modest house that I would soon call home. It was only eight-foot by ten-foot in dimensions with one window above a small bed. The walls were painted a shade of beige with no decorative touches at all. I was allowed to hang some pictures of home on the walls and set them on a small chest.

No one on all of Anthemius had such things as a television set or stereo sound systems. They created their own entertainment by singing or playing an instrument. Many would gather their families round a dining table or in their living rooms and tell stories of when the first robot explorers from Earth arrived. Air conditioning was unheard of, and since electricity was just beginning to be utilized, light at night was furnished by an assortment of apparatuses that had to be ignited. Fortunately there was a form of indoor plumbing that did bring a great deal of comfort when needed.

The next phase of our mission would last six months. During that time we got to know our host families and earned our keep by helping around the home. We also taught English or whatever our native language was to the family members that were interested. All the missionaries looked for ways of mixing with the communities. We were all required to have some kind of skill or education that would be needed on the planet so we could find employment within the communities we lived in. Because the planet was becoming industrialized, I found a high demand for my skills as an engineer. I soon found employment with a small engineering company that was designing and building the first electrical power plants for Aremas. There were differences in math and building ideas, but I was a fast learner and began to contribute some of my own ideas in a few short weeks. Soon I was paying Marcus a small amount for rent for my room and I chipped in for groceries. I felt it would be important to pay my own way.

I knew the most important thing I could do was to get to know the people I worked and lived with and form a relationship with them. I began inviting fellow workers to join me at a local gathering house for dinner in the evenings. From this began a weekly meeting where we ate and shared our lives with each other. After several weeks I started introducing concepts from the Bible during our conversations. When some of them asked where I learned of such ideas, I realized this was an opportunity to share the Gospel and did so whenever this occurred.

During one of our nights at the gathering house we were sharing that some of the homes in the area were in need of repairs, but the people that owned them couldn't afford to do the work. Several of the locals decided they could make the needed repairs on the days they didn't work. That night these natives became volunteers that began helping their neighbors with home repairs, but this soon grew to include many other ways of helping.

After my first year with Marcus and his family, I had made a large number of friends. We started volunteer work for the neighborhoods around us, and we had regular meetings where we discussed a number of life's issues. One thing that I learned was that even though I was millions of miles from home in a foreign place, the problems Anthemians faced daily were just like what we face on Earth. I came to realize no matter where you go there will be problems. I tried to be of comfort and encouragement when needed. The only thing that was missing was no one seemed to be willing to do the one thing that counted the most, accept Jesus as their Lord and Savior. This was puzzling me more every day.

Interplanetary Missions for Christ required each of us in the field to submit a written report every three months on what has been going on in our communities. I would usually express my frustration with the fact that no one had accepted Jesus yet.

William Long was attending one of our meetings and heard me talk about this concern. Afterward he came up to me and explained he had the same frustrations. He had read some of my reports and heard some good things about my work. He wanted me to be part of a delegation from Interplanetary Missions for Christ that would be attending an international and interplanetary summit in the next few weeks.

The first meeting would be there in New Charleston. The summit would be on relations with the various nations on Earth that have been part of the Interstellar Treaty. Very important people from all over Earth and Anthemius would be in attendance. In order to show good will, the meetings would be held in the capital city of all three nations. I guess the icing on the cake was that William was insisting the I.M.C. delegation travel to every capital for this historical event and all expenses would be paid.

Many of the men and women that were coming from Earth were friends with William and were important in helping our mission get started. William wanted several missionaries to attend and meet all of the officials they could. He felt like being present, getting to know the leaders and contributing ideas would do a great deal for both the Missions and to help the progress going in the right direction for everyone. I was very honored that I was asked to be part of our delegation, so I accepted the invitation. This would mean being away for several weeks since we would be traveling with the summit to all the capital cities. I made arrangements with my job, Marcus and Rhea agreed to take over the weekly meetings.

Our delegation was made up of twenty-five missionaries. My old roommate Mark was one of them. The week the summit began, the streets of New Charleston were filled with people hoping to see some important officials along with the usual protesters that no one ever understood, just like on

Earth. All of us moved back into the House while the summit was in session. Mark and I were hoping this would give us a chance to catch up with each other, but events mandated other things to happen.

The delegation from Earth numbered one hundred and fifty, and each delegation from the three Anthemian nations had fifty members. Each delegation had an entourage taking care of all the many needs of each official. Of course there were members of the press from Earth also. This was to be the most important meeting in the history of the universe. There were many topics to cover during the summit, so the organizers broke it up into smaller groups taking each topic to thoroughly discuss. There would be a general session every evening with all delegates in attendance in the largest auditorium that I have ever seen. The sessions we attended were dry and boring, but the food that was served to us from morning till night was not. The greatest surprise was the food the delegation from Earth brought for the Anthemians to sample. I can guarantee you that Mark and all of us in the I.M.C. delegation did more than sample all the familiar foods that came from home.

William had advised me before the summit began to pray for a reception that he arranged that would bring all the delegates from both Earth and Anthemius together in one place. This would be held late on the first evening of the summit at one of the most luxurious meeting halls in New Charleston. He made it perfectly clear that all of us from I.M.C. were to attend. The I.M.C. delegation was going to travel with the delegates, so we needed to get to know them.

Out of all of the important officials in attendance I will only bring up the few that influenced the events this story is about. There were all of the Premiers from every nation of Anthemius, I will offer a translation of the names and hope I do not do dishonor to their memories. There was Premier Macrinus from Comron, Premier Commodus from Ildura and Premier Maximinus from Aremas. The Commander in charge of defending the Shrine of Aremas along with the Joint Head Commanders of all the Shrines of Anthemius. All of these dignitaries were memorable because each was the consummate politician in his and her own right. They seemed to be about making deals with all the delegates from Earth. We wondered who would benefit the most from these, the citizens of their nations or the politicians themselves.

There was the one member of the Aremas delegation that I remember with a greatest amount of fondness. His official title was Historian Emeritus and his name was Severus he was the chief historian of all the Shrines on the planet. Because of the importance of the shrines and his knowledge of the Peace Makers and all the history of the planet Severus was the most powerful figure alive that day. He was an icon that symbolized the peace of the planet. If anything serious were to happen to him there would be chaos on the planet. All of the delegates from Earth as well as his own planet worked to gain his favor. When I met Severus at our reception I was struck by his modest attitude and the simple way he expressed his own thoughts. This was one citizen of the planet that did not have to do any politicking for any cause.

Sir Edward Bennett from England headed the delegation from Earth. His diplomatic skills were well known after resolving serious conflicts that had recently developed between nations on Earth. Maria Lopez from Brazil, Ambassador Guy Lamar from the United States of America and Vladimir Kartsev from the nation of Russia were other leading delegates. Very little was known about Alexander Lermontov, the delegate from a newly organized nation in Eastern Europe called Sargovia. He seemed dark and moody, which did not seem to fit the purpose of the summit.

Each session of the summit had a main theme for the delegates to discuss. The first session's main topic was the selection of representatives to be exchanged between Earth and Anthemius. Before they finished choosing the representatives and agreeing on the arrangements the topic changed to trading goods between the two planets. By the end of the week this became the main topic of all discussions. The Earth delegates seemed to be pushing the issue and were making proposals that did not seem to be fair to the nations of Anthemius. A visit to the international shrine at New Charleston seemed to settle everyone's nerves. Each shrine was considered to be sacred ground and each delegate was to pass through with great respect. With the first week of the summit coming to a close in New Charleston everyone was claiming it to be a success.

Shuttlecrafts from the *I.I. Isomov* were furnished to transport all the delegates and their entourage to the next city, Saudi, Ildura. The main topic of discussion during this week was to be a comparison of the political systems of both the Earth and Anthemius. By some method the topic seemed to be redirected back to trade between the two worlds.

Mark and I were out in the hallway doing our best to mingle during a break. I recognized four people that were aids to Alexander Lermontov. They were talking in low voices while being huddled close together. After pondering on it a while my curiosity got the better of me. All I wanted to do was find out what they were talking about. Mark and I casually walked over to the delegates. I held out my right hand and started to speak in English hoping they would understand. They ignored me and continued with their private discussion so I kept my hand out and gave another greeting in Neo Latin. When they ignored this I decided to push in even more and walked right into the middle of them and repeated my greeting in Neo Latin once again. Their discussion came to a sudden stop and I had all of their undivided attention as they stared at me. After a few seconds there were a few comments in their native tongue that I didn't want to understand. A couple of them bumped into me as they walked away, knocking me to the floor.

While I was picking myself up, I noticed a folded paper on the floor. It must have fallen out of a folder of one of the Sargovian delegates had under his arm. I picked it up and tried reading it. The writing on the paper was in their native language. None of the delegates came back, so I kept it and Mark and I went onto the late afternoon session.

As we sat listening to the next series of speeches, I pulled the paper out of my shirt pocket and tried to make sense of it. For some reason I remembered meeting Nicki, a missionary in our group from Russia. I wondered if he would be able to help me with interpreting what was on the paper. Since Sargovia was located close to Russia Nicki might be able to pick up on a word or two. I went up to Nickis' room that evening and showed him the paper. Even though the spoken language was similar to Russian the written language was very different and there were only two words that he could make out, planet and shrines. I felt uneasy about it but decided to give the paper back to the Sargovian delegation and explain I found it in the area where we met so I thought it belonged to one of them. Nicki volunteered to come along as my translator to see if he could recognize anything they might say.

We found our way to the room for the Sargovian delegates and just went on in where we met two official looking fellows. They began speaking in their native language but in at attempt to help me understand what they were saying Nicki asked if they could speak in either English or Neo Latin. Neither of them could but they found a female member of their group named Nadia that could speak English. It was still difficult talking to her but I handed her the paper and explained I found it in the area where several of the delegates were standing in the hall the day before. She took the paper from me, opened it and began reading the message.

Both of the officials remained in the room and the biggest of them abruptly walked over to Nadia and snatched the paper out of her hands before she had a chance to read all of it. She jerked back in surprise and looked up at the man and began speaking very excitedly in her native language once again. It was like she was asking him what was on the paper but he just ignored her questions and motioned for us to leave. I was compelled to step forward and after mustering my best Neo Latin demanded to see Alexander Lermontov. I wasn't sure what I would do if he came out but I did it anyway. Nadia could understand some of what I was saying and translated it for the two delegates. The bigger one looked very serious at me while he spoke to Nadia. She turned to me and explained that Delegate Lermontov was not available to meet with him and it would be unreasonable for him to concern himself with such a small incident as this. That got me more suspicious of this situation but Nicki and I turned to leave the room. Just before I went out the door Nadia came up to my back and whispered a request of me in English to meet her at the side entrance of the meeting hall after the session that night. I acted as if I did not hear anything and just left the room with Nicki.

Nicki didn't want to come with me, so I went to the only side entrance there was to the meeting hall right after the last speech was given. I had been standing just outside the doors for about ten minutes after everyone had left. It was the time of year that would be referred to as fall back on Earth. The wind was picking up and temperature dropping.

The city of Saudi was known for dramatic lightning storms at night. Tonight was no different with an occasional flash and crack I knew a storm was brewing. Anthemius does not have a moon like Earth so the only light that fills the night sky comes from stars and the sudden flash of the lightning from the churning storm. There were clouds filling about half the sky that seemed to absorb most of the star's light creating an even more dramatic night. Fortunately there were lights on the outside of the building but just as I began to appreciate their bright safety they went off and I felt stranded in the darkness.

Beads of sweat started to form on my forehead as I shoved my hands into my pockets as if to find a sense of security. I started to leave but sounds of foot steps came up along the side of the building. I couldn't tell if they were coming or going but as a flash of lightning struck I could see an outline of a young lady. The tension broke when I heard a friendly, "Hello," from Nadia as she spoke in English with her Sargovian accent.

I was relieved. "Oh, hello, Nadia. I'm glad you made it." She had been followed, but we didn't notice the stranger in the shadows placing us in the sights of the weapon his hands held securely.

"I'm glad you stayed and waited for me," she said as we walked. I could see her face through the darkness now as the lightning flashed around us. She seemed to have a nice warm sort of smile that helped comfort me. I was exhausted but seeing such a face seemed to rejuvenate me.

I finally asked her, "What is it that you wanted to tell me, and why did we have to meet here so late?"

"I'm sorry, but I was not given your name earlier so I do not know what to call you."

"Then I need to apologize for being so rude and not properly introducing myself to you. My name is Curt Casey. I am from the United States and I am a delegate with Interplanetary Missions for Christ. One of our leaders, William Long, asked me and several other missionaries to come to the summit."

Nadia was watching me all this time and just as I finished there was a flash of lightning that lit up her face and I noticed she had very large and dark eyes. She responded to my introduction. "Hello, Curt Casey, you are a member of Interplanetary Missions for Christ delegation who is also representing his home land, the United States of America. I am very pleased to meet you; however, I must end the warm welcome here and get to serious business. I have been wondering about the activities of my delegation for some time now. When you came into our delegate quarters earlier you impressed me as someone I could talk with. Are you someone I can trust with very important information, Curt?"

"Why, yes you can trust me," I said as if in a fog. "What information do you have?"

"I am a junior delegate for my country. They give me a great deal of work to do but I am never included in any of their high level meetings but I have been doing different things to try to find out what is going on. I stand outside the closed doors listening very closely and walk into their meetings with lots of papers in my hands and looking very busy but I listen. I have been able to hear some things before they realize I have entered and I have been trying to piece it all together. The paper you handed to me today was a very important key." She stopped for a moment and looked around and led me by the hand to a bench and sat down.

"Curt, I think our state leader, Alexander Lermontov, has been planning something very large. I am not sure what it is, but I think it has something to do with the shrines and the Historian Emeritus Severus."

I looked at her sort of in disbelief but also with confirmation that I was right about Alexander, he was a dark character not to be trusted. "What do you think they are going to do? Do you think Severus and Lermontov are doing something together?"

She didn't have to think on that one. "No, it is just the opposite. I think Alexander is planning to kidnap Severus. After he has Severus completely under his control then I think Alexander will give his command and steal the international treasures that is at the shrines."

If she didn't have such an intense look on her face and sincere sound to her voice I would have laughed at this, but I did not think it was a good idea at this time. "Nadia, this all sounds a bit too much and possibly a little overreactionary. How did you find all this out anyway?"

"I told you, I've been investigating and found ways of hearing small bits of conversations behind those closed door meetings. Don't you believe me, Curt?"

"Hold on now. Let me think. You have to understand this has caught me a little short. I mean I don't like those guys on your delegation but we have all come here with the idea of having peaceful relationships between all the nations of Anthemius and Earth. What good would it do Alexander if he did this? What purpose would it serve?"

"I have been trying to find out their whole plan but I have been unable to finish my investigation properly. Curt, the last thing I did hear was this afternoon just before you walked in. There was a meeting and I heard something about tomorrow night between ten o'clock and midnight."

Just as she finished these words I heard something move in some brush several yards from us. I was trying to hear the sound again and decide what to do when I heard the clicking of some type of mechanism. Something told me we needed to move fast from the bench. I grabbed Nadia's arm and shoved her toward the ground just as an explosion hit the back of our bench where I had been sitting. As we ran toward a pillar at the side of the building another explosion hit the ground next to Nadia. We just made it behind the pillar when another explosion hit.

I looked at Nadia and asked, "Didn't you notice someone following you here?"

"No, I used every precaution I knew. I don't know where this person came from."

I knew the shooter was still out there and trying to get a better angle on us so I had to be creative and figure out how to get out of this without being killed. The only thing was he had some kind of gun and I had nothing. I said a short prayer asking for strength and ability to do what was needed. I then whispered into Nadia's ear and pointed in a direction for her to go that would take her safely behind another pillar. As she ran to this new position I reached up over my head to a ledge and pulled myself to an opening that led to a balcony above me. The balcony went over the area the shots were coming from so I crawled to that area. I could look over the edge of the balcony and see our adversary looking through the sights of his weapon getting ready to squeeze off another round.

Whatever I did from this point I knew I needed to be quiet and fast or I would be dead and Nadia would be left defenseless. Noticing something that looked like a hardened plaster from the building on the ground. I remembered all those western and war movies that I had watched during my life and suddenly knew what to do. I picked up the fragment from the building and threw it out into the brush. As he swerved his gun to fire I jumped over the edge of the balcony and fell right on top of him.

All that Anthemian food I had been eating for the past months had done a good job of putting more weight on me than I thought because our assailant was completely knocked out from my fall. I grabbed his weapon and swung it around in all directions in anticipation of a partner in the area. After finding no one else I yelled for Nadia to come over then started pulling everything out of the man's pockets to see if there was anything that would help me figure out who he was and who sent him to kill us.

The only thing I could find was a pin that had an insignia printed on it from the inside pocket of his coat. Nadia and I both recognized it as the logo used by the aids for Sir Edward Bennett. We couldn't believe he would have anything to do with this. We figured the man was either acting on his own or was in with Lermonov. The only thing I knew for sure was that we either had to tie our friend up before he came too or get out of there fast. Since we didn't have any rope we chose to run.

We made it to Nadia's quarters in the official Sargovian apartment building that was just a few minutes away. Once we were inside we made sure no one had followed us. Evidently Nadia knew something that someone wanted her dead for. We needed to get to someone that could help us that night. I decided the only person I could trust was William Long. His quarters were on the other side of the complex of buildings that we were all housed in. The biggest problem was that the area we would have to cross to get to him was completely open. There was no way of getting to him without being in danger if our good friend were back at the meeting hall to wake up. We decided the risk was worth taking.

I was knocking at William's apartment a few minutes later and noticed a light under the door as he opened it to greet us as late visitors. "Hello? Who is there?" The light in the hall was dim and he couldn't see who I was.

"William," I replied. "It's Curt Casey. I know it's late, but a friend that is with me, Nadia, with the Sargovian delegation, and I need to speak with you. It's very important."

I could tell he had been sleeping but was now getting focused. "Oh, Curt. It's okay, both of you, please come in."

Once safely in I reached back and checked the door to make sure it was secured properly. William noticed this strange behavior. "What's going on Curt? What are you doing?"

"I know it is very unusual of me to come here like this especially bringing a girl with me this time of night. William, we, well I mean Nadia, has found something out about someone and I am afraid that person now wants her dead. You are the only person that I knew we could trust that would know who to take this to and get help for us and everyone here."

We all sat down and Nadia recited all of what she had conveyed to me earlier that evening. Afterward William asked if the assailant at the meeting hall wasn't a common thief? Anthemius was not free of crime and people that were out late at night were often mugged. He was convinced there was something else to this after I pulled the insignia pin from my pocket. He was also convinced there would be a logical explanation and he would go to Sir Edward first thing in the morning. William allowed us to stay with him that night. I slept uneasy on the couch while Nadia took the bed that was in an extra room.

It would be risky to investigate Alexander or anyone in his delegation but it had to be done soon. If we were wrong this could be a major interplanetary embarrassment. That morning we decided it would be better for William to go to Sir Edward alone and inform him of everything. He did not want to do anything that would disrupt the summit sessions so we all agreed to let him handle this quietly. We parted from each other outside of William's apartment after spending several minutes praying for each other and the peace of the summit.

Nadia decided she needed to go back to her country's office area so no one would suspect anything of her. We went to her apartment so she could ready herself and then we started walking to the Sargovian delegation office area. While walking down a very pleasant walkway to the meeting area I noticed several rather large men out of the corner of my eye to our right walking toward us at a very fast pace. They each had dark suits and sunglasses and a very serious look on their faces. As they came up to us two went in front of Nadia and I, two others remained behind us. Another came to my right and the last rapidly but smoothly made his way over to the left of Nadia. One of them talked to us both in English. "Do not do anything stupid. Just walk with us and do what I tell you. I am equipped with a Lectro with a silencer and I will use it. Now just come along."

These men had us under their control in just a few seconds. I tried to explain what the Lectro weapon was to Nadia in a low whisper. "The pistols these guys are holding on us are Lectros." I turned to the two men behind us and pointed to the ones they held. "It fires a lightweight bullet that has a very powerful electrical charge, that explains the name Lectro. When that bullet hits you it embeds itself into the flesh and a powerful electrical charge runs through the body attacking every inch of the nerve system. This causes an instant paralysis and the person falls to the ground. Since the victim can't help himself he will bleed to death unless another person can get the bullet out quickly. The worst part is you never know how long you have till the bullet explodes inside of you. I would suggest we do exactly what these gentlemen say, okay?"

We walked rapidly to a back hallway then through a door to stairs that took us up to the roof of the meeting hall where a shuttlecraft had just landed. Nadia and I got on board with only one guard being with us. We had no idea where we were going but with a guard with a Lectro, Nadia and I just sat and did not even talk. We were in the outer perimeters of space in just a few minutes and we could see the outline of what appeared to be a larger spacecraft of some type. I didn't recognize the craft at first but as we got closer I saw the name on the side, *I.I. Isomov*. After we maneuvered into the landing bay and the bay doors closed we were led off the craft and into a room that I was never in during all those months on our journey to this new planet. There were large windows on one side that gave a panoramic view of space in all its glory. The guard motioned to us to sit then he left with the door shutting behind him. I ran to the door to test it but it was locked.

Nadia looked up at me with a worried look in her eyes. "What is going on? I have never seen any of those men before. Do you think Alexander is part of this?"

"Well, Nadia, I would think this might be proof that you were correct in what you came up with. What I want to know is who, how, what and why?"

She wrinkled her nose at me and said, "What do you mean by that?"

"I mean I want to know who knows what we know, how did they find out that you know exactly what do they know and why are they doing this? That is what I mean. This is baffling and is not what I was expecting from this summit."

The door came open again and a familiar person walked through. "William," I shouted, surprised to see him on the ship.

He looked over at me. "Curt, when did you two get here?"

"Just a few minutes ago. What happened with you?"

"Well, I was able to meet with Alexander just after you left me this morning. He seemed to be concerned about the information you had. While we were talking two of his men walked into the room and he spoke to them in Sargovian for a few minutes. He then turned to me and explained that he would be looking into all of this and he insisted that I go with the two men. They would be taking me to a location of safety because he wasn't sure what might happen. When I refused to go with them because I wanted to stay with our delegation he ordered the men to pull out a Lectro and force me to go with them and here I am. Now, I have a question for you two. What have you done?"

Nadia answered this quickly, "We didn't do anything, but I think Alexander has. I just figured it out that's all. I know now that he is planning to somehow steal the international treasures at the shrines. If this happens there will be chaos and a disaster."

"I am not sure if you are exactly correct," William interjected. "I saw Alexander speaking with Sir Edward just before I was put on the shuttle and I thought I saw Severus with them also. There is certainly something happening but I am not sure just what it is. I guess now we will have to wait but we can also pray for God's help."

Fortunately there was a fully equipped and stocked kitchen along with the room we were in so we were able to make coffee and something to eat. I hadn't quite gotten into fasting at that point in my spiritual walk so I finally got the breakfast I needed. Several hours passed with no news until the door opened again sometime in the late afternoon. Alexander Lermontov walked into the room along with the Historian Emeritus Severus then we saw Sir Edward Bennett walk behind them. There were four or five other men, crew of the I.I. Isomov that came in behind everyone else. The room became so crowded it took me a few seconds to realize Sir Edward was holding a Lectro in his right hand and he was pointing it toward Lermontov. The ship's crewmen also had Lectro pistols and were now pointing them toward all of us.

William spoke up first in English thinking the bad guy had been caught. "Sir Edward, we've been here for hours. Has anything happened down on the planet? Have you arrested Lermontov?"

Sir Edward answered, "Hello, William. You might say that I have arrested your friend. I am also arresting you and your friends and Severus as well. You are all placed under arrest as of now."

This announcement shocked and confused all of us. William kept the dialogue going a little longer. "I'm not sure if I understand what you mean. Why are we under arrest? I thought the problem was with Alexander and a plot he was involved with."

Alexander broke in and asked very politely, "Sir Edward, may I be allowed to explain it to William?"

Sir Edward nodded approval and said, "It will be alright for everyone to know the whole story. After all, they won't be able to tell anyone?"

Alexander continued. "You see, William." He looked across the room toward Nadia. "She is one of my junior delegates. She has been snooping around trying to find things she had no business knowing. What happened was she found out part of the truth but she didn't hear all of the conversation? What she learned was the shrine here on Anthemius was in danger along with our dear friend here, Severus. What she couldn't hear she assumed but the problem is she assumed incorrectly and let important information out to the wrong people. My people had caught wind of this when we were still on Earth. We have been working to uncover the truth and figure out what to do about it. We have been working on this for years and now one of my junior delegates caused us to fail. I had my men bring all of you up here where I thought you would be removed and safe until all this was over but it looks like it didn't work for you or the rest of us."

"Don't worry about it, Alexander," Sir Edward interrupted. "I'll pick it up from here. What we have is a conspiracy in action. Tonight, for the first time people from Earth will be starting a process of taking over an entire planet. We are about to take a leap into inter planetary history. Yes the great Historian Emeritus Severus has been kidnapped. Next the shrines will be taken and desecrated with of the sacred artifacts and precious treasures disappearing."

William interrupted him, "But what good will this do for anyone?"

"William, why are you so naïve? What I am trying to convey to you is a vision for the future. We have come up with a creative method of a confederation of nations from Earth dominating the nations of Anthemius.

We have men strategically placed close to each of the shrines. They are disguised as soldiers from each of the nations here. When I give the word they will storm the shrines and take them over. Of course the beauty of the plan is that we will have reports of soldiers storming the different shrines of other nations. Then we will let the word out that Severus has been assassinated. There will be threats between the nations and then war will break out. After a few months of this chaos our World Confederation of Nations will step in as mediators. We will have to send a large peace keeping force to help maintain agreements the leaders will be forced to sign."

I had to ask a question at this point. "How do you know this will happen as you planned? How do you know the leaders will agree to anything you want?"

"They will agree," Sir Edward replied. "They will agree because as we come in with our peace keeping forces we will be replacing heads of governments with our puppets. We will be telling them what to do from our command post and it will get done. Don't you see what I am saying? Everything on Earth has been getting used up. When I first learned about what was up here I have to tell you I suddenly saw a way out for all of us. This new planet has everything we need and so why not play the old colonizing game like the old days but apply them to outer space and a planet?"

After listening to this William said, "I am not sure I understand how a man with your reputation would do something like this? Everyone with Interplanetary Missions for Christ prayed for you for years as part of the preparation for this summit. Now what I find is that you have been preparing to continue the same old warn out policies of the past. Conquest at any cost and you will obviously be set up as the ultimate ruler of Anthemius." He sat down in front of a window that looked out over the planet below and placed his face in his hands.

It would be getting dark by now on the surface of the planet so I asked Sir Edward when he would give the word to his men and if everyone in the governments on Earth knew of his plan. I tried to find out how he planned on giving the command to his men but he would not divulge this to us.

He answered the last question first. "My band of men are few, but we're an elite force made up of the best but after the chaos begins I will be able to go back to Earth and convince all the government leaders that my intentions are honorable and noble as they always are. They will follow me and there will be the largest space expedition ever staged in order to help our new space allies. Now I will answer your first question. I have a chore to complete before I give the word but it will be very soon. In fact my troops have full proof instructions. Even if they do not hear from me by the dead line which is in exactly fifteen minutes from now they will begin the attacks automatically."

I was wondering what the chore was that Sir Edward needed to finish when I noticed him bringing his Lectro up from his side as he was looking around the room. His eyes stopped at Severus and I suddenly remembered what he said about Severus having to be assassinated. The Historian Emeritus had been listening intently throughout all the conversation but his English was limited which meant that he had to rely on interpreters but he did not have any of them on the spacecraft. This great man of history and love for all the people of his planet could not understand that he was about to approach his final moments. He was about to meet his own end in a stroke of violence and greed. When I realized what was about to take place it was as if I had gone on automatic pilot. Something in my heart urged me to give a short and quiet prayer for God's help then I took action.

Somehow all of the people that were standing seemed to go into slow motion as I moved to take three giant leaps toward Severus. On the third leap I dove in front of him while Sir Edward squeezed the release of his Lectro. When the bullet pierced my shoulder the electrical current traveled throughout my body in less than a second causing me to fall to the floor unable to move. I was in the process now of bleeding to death. Being rendered paralyzed on the floor all I could do was watch and listen to what happened next.

During the confusion the other crewmen that came in with Sir Edward pulled their Lectros out and started picking out their targets. At this same moment Alexander was able to pull out a Lectros that he had in a pocket on the inside of his coat. He instinctively fired and placed one electrified bullet into Sir Edward's chest. While Sir Edward was falling back he quickly turned the pistol on the other men who quickly shouted, "Who will be next!"

Seeing their leader fall they quickly dropped their weapons. William and Nadia had both jumped up and came to me as the caring friends they had become. Alexander knelt over Sir Edward and demanded that he give him all the information on how to reach his commanders and stop this paramilitary action. If he refused he would be allowed to bleed and ultimately die a horrible death. After a few moments Sir Edward did succumb to the desire to live longer even if it would not be in a world dominated by his own self.

Alexander then pulled a communications device from a pocket and called for medical assistance to come immediately. After calling each commander he held it up to Sir Edward so could he gave the order to abort the attack at once. His plan to create chaos by stealing their most precious and valuable treasures then coming to a false rescue had failed. The all too human sin of wanting power derived from dominating others and colonizing this "New World" had been defeated at least for a little while.

The next thing I knew I woke up in a bunk in sick bay still on board the *I.I. Isomov*. The care I needed came in plenty of time and the bullet was easily removed. Sir Edward was being taken care of in order to go back to Earth for the first trial of interplanetary crime in history. A few days later while I was recuperating the Historian Emeritus Severus paid me a visit.

He came in and stood beside my bed and informed me in his broken English that he had been able to reflect on the actions of that fateful day when I jumped in front of that bullet. He let an interpreter help him with the rest of his message as he thanked me for saving his life. "I have been watching all of you who come here and tell us we should worship a man named Jesus who gave up his life so you can have a relationship with your God. Most of my people have been wondering if any of you would be willing to do the same for us. Now I know the answer to that. Your faith is true. This has touched my heart and I have decided I need this man you call Jesus and I want Him to come and live inside me just like he lives within you. Would you help me with this?"

I suddenly found the energy to jump out of that bunk to pray with this highly revered official. After we offered up the prayer of salvation he quietly sat down for a few moments. He then came back over to my bunk and said, "I now know why you jumped in front of me. I am also ready to follow Jesus because you have shown me he is real. I will issue an official record of all these events. Thank you, Curt Casey. You were my friend but now you are my brother."

After a few days of resting and healing I left the summit to go back to be with Marcus and Rhea to continue working. News of the dramatic events traveled fast and Alexander was quickly placed as head of Earth's delegation. Everything continued as scheduled without any further incidents. It was great to relax with my friends, play with their kids and tell them about the past few days.

One evening after dinner Rhea and Marcus came to me wanting to talk. Rhea spoke first. "I would like to say something I believe you have been hoping to hear for some time. Marcus and I have been thinking about what Severus told you. Even though you lived here in our home and we watched you every day we still wondered what price you were willing to pay for this thing you call faith. We realized you gave up everything you knew back on Earth but we were still wondering if you would be willing to follow your lord in death if called. Like Severus we have our answer and now Marcus and I have decided to ask Jesus to come into our lives. Could you help us?" A few minutes later both were praying to the creator of the universe and every world and creature that is in it.

This was just the beginning of years of service filled with triumphs and failures but most of all adventures for God. Even though it has been many years since my service on Anthemius, I still ponder those times. I never sought attention even to write this account but was truly blessed while being used by God to bring the real meaning of our faith to so many needy souls.